Highland
Deception

Marcia,

Highland Deception

Lori Ann Bailey

May the magic of
Scotland always live
in your heart.

Lori A. Bailey

Entangled Publishing, LLC
2614 South Timberline Road
Suite 109
Fort Collins, CO 80525
Visit our website at www.entangledpublishing.com.

Select Historical is an imprint of Entangled Publishing, LLC.

Edited by Robin Haseltine
Cover design by Erin Dameron-Hill
Cover art by Period Images

ISBN 978-1-68281-280-8

Manufactured in the United States of America

First Edition August 2016

For my best friend, my husband Ken.
Meeting you was the best thing that ever happened to me. You
continue to make all my dreams come true.

Chapter One

Margaret Murray, only daughter to the Duke of Kirk, had done it again. Like she often had in her youth, she had dressed in her brother's clothes and sneaked away from the keep. This time she had no intention of returning. If she wanted to avoid what they had planned for her, she would have to take matters into her own hands.

It had been a long time since she'd been allowed out on her own, and the fresh air was a balm to her soul. She breathed deeply as she cleansed her thoughts of the stifling environment at home. Each hoofbeat farther away brought a relief she'd thought she would never feel again. Giddy that her deception had worked so easily, she hummed a song as she trotted through the lush, green meadow toward a new life. Well, really, the humming was an attempt to pretend she wasn't trembling. Being in the wilds of the Scottish Highlands on her own didn't frighten her—she was more terrified of being caught and sent back.

Pushing the fear out of her mind, she trudged on, but despite her progress, she couldn't shake the dread that clung to her. Her father's last words rang in her ears. "I educated ye like yer brothers, but ye have turned yer intelligence into defiance. Ye will wed Conall."

A life sentence of miserable confinement with a man who turned her blood cold. Conall himself had explained in great detail how he planned to make her suffer.

She had been able to put the wedding off until her twenty-first year, but there was only so much time her family would give her to grieve. Unfortunately, her respite had come to an end.

How long until they discovered her absence? Even now, her father and brothers were meeting with the priest. What would her father do when he discovered she'd kept him from sealing his precious alliance? As long as he had everything he wanted, he wouldn't care. A tear escaped, but she rubbed it away. She had sworn there would be no more tears about something out of her control and no more men to force her into contrition.

After her conversation with her father, it had not taken her long to realize the only option she had was to flee. As she'd played often in the forest, it left her well suited to live without comforts until she reached her destination. If only she knew how to get there. In her haste to leave, she'd not thought to find a map. She only knew to go north.

Her eyes lifted to the heavens. *I promise to be dutiful if I get there safely.*

Luck had been with her, and she'd been able to abscond with a horse that had been tied to a tree just outside the keep, one not from the clan stables. When she'd stopped to run her hand down its long nose, it nuzzled into her as if saying, *take me.* With a quick prayer of thanks, she had climbed on its back, hoping she would be long gone before they thought to look for her.

She shuddered and dug her heels into the sides of the horse, willing herself to stay focused on happy times during the long journey that lay ahead of her, instead of the pain she was leaving behind.

Cherished memories of her grandmother and mother teaching her the art of healing, passed down through the generations, filled her as she cantered through the lush green fields and glens surrounding the castle. Her hand slid down to the sides of the horse, and she rubbed the worn woolen medicine bag that was never far from her side. She sighed at the reassuring texture. It was the only thing she dared bring, in case she was questioned about her destination at the stables. No one had noticed her, however, as she strolled casually out of the gates.

She would never have a daughter to pass her knowledge to. Nor would she get the chance to be the mother she wished to be. It stung to give up on that dream, but she had no choice, so she would console herself in becoming a bride of God. It couldn't be that hard. Surely she could stay chaste with no challenge.

Love between a man and woman didn't really exist. It was for fools and the weak, and she was neither of those things. Reckless and headstrong, maybe, but she would never be someone's fool.

Maggie rode for hours, and she was fair certain she was almost to the edge of Murray land. Her rear was sore from the pounding of her hurried pace, and the horse had slowed to a canter. A short break would suit them both, so she turned the horse toward the stream they'd been following north. She dismounted and found a path the steed could take down the embankment. But the overly long bottoms of the trews she wore quickly became heavy with moisture and muck, her brother's oversize shoes slushed around in the mud, and she wobbled to keep her balance. Most lasses would be horrified by Maggie's current state of dress. She was not. Until her mother's death, she had been allowed to run wild. She was a free spirit, and her mother had encouraged her curious nature, probably just to get her out from under her feet.

Och, she wished her mother were here.

She rubbed her rear and stretched as she guided the stallion to the water.

"I'll call ye Freedom." She patted the gentle creature's head softly. Freedom responded with a nicker, but maybe the happy reply was because he'd eyed the water, not approval of his new name. "We will do well together and then I'll do my best to get ye home," she continued.

The earth shook, and she turned to see movement at the far end of the field she'd just crossed. Horses skirted the edge near the stream.

Her heart lunged into her stomach, and she shook her head in a vain attempt to clear the image of several men galloping toward her. Och, had she been discovered? The riders were gaining fast and were going to be on her soon.

Even squinting, it was impossible to make out who they were. It could be she'd been discovered and her brothers were coming for her. The thought of going home made her heart lurch and sent a shiver down her spine. They would have to drag her back kicking and screaming.

Thankful she was mostly hidden by the embankment, she spared a quick glance over her shoulder to see Freedom's head was dipped to the water, making him hard to see as well. Maggie considered ducking down in the ditch to hide, yet her curiosity got the better of her, and she had to peek over the top of the ridge.

A group of eight men and one young boy of about twelve years of age was going to pass right by her. She didn't recognize the horses or the men, and some of the tension left her shoulders. She said a silent prayer of thanks that the men were not familiar and her family had not caught up to her yet.

The riders didn't appear to be from any of the nearby villages, either, and must just be traveling through. She let go of the breath she hadn't known she was holding. Relief washed over her.

Her gaze gravitated toward the man in the lead. He was one of the brawniest men she had ever seen. Honey-gold, wavy, windblown locks hung loose to his shoulders. The craziest urge to run her fingers through it struck her.

His bearing was confident, almost regal, but at the same time not cocky. Riding one of the finest stallions she'd ever seen, he sat tall and straight. In the early-afternoon sunlight, he looked like a god, golden and brawny, with a rugged but handsome quality, and she caught herself leaning forward to get a better look. The man to his right was laughing at what had been said but the golden-haired mountain beside him looked serious, his brows pinched together as he scowled at the carefree man.

The leader's muscles rippled as he held his hand up to indicate whatever he was saying was important despite his friend's humor. They were so close she was able to make out a dimple as it flashed on his left cheek when he gave in and smiled and then looked protectively at the boy, who drew up alongside them.

She could not pull her eyes away. If she believed in tales of men with honor, Maggie would ask this one to get her to the convent. With his confidence and size, he would be able to protect her. Somehow, she was certain he would never let Conall harm her; just being near the man made her feel safe.

She scowled and chided herself. To daydream was one thing, but to trust that a man would do the right thing for her was like thinking she would one day learn to love someone. She almost laughed out loud, but they were getting closer and she didn't want to give her position away.

As they drew near, the deep tenor of his masculine voice drifted toward her. The vibrations of the husky notes soothed until she made out a few of the words. "…can…have any lass…" There it was, daydream over, and she berated herself for believing there was one man with honor left.

Och, he was just like every other man in Scotland—he would want a woman willing to spread her legs and lie down for him, a lass to moon over him and bear his children while he rolled around under the covers with all the others and broke her heart. She blinked and shook her head to dislodge the fictional image. There was no such thing. Her father and brothers' behavior was testament that men saw women as nothing more than bedmates and property to be bargained away.

Another dark flash pulled her gaze to the side of the field the men had just come from. A second set of riders closed in. Fast. The group in the clearing right above her turned to see the imminent threat, eliciting incoherent shouts and curses as they took in the impending danger.

Maggie's heart nearly stopped at the unmistakable sound of swords sliding out of their sheaths. She turned her back to the embankment and slid down in the muck while she prayed they wouldn't see her.

. . .

"I have told ye before, I will never marry," Lachlan Cameron, laird of clan Cameron, stated with utter confidence and certainty as he rode beside his best friend through the rolling hills on the southern border of the Highlands. Thankful to be out of the Lowlands, he breathed in the fresh air as his gaze took in the full-blooming purple heather and vibrant green foliage of late August. 'Twas lovely, but the scenery didn't compare to the peaceful lochs and vast peaks of the mountains near his land.

"Come now, Lachlan. One bad wench shouldnae taint yer feelings for all the fair lasses," Alan chided.

"I had known her since birth." Lachlan snorted. "How can I trust another woman after what she did?"

"Ye just need to find an uncomely lass. Aileen was too bonny, and she knew it. Stay away from the vain ones and ye will be all right." Alan laughed.

Fine advice, but comely or no', he would never trust a woman with his heart or his life again. "My heart willnae be given to another to trample on. They arenae worth loving." He leaned over the side of his mount and spit then smiled at young Robbie, who drew his horse up next to Alan's.

Lachlan stopped himself from berating his friend. He was happy to bed a lass any time, but that would be as far as he would let it go. "I'll never fight for one again, either. Only the clan, never a woman."

"You are the Lochiel. You need heirs," Alan said, but he should've known what Lachlan's response would be.

"My brother can take care of that." Lachlan spared a glance over his shoulder at his younger sibling. "All the lasses love him. He can have any he wants and will have no problem finding a wife and producing bairns."

A shout rang out from the formation of men behind them. His cousin shouted, "Men approaching from the south. They arenae looking as if they want to welcome us."

"Nathair," Alan growled. "We didnae get away as clean as we thought."

"We cannae let them follow us." Lachlan cursed and turned toward the oncoming riders as the forms of Conall's trusted henchman and nine other men drew near. "Draw yer weapons."

Lachlan caught Alan's gaze, pointed to Robbie, and then

he tilted his head back toward his brother. Alan picked up on the cue and moved to a defensive position in front of both of the lads.

"Can we help ye?" Lachlan drawled as the riders approached.

"Where is the letter?" Nathair's gaze cut from Lachlan's to latch onto his cousin with a foul anger that cut through the air like a torch did the dark of night.

"I dinnae ken what ye mean, Nathair. We're only returning home from escorting my cousin to Edinburgh," he said in a bored tone, his indifference intended to dismiss concern over the accusation. Nathair's glare riveted to Lachlan's.

"I ken ye have a missive that does not belong to ye. Return it now, and ye can go about yer way peacefully." Nathair's eyes drifted toward the lad Lachlan had sworn to protect. Despite the man's assurance, his shifting eyes said he was lying. He couldn't risk letting Lachlan's band leave with the information they had gathered or let Robbie walk away with his life.

Nathair jumped from his steed; his size would be intimidating if Lachlan was not just as large. Those with him also descended and drew their weapons.

Lachlan and his men dismounted and flanked him. It was a practiced position, a team assembled with a skillful precision only gained through experience and an abundance of practice in battle.

His back was to the stream they'd been following north, but the lack of an escape route didn't bother him. They would make their stand here in order to keep Robbie safe and deliver the letter into the hands of the other Highland chiefs. There would be bloodshed, but despite being outnumbered, his men would take this crew without breaking a sweat.

It had crossed his mind that they might be pursued, and if he allowed any to walk away, they would return for Robbie.

There still might be more to come, but he wouldn't allow anyone under his care to remain a target of Conall's wrath. In order to make good time, he'd traveled to Edinburgh with only a few men, but once he had Robbie back at Kentillie, the whole of the Cameron clan would protect him.

To ease his mind, Lachlan's eyes darted to the side, where Alan still guarded the lads. Satisfied, he turned back to Nathair.

"What will Conall's father say when he learns of his own son's pledge of support for Argyll and the Covenanters?" Lachlan asked.

"Then ye do have the letter."

"Aye. How can ye serve a man who plots the death of his own father?" Lachlan snarled and shook his head as Conall's plotted crimes churned in his gut.

"Ye'll never live to tell anyone." Nathair's grip on his iron halberd tightened as he lunged at Lachlan with his weapon. He was well built and strong but sluggish in his swing, and Lachlan could handle a slow enemy. Lachlan was stout, too, but none of his size was from overindulging—it was all training and hard work.

He easily dodged the axe's blow and, because he was too close for a full swing, came down on Nathair's head with the hilt of his claymore. The sickening thud was deep, signaling he'd scored a good hit.

His opponent faltered and stumbled then rolled to the right and jumped back up to land squarely on his feet, his eyes scanning his surroundings as he struggled to catch his breath.

The *whoosh* of a sword sounded from the left, and Lachlan sidestepped in time to escape its range. The man overshot, and Lachlan swung around in one thrust, catching him in his midsection. He fell to the ground in a bloody heap.

Swinging his axe with full force, Nathair was on him again, and Lachlan pulled back, but not far enough. The blade grazed his arm, opening a small gash. It stung like a bee. His white shirt became red, and the coppery smell drifted up to his nostrils.

His wound angered him more. All around him was the sound of men fighting, screaming and dying, although he barely heard it. A concentrated hum buzzed in his ears, his complete focus on Nathair.

When the man turned to recover from the swing of his blow, Lachlan moved faster than his opponent could react and brought his sword down toward Nathair's shoulder. The blade skimmed his chest on the way down.

Nathair grunted. "Is that the best ye have? I expected more from ye. Conall will torture the boy before he kills him."

Lachlan's blood froze as he recalled what Robbie had already been through and the myriad stories he'd heard of Conall's cruelty. The man was telling the truth.

Lachlan's fingers flexed and gripped his sword. He'd never found a use for conversing during battle. It took too much energy and usually distracted him instead of his foe. Before all the words were out, he swung at Nathair's midsection. Blood exploded from his abdomen. He looked at Lachlan, his eyes now blank and disbelieving.

"What were ye saying?" Lachlan taunted as the man crumpled to the ground. "No one will touch the boy while I am alive to protect him." Lachlan squared his shoulders and held his sword high while he scanned for the next man to attack.

• • •

Maggie heard taunts being exchanged but couldn't make them out as she lay pressed against the bank. One was the voice of the well-muscled man she'd been admiring But it had changed, become coarse and dangerous. A shiver ran through her spine at the coolness in the tone.

She was in the wrong place. Freedom had drifted a little farther down the stream, but she could not chance an attempt to reach the horse. This was supposed to be her day of liberation, and there was no way to sneak away undetected. Again, men had interfered with her plans.

She prayed no one saw her.

Unable to control her curiosity, she peeked over the ridge. A couple of the second band of men looked vaguely familiar, and she struggled to place where she'd seen them.

Doing her best to blend in and not be detected, she ducked her head back beneath the embankment. She was dressed like a boy, one who did not belong to either group, and she gulped when she realized she would be cut down for sure if she was spotted.

As she scrambled down to make herself as small as possible, her hands skidded across the muddied earth smelling of dirty water and mildew. She was a mess, but she hardly noticed, because the thud of her pounding heart drove away all other sensations as she contemplated what would happen if she were discovered.

She cringed with each shout and grunt ringing out above her. The clang of clashing swords grated on her as curses flew through the air. A twig scraped her face, and she swatted at it, the muck from her hands smearing over her right cheek and temple.

Shaking and clutching her bag, Maggie cowered and prayed they would leave without finding her. A thud sounding just above her head made her jump.

Moaning came from the source. She had to look, she just had to. Whoever was there would find her anyway. When she looked over the ledge, she discovered a man lay injured and a boy leaning over him with wide, fear-filled eyes. The man on the ground was at least three years younger than she. Barely grown, and he looked so much like her brother. His eyes rolled skyward as he thrashed on the dirt. An unfamiliar pang swelled in her heart.

Blood poured out from a wound to his midsection.

Maggie didn't think; she grabbed her bag, jumped up the embankment, and ran toward the fallen man. The boy's gaze followed her as she knelt down by his friend. His eyes bored into her until something clicked, because he seemed to realize she meant no harm.

By the time she was at the injured man's side, he'd lost consciousness. Mayhap 'twas for the best. She pulled his shirt back to inspect the wound. Once she stilled her frayed nerves, her training kicked in. If it had been a drop higher and just a little deeper or more centered, she wouldn't have been able to do anything.

Hoping to find something that would be of use, she rummaged through the supplies in her bag. Her hand landed on a stray piece of embroidery work. She pulled out the thread and needle and went to work, doing her best to stanch the bleeding and sew up the injury, which was smaller than it had first appeared.

The boy grabbed a sword that had fallen to the ground. He nodded at Maggie and stood, then took up a position to defend them if an attacker came their way. *Brave one.* She concentrated on the wound, her practiced fingers steady as they moved.

She paid no attention as the fighting raged around her and was hardly aware when it fell to just a couple of weapons clanging. As she wiped at the sweat on her brow, she realized blood likely covered the side that had not been muddied earlier, but she didn't care. Some part of her recognized she could not let this man die, and her gut clenched—he reminded her too much of her younger brother, Roland.

When she was confident the wound was sufficiently

stitched and the blood loss had stopped, she took out the small dirk she kept in her bag. She gently sliced off the edge of the sutures, then leaned back on her knees to take in her work and give it a final inspection.

He would be all right; she would just need to get some clean water to wash the gash. Satisfied, she lifted the dirk to assess and wipe it before putting it away, because she always took care to see everything in her bag was kept as clean as possible.

Something rushed her, and she was suddenly soaring backward through the air. The dirk fell from her hands with the force, and her head hit something with a great thud.

Pain exploded in her skull. Blinding white light was all she saw, and then her focus returned. She was choking. Although she reached out to pull the weight off her neck, it was useless.

Maggie stared at her attacker. It was the leader of the first group. Oddly, she noticed his dimple was missing as he throttled her with fury. If she could breathe, she'd laugh at that realization.

His steely eyes were dilated and the most striking blue she'd ever seen, a shade or two lighter than hers. They looked like deceptively peaceful water, beautiful but dangerous. She found herself drowning in them, and then everything went dark.

Chapter Two

Lachlan turned from Nathair's lifeless body to see the fighting was done. He quickly scanned the area and took stock of his men to make sure they were all standing. One was missing. Who?

He cursed. His brother, Malcolm. Lachlan's veins turned to ice — he never should have allowed the lad on this journey. He frantically searched the fallen and found him near a small figure, a boy, leaning over him with a dirk.

Someone was going to kill his brother. Lachlan didn't think, he just ran. Before the boy could bring the knife down, Lachlan had his hand around the murderer's neck and pinned into a nearby tree.

A loud *crack* reverberated as the skull made contact with the trunk. So full of bloodlust, he hardly heard his men calling out for him to stop. Two of them managed to wrestle him to the ground before he could kill the boy. Robbie stood above him and shouted something, but Lachlan couldn't make out the words. He struggled as his men held him down.

"Lachlan. Nae. Stop." He heard but refused to obey.

He tried to get up to finish what he had started, to make sure the murderer would never harm Malcolm again. "Stop," Alan ordered. "He may have saved Malcolm. Ye have to calm down. The lad saved him."

As the words sank in, Lachlan stilled. Alan, Dougal, and Seamus relaxed their hold and allowed him to sit. His fury had been so fierce, it had obviously taken three of his strongest men to take him down.

"This isnae a lad," Finlay chimed in. He stood over the crumpled body.

The well-worn hat lay discarded next to a shoulder.

A girl. Dressed as a man.

Long, jet-black hair had been carefully plaited and pinned up but had fallen free of the silly hat she'd used to conceal the thick braid. Long, delicate fingers and small wrists were exposed beneath the dirty white shirt she wore.

"What do ye mean, Finlay?" Alan jumped up and cautiously ambled over to look at the crumpled figure. "Damn, you're right." He scratched his head then moved in for a closer look.

"She was helping him," Robbie explained as Dougal and Seamus finally let go of Lachlan. He stood and rushed toward his brother.

"Lachlan, ye just tried to kill the lass that saved yer brother's life." He heard Alan but didn't spare a glance in his friend's direction, ignoring the accusation as he leaned over Malcolm to check the sutured wound.

"Did ye hear me, Lachlan?"

He still didn't acknowledge Alan. Malcolm's breathing was relaxed, and his cheeks were still rosy. Lachlan let a whoosh of air from his lungs as relief flooded through him; he would never bring the boy on another mission. Satisfied that Malcolm was still breathing and would recover with no lasting damage, Lachlan finally turned to Alan. "What happened?"

Robbie jumped in with a reply. "Malcolm was down. She popped up from over there"—he pointed to the ditch—"then she ran over and sewed him up. He would have bled out had she not done it."

"I saw a dirk. The boy had a dirk," Lachlan said defensively. He didn't want to believe he had attacked and nearly killed someone who had saved his brother, but Malcolm had been sutured by someone.

"The *lass* was cutting the sutures when ye rushed *her*," Alan said.

With one last glance at his brother to make sure he would be fine, Lachlan reluctantly made his way to the figure on the ground. All the men were gathered around and staring.

"What the hell is she doing dressed as a lad? An English lad, at that," Lachlan scoffed, hoping they were wrong and he had not just attacked an innocent woman.

Damn, it *was* a lass. He'd never seen hair so dark, almost like a raven's wing. She had long lashes and sinfully full lips and was smaller than most of the women of his clan. Her shirtsleeve had been pulled up to reveal a slight hand curled upward, an intricately scrolled metal bracelet circling her tiny wrist. The value of the piece led him to believe she was someone of importance. His gut twisted as guilt assailed him. From the crack of her skull against the tree, he'd not gone easy on her, and she'd be lucky if she would ever be normal again.

"Lachlan, we have to get out of here before anyone else shows up," Alan said.

Glancing around, his gaze studied the open field and well-worn path serving as a road. Movement from the other side of the green and purple expanse caught his attention as a group of blackbirds alighted from the trees as if they had been spooked by something. "Aye, we do. But we cannae just leave her. She'll have to come with us for now." Turning back toward his men, he tilted his head toward the embankment. "Dump the bodies in the ravine. We'll take the horses." Guilt rode him hard—he owed it to her to find her family and see her home safely, but they didn't have the time. "Alan, see to Malcolm. I'll get the lass."

And he needed to get Robbie to safety. His hand rubbed across the leather pouch strapped to his side as he thought of the traitorous words written in Conall's letter. The boy had been through too much already. They wouldn't be safe until he had both back at Kentillie Castle.

Aye, she would have to go with them. *Damn.* Just what he needed right now—to worry about a deceitful lass wearing English trews.

. . .

Riding through the dense, shadowed forest the rest of the afternoon had provided cover from travelers on the main road. Careful of Malcolm's injury and watchful of whether they were followed through the lush greenery left them trotting along at a maddeningly slow pace. When his brother woke, he claimed to be tender where he had been sliced, but showed no signs of anything other than a flesh wound.

Malcolm inspected his sutures and called out to him, "Next time a lass attempts to save me, don't try to kill her. She did a hell of a job."

He flinched. "Ye ken I would never hurt a lass on purpose." If he were being honest, though, he had to admit, "Well, as long as it's not Aileen."

"Will she be all right?" Malcolm's brows drew together.

He looked at the bundle in his arms. Although her face was caked with blood and dirt, she was a bonny lass, even covered in filth and wearing men's clothing. He had the strangest desire to unplait her dark hair and run his fingers through the thick mass.

"I dinnae ken. It was a pretty hard blow." He shook his head as he replayed the scene in his mind. "I had just taken down Nathair when I saw her looming over ye with the knife. I must have been overcome by the fight and not been in my right senses. Looking closely, anyone can tell she is a lass." His gaze fell to the limp form. "I just thought there was a threat to ye and reacted."

"Glad to know ye have my back, brother. She will recover. We'll make sure of it." Malcolm's optimistic tone offered little reassurance.

"Alan was supposed to watch out for ye," he muttered, but not loud enough for anyone to hear. It was an excuse—his friend had been fending off two men when Malcolm was stabbed. In allowing his brother to accompany their party, the blame was all his.

He looked over his shoulder to Alan, who rode several paces behind them, Robbie at his side. The boy had picked up Malcolm's sword and defended him and the wee lass. Where had a boy who had grown up in the care of a priest learned to wield a weapon?

Lachlan turned his attention back to the light weight that fit easily in his arms. Never before had he hit a lass, and the guilt ate at him. She was so small and delicate, and he had not held back when he'd charged her. Even through his enraged fog, he had registered the *thud* of her head hitting the tree. The remembered sound made him wince.

Damn. Why was she dressed as a man? He wanted to shake her for being so foolish. If she had been wearing proper attire, he was sure he'd not have been so rough.

Uncertain such a small woman could recover after what he had done, he nestled the lass to him all afternoon as if his warmth alone could revive her. He had inspected her earlier and felt the bump on the back of her head where it had struck the tree. Some people were never right after a knock that severe. Her head secured up against his chest, he kept it as stable as possible, hoping to minimize any further damage.

She hadn't awoken, and a protective streak he didn't know he possessed kept him holding her close. He prayed she would be whole again. If she wasn't, how would he live with himself or ever compensate her family for their loss? His mistake could also threaten the Camerons—they were not yet back on his land, and the last thing he needed was a war with another clan.

...

Maggie woke on a crude pallet to a pounding head. She was staring up at dark, massive trees looming over her. Just a hint of sunlight was left in the sky. Everything was grainy and unfocused, and it took her a few moments to figure out she wasn't dreaming.

She sat up quickly and wished she hadn't. Pain screamed through her head, and nausea clawed at her belly. She rolled over and swayed a little, but before she could topple over, a strong hand wrapped around her and another stroked her back in a gesture likely meant to be comforting.

It worked. She wanted to let them caress her until the pain went away. The tender touch was the only thing that felt good right now, the only part of her that didn't ache.

Hearing the constant hum of nearby water behind her, she cautiously turned to glimpse lush hues of green with the warm brown bases of towering trees, and it took her a moment to focus. The hands holding her were connected to the man with blue eyes, a mountain of a man almost twice her size. Her hand went to her throat where his hands had strangled her. He had not killed her? She'd been certain he would. Eyes widening, she jerked back, trying to shrink away, but a new wave of pain assaulted her.

Where was she, and why was this man still here? "Are ye going to kill me?"

Her throat was scratchy and hoarse; she sounded like someone else. She shrugged out of his grasp and slowly turned to sit without help. The man had tried to kill her, and yet his hands attempted to calm and reassure her. What kind of idiot was she? She needed to distance herself until she understood what he was doing. Despite craving the soothing touch, she shrank farther away.

"Nae. I didnae intend to harm ye, lass. I thought ye were trying to kill my brother." He sank down beside her, and his hand rose to gently touch her neck. She would have pulled away, but the blue currents in his eyes eased her fear. "Please ken I didnae do this on purpose," the man pleaded. His forehead crinkled slightly as a sad smile quirked his lips.

"Who is yer brother?" she asked. Everything was fuzzy, and she was so tired. Struggling to remember the details made her head ache more. The effort it took to keep her eyes open was overwhelming, and she wanted to lie back down. Nae, she couldn't go back to sleep. She blinked, hoping to clear the haze. It didn't help.

A glance around told her she was in a small clearing in a dense forest, surrounded by a group of the largest men she had ever seen. Other than the man who had tried to kill her and the lad who had guarded her with the sword, she didn't recognize any of them.

"Ye mended him during the skirmish. I saw ye with a dirk and thought ye were going to hurt him." His head dipped, and he frowned. How did he manage to look so intriguing and so contrite at the same time?

A memory dislodged of being bent over a young man as she mended the flesh where a sword had sliced his side. If this man had not known what she'd been doing, she could have appeared threatening. A long-ago image of Robert Ferguson throwing a rock at her brother's cheek emerged. She had charged Robert, knocked him to the ground, and started swinging before her father had pulled her off the much older boy.

Understanding dawned. She nodded, and the relief reflected in his eyes convinced her that he meant no harm.

"Where are we?" She attempted to wave her hand in a circular pattern to indicate the shadowed glade, but her movements were languid and awkward. Her arm barely managed to rise at all. Burning in the clearing was a small cook fire only giving slightly more light than the disappearing sun, but she saw nothing that looked familiar.

"On our way to Kentillie Castle. Ye were out, and we didnae ken how to get ye home. We couldnae leave ye, and we couldnae stay."

When his hands curled around hers, she didn't pull back, and her gaze traveled to where they were joined. His big, callused hands, which had previously been wrapped around her neck, were now impossibly comforting. She should be terrified of him and didn't try to analyze the irony as the thought flitted through her head.

"Home…" she said, testing the word on her tongue.

They hadn't taken her home. They were taking her somewhere else. Despite her confusion, a spark ignited somewhere in the fog, and hope lightened her chest—she wasn't being returned to the keep.

He must have taken her reaction as fear, because he continued quickly, "I promise we will return ye to yer home as soon as we can." His earnest blue eyes were mesmerizing, but what had he said? He was going to take her home.

She tensed and could feel whatever color was left drain from her face. *Nae.* That's not what she wanted. She wanted to go anywhere but home. The convent…aye…she'd been on her way there.

"What direction are we headed?"

"North."

The breath she'd been holding whooshed out. She had no idea where they were, but at least she was headed the right way. Away. And that was a start.

"Can I have some water?" she croaked as she gently fingered her neck.

"Aye, I'll get ye some, lass. What's yer name?" he asked as he rose.

She was so focused on what she had to do next, she answered automatically. "Maggie."

Then her senses came to her. Och, she couldn't tell him who she was. No one defied her father, the powerful Duke of Kirk, and no matter how she protested, this man would march her back to the keep once he learned her identity.

While he was gone, she formulated a plan—she would forget where she was from. Only her family called her Maggie, and everyone would be looking for Margaret. With her head injury, no one would ever know she wasn't telling the truth.

These men circled the camp as if they expected another band to attack at any moment, yet not a one made a move she could construe as threatening; the boy had even protected her during the skirmish. Mayhap she could find a convent near their home, or better yet, just blend in with their clan and start over. Her head was starting to feel better already. She was saved.

The leader handed her a cup of water, and her fingers brushed his as they made the exchange. They were long and lean to match the rest of his sculpted physique. An unexpected shiver ran through her at the touch.

She must have lingered too long, because he cleared his throat, and she pulled back abruptly and caught his gaze, a subtle hint of interest buried deep in his eyes. Whether it was for her as a woman, or he was just curious about how to get rid of her, she wasn't sure.

She rubbed at her face and noticed something on it. Och—clumps of crusted mud from the embankment covered her hand. She must look awful.

"And what is yer name, sir?" Her voice sounded so formal and cold. She wanted to cringe at the words as soon as she said them, it was so unlike her. Mayhap it was her reaction to his touch, which had oddly made her body respond in a way that puzzled her. She shook her head, hoping to forget the warmth it had evoked.

His brow quirked, and she saw a shadow of a smile. That intriguing dimple hid just below the surface. "Lachlan" rolled off his tongue and washed over her.

It figured he would be named for the lochs that matched those blue eyes. Nae, she was wrong. Those eyes put the waters of Scotland to shame. She'd never seen anything more beautiful.

Damn, she was staring, and she was having strange stirrings again. It was probably a good thing she was caked in mud and wearing boy's clothing, and she prayed the grime hid her blush.

"Who's yer clan, Maggie?"

She was not ready to answer that yet.

When she opened her mouth nothing came out, and he studied her intently. Oh, God, she hadn't thought it through—she was not good at lying. Her inability to keep an impassive face was why her brothers always let her play games with them. She was an open book, her emotions and thoughts always evident in her expressions for the whole world to see.

She bit her lip, and her eyes shifted down. He would likely know she wasn't being completely honest, but she couldn't look him in the face. "Everything is so fuzzy." After a swallow she peeked up at him. "I think 'tis my head." Mayhap he wouldn't confront her if he thought it was his fault. It was cruel to play off his chivalry, but it was the only option she had.

His pupils flashed and eyes narrowed. His jaw hardened, and his dimple was nowhere to be seen. He knew, all right. Why had she never learned to lie? She took the only path open to her and changed the subject.

"You're wounded. If ye have my bag, I can look at it." The ploy didn't seem to work, because he continued to appraise her with suspicion.

"'Tis a scratch," he said coolly.

His gaze cut through her, and she felt cornered, about to break, until she thought of the one thing that might distract him. "I need to see to yer brother's wound as well, and it needs to be washed. If it doesnae heal properly, he could come down with an infection."

It was the truth, and he must have recognized it, because his appraisal of her lightened as his eyes warmed and he called out, "Finlay. Where is the satchel the lass had?"

A man almost as formidable and almost as attractive as Lachlan—Finlay, she assumed—appeared at her side holding her bag. He avoided her gaze and gently set it by her side as his face flushed. He looked at her through lowered lids then nodded before he walked away. Finlay must be shy around women.

"Malcolm." Lachlan interrupted her thoughts. "Maggie is going to inspect yer wound."

The man she'd tended earlier sat down so close to her, he could have almost been in her lap. He grinned and winked at her as she pulled up the edge of his shirt. Unlike Finlay, he didn't seem to have the same qualms about a woman's attention.

One of the men set a bucket of warm water, a cup, and some rags down beside them. Scooping some of the liquid out, she poured it over her hands until the water ran clear. She repeated it with another cupful to be certain they were sufficiently clean, and because the warm fluid was soothing.

While she inspected the sutures, she glanced up at Lachlan, who still watched her with distrustful eyes, and she had the urge to hide behind his smiling brother when she asked, "What clan are ye from?"

"We're the Camerons," Malcolm answered while Lachlan's gaze openly examined her. "Lachlan is our laird."

So she had been correct in her assessment—he had the bearing and temperament of a leader, including his ability to judge people. No wonder he knew she was lying.

"Then ye were just traveling through?" She directed the question to Malcolm this time, then reached down and dipped a cloth into the water.

"Aye, we took my cousin to Edinburgh, and we're on the way home." She liked this man. Before, he might have reminded her of her younger brother, but now she saw some of her eldest in him.

"And who were the men that attacked ye? They seemed to know ye." She dabbed the wet, warm cloth over the wound.

Silence met her question. She glanced back over to the man whose gaze she'd been trying to avoid. He shook his head.

It didn't bother her. They had their secrets, and she had hers. Pushing for answers might be a mistake, so she put the rag down and continued her work.

After seeing to Malcolm, she turned to the man who had loomed over her when he wasn't pacing or studying her intently. He appeared tense and on edge, and she struggled with how she would reach across the impenetrable distance between them. If she didn't put him at ease, and soon, his scrutiny might cause her to stumble and confess more than she wanted.

"Come, Lachlan, sit. Let me look at yer wound," she said as she motioned for him to take the place Malcolm had vacated.

He silently did as she commanded. She reached to pull his sleeve up. When her hand gently touched his arm as she grabbed the cuff, he flinched. Oh, he really didn't trust her. She reached to grasp the cloth and dipped it in the water, then wrung it out again—anything to keep at bay the urge she had to confess all.

Once she had steeled her resolve, she returned her gaze to see his breathing had become heavy and his pupils were dilated. It was an odd reaction. She didn't feel mistrusted— she felt like prey, like he wanted to devour her. Mayhap her mind was still foggy from the knock to her head, and she misinterpreted his response. Water dripped down her wrist as she held her hands palm up and said, "Yer wound is too high up on yer arm. I cannae look at it with yer shirt in the way."

In one swift move, he pulled the garment off and raked her with burning eyes. The wet rag fell into her lap. A wave of dizziness rushed at her, but she wasn't sure if it was from his proximity or her pounding head. The air turned warm, and she swiped at her brow with the sleeve of her shirt. Some of the dirt flaked off, and she was reminded how pitiful she must look. She swallowed hard.

Muscles rippled as he held his arm out for her inspection. Her hands trembled, but she mustered up what nerve she could and inspected his cut. It appeared clean enough to not need washing; either his shirt had protected it or he'd cleaned it himself before she woke.

"'Tis no' so bad. I dinnae think it would have even needed sutures," she said as her fingers rubbed against his taut skin.

"I've had worse." Tension left his shoulders as he watched her hands glide across his arm while she rubbed ointment on the wound.

She continued, "Ye were lucky 'twas only a small cut."

"Nae," he grunted, but it sounded more like a growl. "'Twas no' luck. 'Twas skill."

Och, she'd wounded his pride. "Ye handled yerself well against so many." Confidence radiated in the slow smile he turned her way, and she saw why these men would follow him, because the pride and knowledge that flowed through his words indicated he indeed knew how to engage in combat and win.

He must have seen the appreciation in her eyes, because his gaze moved from her head to her feet in a slow perusal. Her pulse quickened, and her skin heated.

She had to get herself together. This man who had scrutinized her with wariness just moments earlier now stared at her with a lazy, hooded look, as if he wanted to lay her down and take her right here. The bump to her head must be worse than she had first imagined.

"What of yer head?" The fingers of his free hand forked into the loose weave of her braid and gently brushed the tender spot as if she were a flower whose petals were on the verge of falling off. Fire ignited in her breast, and she found it hard to breathe as his gaze returned to hers with what she believed might be genuine concern.

"'Twill be fine." Somehow, she managed to get the words out, but the breathless, raspy reply shocked her. "I have some herbs I can use as a tea. It should help."

He pulled back and broke the spell. "Dougal, can ye fetch the lass more hot water for her tea?"

She busied herself putting away the salve and retrieving a bandage, but a strange hum continued to vibrate through her limbs, making her movements clumsy. She cursed silently; she was never awkward.

Bandaging him up was pure torture. She tried to avoid looking at the broad expanse of his chest, the muscles that rippled and the tautness of his belly, but she couldn't dodge the trace of his sensual, earthy male smell, which hung in the space between them.

While she worked, he spoke to the man who had been riding beside him in the field. Then his gaze strayed over to Malcolm and to watch the boy who had taken the protective stance over her during the battle. The lad had the same regal bearing she'd noticed in Lachlan. "'Tis yer son?"

"Robbie?"

Lachlan looked too young to be the father of someone on the verge of becoming a man, but the protective way he watched the boy made her question her judgment. She nodded as she covered the wound with a clean cloth.

"Nae. He's just a boy in need of a home." His dimple appeared as he observed his friend show Robbie how to light a fire in the middle of the makeshift camp they had made.

"Yer friend is good with him." She remembered overhearing talk in the kitchen about Conall beating a lost boy he'd found in the woods merely for asking directions. A shiver ran down her spine. Lachlan didn't seem to notice as he continued to smile at the pair. These men were nothing like that monster.

"Aye, Alan lost his parents young, too. My parents took him in."

"Do ye make a habit of taking in strangers?" she teased and smiled. It was the first time since waking she'd felt at ease.

"Aye, it does appear as if I have developed a distasteful habit." His eyes returned to hers. He smirked, then looked down to her hand, which still rested on his arm. She hadn't even realized she had lingered too long, but touching him gave her an odd sense of safety. It took some effort, but she slowly pulled her hand back into her lap to discover the wet cloth dampening her trews.

"See? 'Twas just a scratch." He pulled his arm away quickly, almost as if he was purposely putting as much distance between them as he could, but mayhap she had read him wrong. It was just her head, nothing more.

The thrumming in her ears continued when she settled back to pull the herbs needed for tea from her bag. While Lachlan asked her about the mixture, she tossed the rag back into the bucket.

Moments later, she sipped a tea made of a mix of herbs she had thought might help with the relentless throbbing in her head. As she drank the pain lessened, and she did her best to answer his probing questions, but a sleepy, contented fog washed over her.

Maggie tried to stay alert, to make sure she didn't slip and tell him who she was, but she could barely hold her eyes open. Before she knew it, she'd set the cup down and rested her head on her hands. Surprisingly, although she was surrounded by men she barely knew, she allowed a deep sleep to claim her.

. . .

As he sat on the ground near her, Lachlan analyzed his conversations with Maggie for any clues to whom she might be. After she'd bandaged his scratch, her small hand had lingered on his arm, and he had been tempted to invent other injuries so she would touch him in other places. He had fought the urge.

He'd had worse wounds and had done nothing for them, but if she could relax and become comfortable with him, she might open up about who she was. It had worked until his reaction to her touch startled her. She then sat back and swirled some dried leaves into her drink.

He wrinkled his nose at the concoction she drank. "Och, it smells like wet grass."

"'Tis no' so bad," she said.

"What is it?"

"The herb is called meadowsweet. It should help my head." She blew at the steam.

"How did ye learn healing?" he asked.

"My mother and grandmother taught me." She smiled and sat up straighter.

"How did they ken it?"

"My grandma is from Ireland. I dinnae know when it started. She learned from her ma. 'Twas just always that way."

He found it refreshing she had been honest with him. He liked how easy she was to read, despite half her face being obscured with grime. She was probably bonny under all of it.

Her eyes lit, and she smiled. "Freedom," she whispered.

He cocked his head, then followed her gaze to see what she was looking at. It was the horses.

"Is one of them yers?"

"Aye, the brown one with the star. I thought he was gone when the fighting started."

He studied the animal. The white mark on its face did look like a star, which meant the horse was easily identifiable.

He had glanced back to Maggie and was surprised to see she was swaying with fatigue. He scooped her into his arms and looked down, but her eyes were already shut. "Is Maggie yer real name?"

She nodded and snuggled into his arm. Her expression was relaxed, and he could see her reserve slip away. "Who is yer clan?" This time she didn't answer. All the tension had left her body, and she was gone to the world.

As Lachlan laid Maggie on a pallet on the ground, he ran his fingers through her loosely woven braid to inspect the knot again. It was still there, and she flinched in her sleep when he touched it. His sister, Kirstie, had slept for days once when she'd fallen and hit her head. The overpowering helplessness he'd been forced to endure while he'd waited for her to heal had left its mark on him. A wave of guilt mixed with a strong need to protect this lass washed over him.

After Maggie was secured neatly under a wool blanket, he sought out Dougal. "First thing in the morn, take this horse and see if someone recognizes it."

"Why this one?" Dougal scratched his head.

"It belongs to Maggie. If we find the owner, I'll be able to get her home."

"Aye," Dougal said.

"Despite our slow pace, we covered a good distance, but if ye go back tomorrow, ye can catch up to us in a day or two."

After speaking with Dougal, Lachlan claimed a spot on the ground near Maggie and watched Robbie, who rubbed at the cross around his neck as if it were some magic key that would bring back everything he had lost. Maggie wasn't the only one keeping secrets. The lad, wise beyond his years, had an awareness in his eyes, and if he'd not found the boy crying over the corpse of the priest with the church still burning nearby, Lachlan might have even questioned his story of being raised by the religious man. Sure, he was well educated, but there was more to him than the lad was willing to share.

He ran his fingers over his sporran with the letter ensconced safely inside. Another puzzle to be solved. If he was lucky, the missive would be enough to condemn Conall in the eyes of the other chiefs and bring the bastard to justice without having to use the lad's unfortunate connection to the blackguard. In fact, 'twas best Conall not ken where the boy was, and even better if Robbie could avoid being called in front of a council of men to relive the horrific sights he'd seen.

When they'd stumbled on Conall in Edinburgh and Robbie had accused him of murder, the man's eyes had blazed with a bone-chilling hatred. Lachlan shook the image from his head. Robbie was now with the Camerons, and there was no better person to watch over him than Alan. The boy was safe for now.

Chapter Three

Opening her eyes, Maggie listened as birds chattered in the towering pines and oaks while the first rays of light peeked through the moss-covered branches. Morning came too soon. Maggie's head still hurt, but not as badly. Wiping the sleep out of her eyes, her fingers rubbed speckles of blood and muck from her face. She needed to wash—she must look like a sow. The burble of a stream nearby was tempting, and a quick glance told her the men still slept, so she decided to go clean herself and be back in time to break the fast. From the steady gurgling, she guessed it wouldn't be much of a walk.

She slipped out from under a warm woolen blanket someone had draped over her and tiptoed toward the soothing rumble of the rushing water. When she came upon a river and not a small babbling brook, she was delighted—she could wade out and wash her body, too. She was sticky and sweaty and would welcome the cool wetness. Unfortunately, she would have to make it quick, before anyone thought to come looking for her.

She undressed and waded out into the river. The glorious

water slid over her skin, and gooseflesh rose on her arms, waking her senses. Peace filled her as she washed the grime from her face and body.

All the fuss over her imminent marriage had been drowning her, threatening to pull her into a deep sea of misery. If not a death sentence, then she had been given a life term of miserable confinement and torture when her father had pledged her to Conall. The man had promised her just as much on his unwelcome visits over the past few years.

Although she had been able to delay the wedding until her twenty-first year, due to her mother's death, there was only so much time her selfish family would give her to grieve. She had tried to tell them what a snake Conall was, but they would not budge. Just like they'd treated her poor mother with disregard, they didn't care what happened to her as long as they had everything they wanted.

Thus her decision to join a convent. If she pledged her life to God, no man could force her to do his bidding ever again. She had always loved her Catholic faith, and if she couldn't have a happy home, at least at a nunnery she would have a safe one.

She was on her way north. She was free. This would be a new start for her, and there was nothing to fear.

· · ·

Waking at first light, when Dougal had taken Maggie's horse and set out on his mission, Lachlan stayed where he was and contemplated his next steps. Lying on his back, he studied the gently swaying canopy overhead as he thought on how best to protect Robbie and expose Conall's plot. He had come to the conclusion the lad would need to be hidden away, and the knowledge of the letter's contents would be best shared among other Royalist lairds, who had an interest in ensuring the Highlands weren't forced to bend to the will of the Earl of Argyll. The earl might be laird to the Campbells, but he didn't speak for the rest of the Highland chiefs.

Motion caught his eyes as Maggie left her bed and wandered off. He frowned, tossed off the blanket, and hastily dressed.

A branch cracking beneath her foot gave her position away, and he moved to trail her. The lass was not to be trusted, but neither were these woods, as he wasn't certain whose land they were on. They might be somewhere between the Murrays' and the Macnabs' territories. Both clans were friendly enough, but his band still could have been followed.

Maggie didn't notice she was being watched as he walked several paces behind her through the trees. He told himself he had followed the deceitful lass not knowing what she was up to. Now he questioned his motives. Did he just want to get her alone? Damn his cursed male parts for not listening to his head.

As she stepped to the edge of the river, she reached for the end of her braid and unwound the binding she had there. Her hands went to work unplaiting her hair. Long, dark tresses fell free from the loose weave, and she ran her fingers through the length of it while he imagined his hands fisting in the silky strands and pulling her full lips to his. Closing his eyes, he shook his head to dislodge the wayward image.

As his lids opened and gaze returned to her, Maggie scanned her surroundings quickly. Then in a blur, she pulled off her boots, shirt, and breeches and ran for the water. Lachlan's mouth fell open, and his treacherous cock jumped as he took in the curves the oversize boy's clothing had hidden so well.

Her head disappeared beneath the surface before he'd had time to register what the lass had just done. Was she insane? They were God knew where and she didn't know any of his men. Who in their right mind would bathe naked near a band of strangers?

When she emerged from the water, it was as if she had been transformed by a sprite. Her black tresses clung to her shoulders and back, and the water came just above her waist. She swam out farther, and he considered giving her privacy. But when she resurfaced, he thought better of it. She needed him for protection. What if some real stranger came along? Oh, damn, was she safe from him?

It wouldn't hurt to peek. To ensure no one was lurking about watching her, of course. Besides, she had invited his attentions by sneaking away.

She turned about, her face no longer coated with grime, and he noticed for the first time how truly bonny she was. He had suspected her to be fair, but he stood mesmerized. She was lovelier than any lass he had ever seen.

She put Aileen's beauty to shame, but he had learned the hard way that looks meant nothing without trust, and Maggie had lied to him last night. She could use some lessons from Aileen, because she'd not even been able to look him in the eyes as she spoke.

Just what he needed in his midst—another beautiful, devious woman. He chided himself and started to walk away when he noticed something floating in the river. A massive log glided downstream straight toward the lass, and she had no idea. Damn, he had to do something—he couldn't be responsible for her becoming injured again. She was going to know he had been watching her, but if he didn't warn her now, she wouldn't be able to get out of the way in time.

"Maggie!" he shouted as he ran toward the bank. She looked over at him, startled, then attempted to cover her bare shoulders by sinking down farther into the fast-moving water. A little late for modesty.

"Och, can ye no give me some privacy?"

"Ye have to move," he yelled louder.

"Go away," she scowled.

"Look behind ye, lass." She turned and her eyes grew large, then she shrieked and started to wade toward him.

She slipped on something and went under.

* * *

Maggie burst up through the water and pushed toward the shore. She looked back to see if she had made any progress, but she was still in the path of the ominous-looking object rushing toward her.

Just a little farther. Swimming would be faster than wading, and she leaned into the water and kicked, stroking faster than she ever had. She paddled right into Lachlan's waiting arms, his body wrapping around hers as he pulled her closer to land. Her breath was ragged and shallow from the exertion, but the warmth of him chased away the chill of her fear.

"Thank ye," she rasped out before her senses came back to her. She had made it to safety. But had she? Flowing water continued to glide across her ankles, but the rest of her was naked and vulnerable with a man who only the day before had tried to kill her.

"Are ye mad, lass?" The disapproval in his voice caught her off guard. He was rigid, and she peered up to see a gaze that danced with flames. Och, he was fuming, but then his eyes softened and tone lightened. "Ye could have been hurt. Someone else might have found ye."

He then searched the shore, but the only thing she saw were thick trees standing sentinel and the vibrant violets of thorny thistle bushes dotting the bank. A flush ran through her—he had been watching her. Now her own blood heated with embarrassment. She started to pull away, then she changed her mind and quickly circled her arms around him.

As soon as he let go of her and backed up, he would see her in a way no man ever had before. Why hadn't she just washed her face and gone back to the camp?

"Were ye spying on me?" She risked a glance up only to be met with his chin as he stared off in the distance.

"I followed ye," he stated smugly, with no hint of remorse.

"Why?"

"I dinnae trust ye." His head tilted down, and she was met with an unyielding stare.

Aye, that stung. But she had not been honest with him. "That doesnae give ye the right to watch me while I bathe." She pinned him with all the exasperation she could muster, because it was easier than to admit he'd wounded her pride.

"I was concerned for yer safety." His gaze softened.

She'd bet he was.

His arms stayed wrapped around her, and his hands were hot on her chilled skin. She turned her face down so that he wouldn't see the blush she imagined crept up her cheeks. Chill bumps erupted on her arms and legs, and her breasts tingled as they pressed against his shirt.

"We should get back," he said, but his voice was deeper and strained. When she looked back up at him, he avoided her gaze. She could feel his heart beating fast—or was that her own? Or was he repulsed by her?

"If ye let go, ye will see me," she whispered. The words were hoarse and throaty, and she hardly recognized her own voice. Mayhap her head was still reeling from the blow yesterday, because her knees were suddenly weak and unresponsive to her command for them to move. Wobbly, as if she would fall any minute, and he was the only person who could catch her.

"What if I want to see you?" he rumbled.

She gasped, and something in her chest fluttered. His gaze had returned to her, and his eyes were dilated and glazed over. She'd seen the same look in her brothers' eyes as they'd evaluated women—he was appraising her in the way a man would when he wanted to take a woman to bed. She looked away.

His hand skimmed up her back and left a trail of sinful sparks in its wake. His fingers splayed through her wet hair and cradled the base of her skull. Chills ran through the length of her body as he pulled back on her head to force eye contact. His blue eyes were mesmerizing, and she imagined drowning in their watery depths. She moistened her dry lips with her tongue, and he groaned.

"I'm going to kiss ye," he warned as his mouth came crushing down on hers.

Fire seared her. It was alarming but exciting at the same time. His tongue jutted out and delved into her mouth, and she gasped in surprise. It was totally unexpected and sent shivers down her spine. She tentatively reached out with her tongue and was instantly rewarded as he pulled her body in closer to his masculine frame. She was lost to the thrill of her first kiss.

He pulled back and seared her with penetrating eyes, desire pulsating in his gaze. Without warning, his stare turned distant. What had she done? As if being near her made him uncomfortable, he moved away and spun around so quickly she almost lost her balance. He didn't even try to get a view of her naked body.

The loss of his heat made her shiver. His rejection stung, but that was all right, because she would never have let him into her heart. No man would ever take from her what her mother had given to her uncaring father.

While he strode farther into the trees, Lachlan called over his shoulder, "Get dressed and return to camp. We need to be on our way."

As soon as he was out of sight, Maggie yanked on her clothes. The moldering smell of the dirty rags assailed her, but she had nothing else—these would have to do. Once she got to the convent, she would be trading them in for robes.

Her fingers rose to trace her tingling, swollen lips. How would she manage in a confined place like that after Lachlan had awoken her to the enjoyment of a man's touch? Her body still thrummed, and her knees were weak. His rebuff hurt more than she cared to admit.

Aye, she'd been told her whole life she was a beauty, but mayhap all the men who asked for her hand were only interested in alliances and hadn't been honest. She had hoped some of them might have seen her for herself as a woman, but now she doubted all their words.

She plopped down to pull on her shoes.

I amnae completely naive. Need had shown in Lachlan's eyes, and for a moment he'd lost himself in her, but he must have decided he had nothing to gain and had pulled back— she wouldn't further his position, so she was useless. With a curse, she picked up a stone and threw it into the water.

The corners of her mouth turned up as a thought bloomed. Why not lie with him while she still had an opportunity? Her body had never reacted so strongly to a man, and she wanted to experience the pleasure her mother had told her of before she gave her life to God. He would be perfect. He wanted nothing but to get rid of her, so didn't that make him the best kind of bed partner? And if she slept with Lachlan, should Conall catch up to her, mayhap he wouldn't want her, as she wouldn't be pure. Another reason to invite Lachlan into her bed.

But he'd pushed her away. Men seemed so fickle, with their affections and moods that changed as often as the weather.

'Twas better this way. She seemed to so easily lose her mind around Lachlan, which could get her into more trouble than she could handle. Her only goal should be getting to the convent as quickly as possible, although she needed him on her side to keep her safe from Conall.

. . .

Lachlan cursed himself as he stomped back to the camp. Maggie was a siren, and he had been trapped in her spell. Her beauty had bewitched him, and what was worse, he had allowed her seduction even knowing she was lying to him. Damn, it was Aileen all over, only more disastrous, as his body yearned for Maggie in a way it never had for Aileen. He had to stay away from her, because he couldn't go through the pain and humiliation again. He didn't even know who she was. Och, he was a fool.

He readjusted his cock. It was still stiff as stone and ached with a throbbing need for release. If he'd not come to his senses, he might have taken her standing at the edge of the water. In fact, his cock begged him to go back and do so now, but his head disagreed. What was he going to do?

If she stayed with his clan, he wasn't sure he would be able to resist those blue eyes and the full lips that had so eagerly parted to let him in. There was only so much temptation he could resist. Maggie had to go before he made more mistakes he would regret. Currently, she was untouched and her family could make a good match for her, but he wouldn't be able to keep his hands off her for long. The faster she was sent home, the sooner he would come back to his senses.

She must be a spy of some sort. Why else would she have appeared when she did, to save them and gain the confidence of him and his men? And she had shown an unusual interest in Robbie. If she were one of Conall's spies, the boy could be in danger.

Once she had fallen asleep, he had checked her bag for weapons and not found anything inside that appeared dangerous. But poison was a woman's weapon, and he didn't have the knowledge to analyze all the herbs and small bottles of liquid she had tucked away. He would have to watch her closely when she mixed up whatever concoctions she was making.

Shaking his head, he knew he couldn't fault the men for the appreciative glances aimed her way when she returned to the clearing. Her midnight-colored hair was down, still wet and clinging to her as she swayed seductively into their midst. Her shirt was slick with water from her swim and hugged her body, showing off her curves. He had held those curves in his hands and wanted to again, but she might be the enemy. Every eye was on her, but she didn't notice, because she fixated on him. His groin tightened at the thought, but he quickly squashed down the lust.

Mouths watering, his men gaped. Judging from their reaction to her, there was not a chance in hell he could keep them away if he didn't secure her by his side. His fists clenched and urged him to knock sense into them. Although Lachlan was hesitant to be near this bonny but dishonest female, if he did not keep her close, one of his men would take her and might spill all the clan's secrets—something he could not allow, given the letter in his possession. Spy or not, she was his.

No one else would lay their hands on the pale flesh he could still feel under his fingertips. Still tasting her on his tongue, honey and innocence, he growled as his men continued to ogle her. Damn, why did she have to be so comely?

Maggie looked at him with penetrating sapphire eyes that beckoned him to touch and taste her. They seared him and heated his blood. If he didn't know any better, he would think she wanted him, that she was skilled in the art of seduction. That couldn't be true. The way she trembled in his arms spoke of someone terrified of being in a vulnerable position with another. She had returned his kiss in the water, but it was unskilled, leading him to believe she had never been kissed before.

Spy or innocent, he was guided by his values and honor to protect her until she could be returned safely. Especially after his rough treatment of her—faint bruises marked her neck where he had nearly… God, he did not want to think about what he had nearly done to her.

A male form swaggered toward her, and Lachlan's shoulders tensed. As Finlay, the shyest man of his group, blushed and drooled over Maggie when he held out a trencher filled with cheese and bread, Lachlan found his own breathing deepen and his chest tighter. She accepted the proffered plate and smiled at his cousin. Her eyes lit, and Finlay reached out to pat her arm as Lachlan ground his teeth. Bashful or no', the man would be one of the group he sent to find her clan.

Next to saunter up to her was his brother, then the rest. Suddenly she had an audience. The only ones who stayed away were Alan, Robbie, and Seamus, the lone married man in the bunch. They all still watched her, though.

"Enough," he called. The startled men took a step back and riveted their gazes on him, while Malcolm studied him, perplexed.

What had the wench done to him? He'd never before lost his senses over a woman. For Christ's sake, he was bothered that his men were just looking at her.

After clearing his throat loudly, he said, "Time to be on our way," his words clipped. The men gathered around her quickly dispersed, although Alan grinned and gave Lachlan a defiant smile. The bastard knew he desired her. Of course, after his outburst they would all know, while he hadn't yet had time to analyze the strange emotions swirling in his head. He did, however, understand the ones that caused his shaft to tighten and ache.

"Alan," he called. Once his friend strode up, he pulled

him over to the side and muttered, "Keep an eye on her."

His friend's brow rose. "Ye want her."

Lachlan caught the man's arm as he turned to go. "Dinnae let anyone touch her." Alan just winked and gave him a mischievous, lopsided grin. They had been friends far too long, and Alan knew him better than he knew himself—Lachlan was staking a claim on her whether he'd intended to or no'. It was the last thing he needed, but he couldn't stand back and watch his men become infatuated with her. Clan Cameron was in a precarious position, and he couldn't afford any wagging tongues loosened by lust. Aye, that was the reason for his agitation.

"Finlay, Gillies, come." He grabbed a satchel and tramped into the woods without looking to see if they followed, because none would question their laird. "Double back and find where she came from. She doesnae belong here with us. Either she is a spy, or her clan will be looking for her. We need to know the truth."

The men nodded, and Lachlan continued, "Start with the Macnabs, then the MacLarens, and branch out from there. She was on Macnab land when we found her. She's well educated. Someone will ken who she is." He didn't have to remind them how bonny she was.

"They all support the Royalists, so we have nothing to fear from her." Finlay's relieved tone gave Lachlan the impression his cousin had already developed a fondness for the wench. "Should we tell their chiefs of the letter?"

"Nae, 'twould be best coming from me, along with an invitation to Kentillie. I will arrange a meeting to discuss how we should proceed. Argyll's support to weaken King Charles's reign is strengthening—Conall is a prime example of the traitorous bastards—and I fear the earl's drive to push his beliefs on the rest of our country is growing. Our best chance at squashing their efforts will require caution."

"Do ye think the Macnabs and MacLarens can be trusted?" Gillies asked.

"Aye, but best ye dinnae tell anyone Maggie is with us, not until we ken she isnae a threat."

"I dinnae see her as a danger. She saved yer brother," Finlay continued to defend the lass.

"Aye, but she could also be a Covenanter spy. Mayhap Conall's spy. She came out of nowhere when Nathair showed up." The swirling doubt in his own mind was echoed by Gillies's words.

"Do ye think Conall will send more men?" Finlay asked.

"Aye, he will be looking for Robbie, along with his letter. Did ye see the menace in his eyes when the boy identified him?"

"Aye, 'tis the only safe place for him, being with the Camerons. At least until Conall's dead or rotting in prison," Gillies said.

"He'll have noticed by now Nathair is missing." Finlay said.

"That is why I want both of ye to go. There is safety in numbers. Be careful where ye ask questions. Ye never know who is listening." Lachlan paced as he gave his instructions.

"What if our activities are questioned?" Finlay asked.

"Take this." Lachlan tossed a bag to him. The cousin they had escorted to Edinburgh a few days earlier conveniently provided them an excuse. "It's some of Fiona's things she was sending to her sister. It can be a ruse to give ye reason to travel back through the area. Ye can say some of her belongings got mixed in with ours, and ye needed to return to Edinburgh to give it to her."

"Didnae ye send Dougal to find Maggie's family?"

"I only sent him to ask who owned her horse. He's just to say he found it wandering and nothing of her. I dinnae think he will be recognized, anyway. He was not with us when we came upon the letter or during the altercation." Lachlan shook his hand out. His knuckles were still bruised from the punch he'd landed on Conall's jaw.

"We will take care," Gillies said.

"And take only horses from our stables. Ye don't need to be seen on any of Conall's." They turned to walk back to the camp, and Lachlan continued, "Return as quickly as ye can." He wasn't certain how long his resolve would hold out. Maggie was a distraction he didn't have time for, especially as his clan became increasingly mired in politics.

He not only had an obligation to protect Robbie—he was sworn to the Catholic Royalists. If he was able to thwart Conall's plan to align with Argyll, he might be able to stop the fanatical Covenanters from forcing their religion on others. King Charles shouldn't have tried to impose Catholicism on the Covenanters, but he didn't see that his oppression had sparked their movement. There would be war soon if something couldn't be done, and the last thing he wanted was to send his men to fight.

Nae, the bonny Maggie, with curves his fingers itched to feel again and innocent lips that had been sweet and willing, was a diversion he didn't need and couldn't afford. Neither could his clan.

Chapter Four

After returning to the glade, Maggie let her gaze drift to Lachlan. But he took one look at her and, as if nothing had happened between them, turned away and strode off through the thick green shrubbery and lavender heather into the opposite woods with two of his men.

"Why does he find me offensive?" Maggie asked, discouraged, when Alan came to stand beside her.

"Ye misread him, dear lass." Alan laughed, his eyes twinkling with mirth.

"How so?" Lachlan's changing currents of emotions had utterly perplexed her.

"'Tis no' ye he finds offensive. 'Tis the thought of a beautiful woman, which fortunately or unfortunately for ye, puts ye into the untrustworthy wench category."

This man only confused her more. Maggie's head quirked to the side. "Why?" she asked.

"Lachlan overheard his betrothed plotting his murder. She was a bonny lass he had known all his life. Now he doesnae trust women. But he wants ye. I can see it. He's trying to deny it, but we all saw it just now."

"What did ye see? I see him avoiding me like a leper." Her gaze wandered restlessly to the woods where he'd disappeared.

"In his own way, he just warned us all to stay away from ye." Alan laughed harder. She didn't see anything humorous in the matter. "Watch yerself, lass. He's sworn to never marry. Dinnae hope for that outcome."

She didn't want marriage, either, but she wasn't about to tell Alan—all men assumed that was a woman's goal in life.

"Are ye Presbyterian, lass?" His good humor had fled, and she blinked at the change. His face had become granite, and his eyes met hers with a steely challenge. Like Lachlan, he had obviously hoped to trip her up by pretending friendship. She got the sense her answer would tell him much, and whatever he learned would be passed on to Lachlan.

"Why does it matter what my religion is?" She crossed her arms and tilted her head.

"The Camerons are Royalists. If ye are a Covenanter, ye will have to seek refuge elsewhere."

"I believe everyone has the right to worship in whatever way they please."

"'Tis noble of ye, but where are yer clan's loyalties?"

She looked away to avoid his scrutiny, fighting back the bitter feelings from years of being told her fate was for the good of her clan. Despite that, she would not betray her people by speaking about them to a stranger.

Lachlan had probably told all of them his suspicions about her, so she considered what she could say without confessing too much. Giving up the pretense that she couldn't remember who she was, she eyed Alan. "I willnae tell ye of my clan. But if ye must ken, I am Catholic." She squared her shoulders, and his features lightened.

"'Tis enough for now. He'll no' send ye away." Alan

smiled and nodded toward Lachlan, who strode back into their midst. "So ye best decide if ye want his attentions. He's already decided he wants ye, even if he won't admit it."

Lachlan motioned, and Alan left her side. She turned her back to think about what she should do next—stay with these men or sneak out and continue on her own. Then she remembered she was free of her betrothal, and soon she would be done with all the politics. Although Lachlan and his men regarded her with wariness, they were her best chance to reach the north safely and stay out of Conall's grasp. Before long, she would be ensconced in a colony of women who wouldn't care about her family's allegiances. Really, it didn't matter what these men thought of her, because she would be where no one could use her—unless she stumbled and told them her father was the Duke of Kirk.

As a Royalist, Lachlan would approve of her marriage to Conall, who was the Earl of Lundin's son and would someday be the governor of Edinburgh. He would want to keep the Royalists in power there. Her heart sank. If he knew whom she was betrothed to, there would be no hope—Lachlan would treat her just like her father had and turn her over to that monster.

If Lachlan was prepared to go to battle for the Royalist cause, he wouldn't hesitate to hand a stranger over to someone who fought for the same side. It had just become even more important she keep her identity secret.

•••

Lachlan walked into the clearing to Alan's laughter as he stood near Maggie at the edge of their camp. His shoulders tensed at his friend's close proximity until he noticed how Maggie watched the man dully, her eyes solemn and troubled. Her pale skin had turned a light gray, and her distressed state made him forget his plans to ignore her. What the devil had he told her? She looked away and refused to meet his eyes.

Lachlan pointed to Alan and crooked his finger in command.

"Excuse me, Maggie," Alan said, loud enough for Lachlan to overhear as he gave her a mischievous grin. Lachlan didn't miss the wink Alan shot her way as his friend strutted toward him.

"What did ye say? She doesnae look pleased." Irritation rumbled through him.

"I told her that ye despised beautiful women. She seemed disappointed. I think she wants ye. I told her not to expect anything from ye." The smirk on his face said he was stifling another laugh.

"Were ye trying to do me favors? Because if I wanted to bed her, she probably willnae want me now." He'd not thought about her rejecting him and pushed the unpleasant idea from his mind.

"Nae, she wants ye. She just doesnae seek a broken heart. I warned her to guard it. What she does with the information is up to her." Alan patted Lachlan on the back.

He didn't want to analyze why his friend's words bothered him. They talked about wenches all the time, but something was different. He was compelled by an odd need to protect Maggie from anything, or anyone, that would hurt her. Mayhap it was because he'd caused her enough pain already.

Lachlan growled at Alan, then glanced over to the lovely nymph. He had carefully crafted secure walls to keep himself guarded, but he feared somewhere down deep she might be the one to break through those walls and lure him into more than casual bedsport. "We dinnae even ken who she is."

"Does it matter?" Alan asked.

"Aye. She's educated. I dinnae think she's a simple farmer's daughter. If being with her brings war with another clan, 'tis no' worth it." Lachlan kept his eyes locked on the woman in question. With her back to him, his eyes could trace the dark curls reaching to her waist.

"And if she isnae so important? Would ye want her then?"

Maggie slowly spun toward them and met Lachlan's gaze with sad blue eyes that turned heated within an instant. A fire sparked, and her defiance blazed. She glanced away, her rebellious curls swinging around her shoulders in subordination. He took it as a challenge.

Lachlan had been with others since his betrothal had been dissolved, but he couldn't deny the desire coursing through him. It was only a matter of time until he gave in to the growing need. "Aye, Alan. I want her."

He had just become the predator and she the prey.

. . .

Frustration beat at Lachlan's chest because she wouldn't look at him. They had been riding for hours, but she sat stiff on the back of one of their newly acquired horses, not sparing a glance at him. Alan's warning had scared her. When he'd met her, she had seemed fearless to the point of putting herself in danger. Could it be true she was afraid of nothing but a broken heart? Or was there something more?

"Where's Freedom?" she had asked as he'd put his hands out to help her mount.

"I sent Dougal ahead with him. Wanted to make sure there were no more surprises." *Now you are the one lying.* He had justified it by thinking, *It's only half a lie and to protect the clan.*

She'd frowned. "Why Freedom? Does Dougal no' have his own horse?"

"Aye, he does, but I sent him with extra, so he could make better time."

She'd stepped up into his hand like she was a princess, mounted, and then turned her head to ignore him.

She had a defiant streak in her. A lass who would goad him and ignite a fire in his blood. It was refreshing to see a woman who didn't jump at his command. But her recklessness was unnerving—she had jumped into a battle to save a man she didn't know and run into a river naked in an unknown area with unfamiliar men close at hand.

Now she challenged him in front of his men. He slowed to ride beside her, and she sped up. When he sped up, she slowed down. The men snickered, and Alan was openly amused at his plight.

Maggie was making herself unavailable to him, and strangely, her curt dismissal of him made him want her more. Aileen had always been the one to initiate their interludes. This lass was making him work for her affections.

He dropped behind again and studied her regal bearing. She obviously had some tutoring, and she rode a horse well. Why would an intelligent, definitely innocent lass be going away from her home instead of toward it?

She had not protested last evening when he had told her she would have to travel to Kentillie with them before they would be able to return her—he'd expected her to argue and insist they take her home immediately. Shocking that instead she'd looked relieved, even happy over the idea of not being reunited with her family.

They stopped for a rest. Dismounting, Lachlan frowned at her. "Maggie, come," he ordered.

His voice was harsher than he'd intended, yet how was he supposed react to the defiant stance she'd taken with him? Her eyes pinned him with suspicion, but she slowly obeyed and walked a few steps behind.

He took her hand and was surprised at how it molded into his, although she eyed him suspiciously. "Come. 'Tis good to stretch while we're stopped."

"Aye," she said as she smiled innocently up at him. "I am stiff. I dinnae ever remember riding so long."

"Do ye ride much?"

"I used to, but no' so much anymore. I miss it." After a sigh, she continued, "There is something liberating about riding."

"Is that why ye named yer horse Freedom?"

Instead of answering, she stared off into the distance. His temper flared as it dawned on him she was not going to answer such a simple question.

He rounded on her. She stopped short to avoid colliding with his chest and jerked her hand from his as she backed a step. The whites of her eyes were large as she swallowed.

"Why are ye in men's clothes?" Fingering the edge of her loose-fitting white shirt, he raked his gaze downward to her trews. He pinned her with a steady gaze, but her eyes shifted to the side. She would lie, then. How he wanted to growl in frustration.

"I—I dinnae recall," she stammered. He grabbed her hand and towed her along.

"Ye arenae good at lying, lass."

They had made it to a copse of trees, and he continued on, pulling her when she hesitated. Her trembling fingers led him to believe leading her away from the group scared her, but he wanted to touch and taste her. If he got some honest responses from her in the process, it would be worth it.

"My answers may not be what ye want to hear, but if I am less than honest, I am doing so in order to protect myself. I swear my intention is no' to harm anyone." She held her shoulders back and head high, but the hitch in her voice belied her confident resolve.

He stopped short and turned to face her. She sucked in her breath sharply. A glimpse of the tops of her breasts as they rose and fell under the material of the shirt caught his eyes, and his gaze drifted down and lingered momentarily. Before she could react, he had snaked his arm around her waist and pulled her in close.

He huffed out a breath. "Maggie, I dinnae ken what kind of game ye are playing, but ye are going to get burned."

Through his shirt, he could feel her heart beating like a scared rabbit's, and he lowered his head to give her a punishing kiss. As soon as their lips touched, he remembered her innocence and he slowed. He gentled the caress until she tentatively matched his pace. She moaned, inciting him and urging him on.

One hand came around to knead her breast. She gasped in his mouth, and her eyes flew open. She was shocked, but her pupils dilated and begged for more. Her lids closed, and she pressed into his touch.

His groin tightened, and he leaned down farther as his mouth closed on her neck and suckled, gently biting down and pulling back. As she melted into him and moaned, her head tilted to give him purchase. He nibbled on her ear and then blew hot air gently into it.

"Oh, sweet Maggie, I do want ye," he whispered, his voice husky.

He nipped again then eased away to see his desire mirrored in her eyes. Never had he seen a more alluring sight than the wanton woman who had sprung to life with nothing more than his kisses. Her windblown hair, flushed cheeks, and swollen lips enticed him to take more. She might be lying about who she was, but the yearning in her eyes was real. She wanted him.

Blushing, she bit her lower lip under his scrutiny, and he wanted to surrender and take her. But he was laird. He was stronger than that. He couldn't have her if it would bring war to the clan. "I have to know first. Where are ye from?"

She stilled, and her breath caught. Instead of answering, her gaze drifted away from his.

"Where are ye from?" he insisted as he splayed his hands into her hair, grasped her head, and forced her to look up at him.

"I cannae tell ye." The passion that had reflected in her eyes moments ago vanished. It changed to fear.

"Why, Maggie? Why will ye no' tell me?" His ragged voice tinged with frustration, and the question came out harsher than he intended.

"Because." She shut her eyes. When she opened them again, they pooled wet with moisture. "If I tell ye, ye will send me back."

One tear escaped and trailed down her face, but she ignored it. The little lass pushed off him with a strength he wouldn't have thought possible as her defiance reared. "Ye willnae soften me with yer kisses. Ye dinnae have to take me with ye if ye do not wish. I will go on my own. I am no longer yer concern."

Faster than he could blink, she had ducked around him and was darting through the thick woods. Never had he seen such a small lass move so quickly. Stunned, he'd not expected her to reject him and take off, especially after experiencing the passion he'd stirred in her.

"Maggie, stop."

She easily skirted several trees, jumped roots, and dodged thickets. It became obvious she had spent a lot of time outdoors. Most lasses would be terrified of being here on their own, away from their home. What was she thinking? She needed protection. It wasn't wise for a woman to roam without a guardian in these woods, and he again cursed her reckless streak for the havoc it played on his nerves. With a groan, Lachlan gave chase.

He slowly gained on her, but only due to his longer legs.

To catch up, he took the brunt of all the twigs and branches, and he winced as one scraped across the arm she had mended. He didn't want to have to tackle her. His frame would crush her, and he'd already hurt her enough.

"Maggie!" he shouted. "Stop, lass." She didn't answer. She kept running.

Damn, he had wanted to scare her, but not enough to make her flee; he had only wanted the truth. *What fool woman would want to be out here far from her kin?* He answered himself. *One who is more afraid of something, or someone, than the uncertainty of the forest.*

She ducked under another branch, but it hit him squarely in the chest, nearly knocking him off his feet, and he lost a couple of steps.

Unexpectedly, she slowed then stopped. The move took him by surprise. She swayed back and forth, and her arms shot out to the sides like she was trying to get her balance.

He almost ran into her and had to swerve to avoid plowing her over. Forward then back, she wavered on her feet. As Lachlan maneuvered around to her front, her eyes became unfocused and glazed over.

He had seen it before in battles, men who had been hit in the head. Running had reinjured her. She fell to her knees before he could catch her. One hand rose up to cover her mouth while the rest of her body continued to move in unsteady circles. Guilt assailed him.

He lowered himself to the ground and gently pulled her into his lap to cradle her. Her eyes remained unfocused, but trails of tears had run down her face as she'd tried to make her escape. Using his thumb, he wiped them away.

"I willnae send ye back, lass. I willnae send ye back."

She said nothing, just stared off blankly, occasionally blinking. After several moments, her bleary eyes closed, and she fell asleep in his arms. He was afraid to move her; she seemed so fragile and breakable. Not the defiant girl who had just pushed a man nearly twice her size.

When he eventually made his way back to the waiting men, he was greeted with slack jaws and inquiring eyes, but none dared question their laird. His solemn expression and Maggie's limp form in his arms apparently shocked them all into silence.

Alan raised his eyebrows, but Lachlan just shook his head. "We need to move on to somewhere safe. We will stop early for the night."

"We aren't far from my home," Robbie stated.

"Are ye sure ye wish to go back there, lad?" Alan asked.

"Aye, we can stay in Father Ailbert's cottage." If Lachlan hadn't become so attuned to the lad's steady tone, he wouldn't have noticed the hitch in his voice as he said his mentor's name. Robbie's thumb slid back and forth over his shirt above the spot where the cross he wore was hidden. "We will all fit inside for the night." The lad's eyes were hopeful.

'Twould probably be the last place Conall would think to look for them.

A warm fire inside a cottage was appealing, but the boy had been through so much, and Lachlan didn't want to subject him to any more pain. "Ye are certain?"

"Aye. I would like to collect more of my things while we are there."

Lachlan's eyes dipped to the woman in his arms. She could use a comfortable place to spend the night. He glanced back to Robbie and nodded. "Can ye lead the way?" Last time the group had been there, they had been guided to the site by the ribbons of smoke that rose from the burning church.

"Alan, take Maggie while I mount." His friend looped his arms under the lass and took the light weight. "Cradle her head," Lachlan instructed. "The priest's cottage will be a good place for her to rest if 'tis her head. Remember when Kirstie hit her head?"

Alan visibly shuddered as his gaze took on a faraway quality, making Lachlan think his friend might be longing to see Kirstie again. Lachlan had always known Alan had feelings for his sister, but the man would never admit it. He suspected Kirstie's real reason for leaving home revolved around Alan as well, but they were both stubborn and neither would ever acknowledge the truth.

Once on his horse, he reached down and Alan handed Maggie to him. He tucked her head into the crook of his arm and secured her close to his chest then trotted after Robbie.

Late in the afternoon, as they reached the familiar clearing, the sun cast warm beams on the cool violet and blue hues of overgrown heather surrounding the glade. A quaint, peaceful cottage sat near the center, marred only in beauty by the remains of the burned church. It presented an ominous picture of the events that had unfolded just days before they'd reached Edinburgh. Robbie had been huddled on the ground a short distance from the roaring flames of the structure, with the priest lain over his lap. His clothes were singed, and soot marks streaked his face from his heedless rush into the burning structure to find his mentor.

Cousin Fiona had screamed when she'd seen the battered and bloodied body of the holy man, and Dougal had escorted her away from the horrific scene while Lachlan knelt down next to the lad, who sat motionless, staring at the flames as they consumed the last vestiges of the small building. "What happened, lad?"

The boy swallowed then turned his tired eyes toward Lachlan as if to assess him. He either approved of what he saw or just needed someone to talk to, because he confided, "Covenanters."

Lachlan's blood froze; he'd been hoping the fire had been some horrific accident. "Did ye see them?"

"Aye. They were leaving when I got here." He pointed toward the road south.

"Did they kill the Father or was it the fire?" Lachlan gulped and held out hope that no one could be so cruel as to murder a defenseless priest.

King Charles's wish to unify, England, Scotland, and Ireland was admirable, but people had to have the right to choose their own religion. Lachlan didn't have a problem with the Covenanters' desire to practice as they wished, but that they forced others to convert to Presbyterianism through threats and by burning churches and killing priests maddened him. Their demands were no better than the king's.

As Catholics, Lachlan and his clan were Royalists who supported the king and were not allied with the Covenanters elected to Parliament who claimed to represent all of Scotland. They did not.

"'Twas no' the fire. It was the man with the twisted smile. He still had the bloody knife in his hand. I will never forget his face." On the verge of going into shock, the lad lifted a bloody hand that covered a wound on the dead priest. "He was still alive when I pulled him out."

"Did Father tell ye who they were?" Lachlan asked.

"Nae, he just said, 'Covenanters took everything, took your cross.'"

"What's yer name, lad?"

"Ro…" He hesitated and turned his eyes back to the flames. "Robbie."

"Where's yer family, Robbie?" The lad shook his head.

Although the area was soaked from an earlier rain, they had spent the next several hours ensuring the flames didn't spread to the nearby woods. Lachlan and the rest of his men took turns digging the grave.

When all was done and they were ready to leave, Robbie surprised them. "May I come with you? I have nothing left here."

Alan chimed in before Lachlan could reply. "Aye. The Camerons have room for ye."

There had been a fire the night Alan's parents had died, and Lachlan couldn't deny his adoptive brother the opportunity to help a boy who found himself in similar circumstances. He nodded at the pair, and shortly after, their band continued on to Edinburgh, not knowing they would soon find the monster responsible for the senseless murder.

Chapter Five

Maggie blinked. She looked up at Lachlan's strong chin as he talked in hushed tones to someone nearby. She lay cradled in his arms in front of a blazing fire in some home she'd never seen before. She felt safe and treasured in the warmth of his strong, protective embrace, and och, he smelled of the fresh outdoors and wood and all things comforting.

In an attempt to remember how she had come to be here, she blinked a few times. The man had kissed her in the woods near the encampment, turned her insides to mush, and she'd been so attuned to the sensations of his touch she lost all sense. Connected to him in that moment, she'd wanted to give him the truth, not keep anything from him. But when he questioned her, she came to the realization that he'd only kissed her to lower her defenses, learn who her family was, and send her home. He hadn't been moved by their embrace the same way she had.

She had gone from such pleasure and trust to being hurt and scared at the same time and had done the only thing she could think of. She ran. It might not have been the smartest move, but she'd had no choice.

The memory of what happened next eluded her. No matter how she tried, it wouldn't come back, and a pain throbbed in her temple. The head injury had done this to her, and she needed to get to her bag and mix some tea. If she was going to survive and get to safety, she had to take better care of herself.

Again Maggie blinked and focused on the man holding her. His skin glowed a warm caramel color in the dim firelight.

Conversation stopped, and his anxious gaze tilted to her.

Had he been worried about her?

His free hand wound around her to massage and knead her temple and skull, and she sighed.

"Maggie."

As she gave him a small smile, his shoulders relaxed.

His hand started to fall away, but she caught it. "Please, it feels nice." His lips curved up, and he continued. A slight shift in the air gave her the impression the person he'd been talking to left to give them some sort of privacy.

"Where are we?" She found it disturbing that it was the second time in two days she'd had to ask that question.

"We only rode a little farther to a safe place after ye fainted." Concerned eyes studied her.

Now she was confused and annoyed. She was no wilting flower who fell at any sign of danger. "I have never fainted."

"Ye did today." He looked away then back down at her. "Ye were running from me. What are ye so afraid of?" She stiffened, and his hand moved to cradle her cheek softly.

"I cannae go home. If ye dinnae want me here, I will find a convent on my own."

"A convent?" His lips quirked. It didn't matter if he believed her—she was done defending herself, and she was perfectly capable of navigating through the Highlands without the assistance of a man.

"Ye wouldnae be happy at a place like that." His fingers slid back into her hair, and her scalp tingled. "Ye have too much fire in ye." It surprised her he could read her so well. She knew she would never be happy there, but she would settle for whatever kept her safe.

"'Tis the only option I have." She turned her eyes toward the flames and hoped he would drop the subject. "I need my bag. There are herbs for my head." Now she pushed his hand away and cautiously attempted to rise. He stopped her.

"If ye cannae trust me, then I will go my own way. Ye are free from any obligation." She attempted to look stern and unbendable, but in his arms like this, it was doubtful her determination came across.

"Ye cannae be out here on yer own." His head slowly shook.

"Will ye keep me against my will?"

"If that's what it takes to keep ye safe." His hand rested on her cheek again, and an odd look came over his face. Could it be he felt protective of her as a woman and not just a piece of property?

"I willnae go back."

"Promise me ye willnae run, lass. I willnae send ye home." His eyes were sincere, and she breathed a sigh of relief. She had to trust him, not that he was giving her the same courtesy. "Promise, Maggie."

She nodded, then asked, "Do ye have my satchel? I'd like to make some tea for my head."

Rising with her still in his arms, he turned and gingerly set her on the chair. The wood was hard, and she missed the comfort and warmth of being held in his gentle embrace. "Stay. I'll get yer bag and some water."

Soft, relaxed male voices floated around the room. Her gaze shifted from the cook fire, which doubled as the cottage's only source of warmth, to take in the scene. She skimmed the comfortable room that consisted of a kitchen and gathering place. A small table sat between her chair and the one that had been vacated, while the group of men congregated around a slightly larger table with empty plates as they conversed. The only man not in the room was Seamus, the quiet one she'd not had the chance to get to know yet.

Lachlan reappeared and passed her the bag as he sat next to her. Peering in, she noticed immediately its contents had been rifled through, and her fingers froze as her mind turned over the fact he had searched her things. Resentment blossomed in her chest.

"Ye went through it." She was surprised how calmly the words came out, because her bottom lip quivered; she didn't know if it was from anger or fear he might have discovered her identity. She wanted to shout, but her head still hurt.

Was there anything in there he shouldn't see?

She searched her memory and came up with an answer that made her heart skip a beat. Her ma's cuff—the only thing of any value she had brought with her. Surely he would not deduce her identity from it, but her hand moved to cover the matching bracelet she wore. If he noticed, he kept it hidden. She knew the inscription by heart: *Beloved wife and mother, S.M.* How often she had dreamed her father had cared for her ma. She'd held onto the silver bangle because it was proof at one time he had loved her enough to have those words etched.

She pulled the bag farther into her lap and reached in casually. Relief flooded through her as her fingers skimmed the cool metal in the same pocket where she'd left it. There was still hope he wouldn't send her back.

His gaze drifted down, and he had the nerve to look repentant and way too handsome. Why was she even thinking about how bonny he was?

As he sat there quietly and bit down on his lip, she

remembered how those lips had made her quiver and how she had melted into his embrace. His continued silence made her imagine he was trying to come up with a good reason for violating her trust or attempting to lure her into some trap to divulge her identity.

She shook her head and tore her gaze from those luscious lips. "Ye had no right." Her fingers tightened on the bag.

"I had to ken ye wouldnae harm any of my clan."

"I bandaged ye and Malcolm. Why do ye think I would harm someone?"

"'Twas no' about ye. I would have done it to anyone. I'd rather be distrustful than dead." His eyes became hard, and the relaxed manner he'd had with her moments ago disappeared. He was rigid and on edge.

She opened her mouth to tell him he was foolish, but she stopped herself, because she realized his mistrust was a reaction to the betrayal Alan had alluded to. Lachlan had been hurt deeply. He didn't trust women because he didn't want to experience that pain again, and he had set up walls to protect himself, so she couldn't fault him for fortifying his heart against further hurt. More than that, she was a stranger, while, as laird, his job was to guard his clan. She would probably feel the same way if she were in his place.

"I'm sorry."

Her head tilted. Had any of the men in her life ever apologized to her?

His eyes peered directly into hers. The stony tension in him had softened, and he continued, "I was careful no' to damage anything."

Her shoulders relaxed, and she nodded, surprised at how easy she found it to forgive him. The Cameron laird valued her enough to apologize for upsetting her.

"Some water for yer tea." Malcolm set the cup down on the small wooden table between the two chairs.

Before her gaze shifted to Malcolm to thank him, she smiled at Lachlan. For some reason, it was important he knew she had accepted his apology. He answered with a small grin of his own.

After she finished her tea and had a piece of bannock with honey, she swayed with weariness and almost fell from the chair. Lachlan took her arm, helped her up, and guided her to the larger of two small beds in an adjoining room. It was cooler here, despite the door left ajar for heat from the cook fire.

"With the rain, 'tis good we have a place to stay inside tonight."

She didn't attempt to clear the fog in her head and hadn't even known it was raining. "Whose bed?" Her lids fought to close before she could lie down.

"'Twas Father Ailbert's. The other is Robbie's." Lachlan pulled the blankets back and eased her to sit on the mattress.

He knelt down in front her, and her heart beat faster at the nearness and intimacy of the position. If he'd looked at her she might have come undone, but he was unlacing the dirty, old man boots she wore. A sigh escaped. He set her shoes aside and rose to his full, intimidating height.

"Robbie has found ye some clean clothes." Pointing to the edge of the bed where a white shirt and some trews similar to the ones she wore lay folded, he shrugged. "'Twas that or priest's robes."

The idea of clean garments of any kind had her smiling. He nodded to a small bowl resting on a table in the corner.

"There is water in the basin for washing. Mayhap 'tis still warm," he called over his shoulder as he left the room.

She went to the basin and picked up the cloth beside it to wash the day's dirt from her face and hands. A brush lay on the table as well. For all that he didn't trust her, he had still thought of her comfort. Odd for a man to consider her needs.

After washing, she spent several moments running the bristles through her tangled hair. Undressing and placing the dirty clothes in a pile at the side of the room, she put on the crisp shirt and laid the clean trews and stockings on a side table. Lachlan came back through the door and froze, his gaze fixed on her. Comfortable but exhausted now, she didn't try to analyze what he was thinking as she sat on the bed.

"Climb in and move to the other side." His voice sounded strangled, almost as if it were a plea instead of a command, but she was so drowsy that she did as instructed and shut her eyes before thinking to ask, "Why?"

"'Cause we'll be sharing the bed," was what she imagined he said, but she was nearly asleep.

At some point during the night, Maggie woke with Lachlan's arm around her. It was comforting, and she nestled into the warmth of the embrace as she relished the security of his hold. He hadn't attempted to woo her, only kept her encircled like a treasured possession in his strong arms, and that's how she knew it was just a dream.

No one has ever valued me.

. . .

Maggie woke to the sound of deep male laughter and voices not belonging to her brothers. Early-morning light streamed in through threadbare curtains, and a cross hung on the wall, reminding her where she had slept. She rose, pulled on the clean clothes and her boots, and walked into the other room. Seamus had reappeared, but Alan was missing. Lachlan stood near the fire, and his gaze met hers as she crossed to sit on the only open chair at the larger table.

"Good morning," she said and was greeted with a chorus of the same. Talk continued, but she found it impossible to concentrate on the cadence of the conversation because she could sense Lachlan's stare penetrate her as he studied her from the side. Her face flushed as she remembered they had shared a bed the previous evening, and every man in this house knew it.

Robbie jumped up from the seat beside her but returned shortly with a bowl of oats with cream. She focused on it until she mustered the courage to look up and noticed early-morning rays of light streamed in from a nearby window, and clear skies showed no hint there had been rain during the night.

After eating, she followed Lachlan and Seamus out of the cottage to finish their journey north but stopped in her tracks. "Blessed Mother" escaped her lips as Malcolm bumped into her from behind. The burned remains of what had once been a church moldered just outside the door.

Lachlan turned, and his perceptive scrutiny bored into her. Her hand had flown to cover her heart, and a shroud of darkness seeped into her core. "'Tis a church?"

"Aye." Lachlan took a step toward her.

"What happened?"

"Covenanters." His eyes darkened as the words passed coolly through his lips, almost as a hiss.

"Why would someone do that?"

Lachlan's eyes shifted only momentarily toward Robbie, but she caught the slight movement. Her gaze darted in the same direction, and she saw the lad trudge toward a fresh mound of dirt. Her eyes watered as the implications hit her.

She made the sign of the cross and shook her head. 'Twas why Robbie had been given the other bed—it truly was his, and the priest he lived with must have been killed in the fire. Her heart broke for him because she understood loss. The grief never went away, just mellowed with the passing of time.

"Ye took him in?"

"Aye, he is under Cameron protection now."

Lachlan's arm wrapped around her waist and pulled her close. "Come, lass. We'll give him some time." He drew her toward the horses.

A tear slid down her cheek. "Why?" she asked again as her gaze returned to the scorched ruins.

"No one can explain evil men."

She nodded as another tear trailed down her cheek. She knew that all too well. She'd only known one truly evil man, and she would say a prayer of thanks every day to never see him again.

Maggie was grateful they traveled at an unhurried pace through the morning, since Lachlan kept looking over at her as if he expected her to fall off her horse at any moment. It was a good thing, because she might. Her head still pounded, and she could barely keep her eyes open even though she had slept well. Och, she wanted to lie back down. She wished she were still in the soft bed and the safety of Lachlan's strong arms, but at the same time she tried to fight the guilt of how comfortable that had been. Her time with him was only a temporary solution and she'd be on her way soon, besides she couldn't let down her guard and risk her heart.

Maggie swayed and caught herself. She forced her eyes wide and took a deep breath.

"We break." Lachlan's voice came from right beside her as he pointed to a spot up ahead she couldn't focus on. He was suddenly unnervingly close.

She furtively glanced through her eyelashes at the man riding near her. He made her feel safe and had awoken a desire inside her no other man ever had. Her mind battled with her body, which yearned for him to touch her, kiss her again.

His gaze drifted her way and caught her eyes. A crooked, mischievous grin slowly emerged. An intense, heated stare made her ache with a desire she was becoming all too familiar with, and she blushed.

The smoldering glance he returned said he was aware of what she was thinking. She didn't see revulsion in his eyes—he looked interested. Mayhap she'd mistaken his intentions yesterday when she'd run from him.

The blues of the vast clear sky blurred by with occasional white puffs of clouds, and she found herself relaxing into the rhythmic *thud, thud, thud* of the horses' hoofbeats and the men's silence as they worked their way home. As the greens of dense shrubbery, pines, and oaks, the deep purples of the heather, and violets of thistle dotting the hills drew her into their beauty, she found it increasingly difficult to keep her lids open.

Before she knew it, they'd stopped and Lachlan was at her side, pulling her down from her horse. Thankful she didn't have to expend the energy to stay upright on her own, she leaned into his body. He steadied, then guided her over to a large rock and gently nudged her to sit. He turned and left, so she stood and stretched, because sleep would overtake her if she didn't move around.

As the life came back into her limbs, they started to revive, and the fogginess in her head abated. When he returned with bread and dried meat, he held some out to her.

"Sit," he ordered, and she did, because she was no longer afraid she'd tumble over with weariness. She was struck by how small and vulnerable she felt next to him, but at the same time how at ease she was in his presence, despite his massive build.

"Eat," he said. He broke off a piece of the bread and handed it to her then bit into a piece of the meat.

"I'm no' so hungry," she said, but she took a bite anyway.

"Does yer head still hurt?"

"Nae, I'm just so tired."

"It may take ye some time to recover. My sister was

always tripping over something and hitting her head. Once she was dizzy and in bed for a week."

"Ye have a sister?" She popped another small piece of bread in her mouth. Mayhap she was hungry after all.

"Aye. She's just a wee bit older than Malcolm. Ye remind me a lot of her."

"How?"

"Kirstie is just as stubborn as ye and always gets her way." Lachlan's smile gave her the impression his love for his sister ran deep.

"I'm no' stubborn." She pouted.

"Aye, ye are. Ye have a way of turning things to get what ye want. She could always talk me into the craziest things, too."

"I always wanted a sister. Will I get to meet her?" Mayhap a sister wouldn't have been a good idea—she wasn't certain she would have been able to keep one safe from Conall.

"Nae, she isnae at Kentillie." A cloud covered his eyes.

"Is she married, then?"

"Nae, she went to live with our cousin. She's been there for a couple of years now." Lachlan's smile faded, and he looked off into the distance.

"Ye let her go?" She couldn't wrap her mind around a man who would allow a woman to choose a path he'd not planned for her.

"She has her own mind, and I couldnae temper her spirit by forcing her to stay somewhere she didnae want."

"Most men wouldnae let a woman make her own decisions."

"That may be so, but I've kenned women more intelligent than most men. 'Twas no' my place to stop her."

"Ye are her laird."

"Aye, but I have a heart and wouldnae see her be miserable."

"My father and brothers dinnae share yer views."

"Then they need to open their minds and hearts."

She was astonished. She'd probably found the only man in all of Scotland who could find his way into her soul.

Even if his touch had not set her ablaze, now she wanted to give herself to him before she was forced into seclusion. Her one taste of intimacy would be with a man who valued her not as a woman who could be bartered for his own gain, but as a woman to be respected.

Out of all the men she'd known, he was the only one that threatened to tear down the fortress she'd built around her heart. It was a shame he didn't want to wed, because if she could ever see herself with anyone, it would have been a man like Lachlan Cameron.

· · ·

As the sun sank, it cast pink shadows on the clouds, and the beauty of it, as Lachlan held her close, gave her a calm reassurance that warmed and comforted her. It had been years since she'd had a sense of security so strong that flashes of her friend's broken body didn't intrude.

'Twas blessed peace to be out in the fresh air of the pines and see the changing landscape as the mountains rose to touch the heavens. They wove in and out of glens and open fields littered with fragrant heather. Traversing the forests had become difficult with jagged, uneven earth posing a risk to the horses, so they had moved onto well-trodden paths. Lachlan had insisted she ride the remainder of the afternoon with him, and she was secretly grateful he had, because shortly after they had set off again, she had nestled into his arms and fallen asleep with the steady movement of the horse.

She was refreshed after the afternoon nap, and clarity had returned. Her head hadn't even hurt.

They stopped and set up camp at the edge of a clearing. Once again, Lachlan helped her dismount. *I could get used to this*, she thought as her body slid down his solid chest and a flutter started in her stomach.

They sat quietly in a circle while Malcolm started a fire. Seamus, the quiet man with his intimidating size, carved a little wooden dog out of a piece of wood for his youngest son.

Movement out of the corner of her eye caught Maggie's attention. A large buck emerged from the trees. She didn't want to scare it away, so she put her fingers to her lips to signal the men to silence.

They watched intently as she reached over for Malcolm's bow and silently pulled an arrow from the quiver. The deer was a good distance away and it would be a tough shot, but she focused on the buck and moved soundlessly into a perfect, braced stance.

She pulled the bow up and notched the arrow. Pulling back, she tested the tension of the string, and when she was comfortable, she placed her head close to the bow and squinted, carefully aiming, then releasing the arrow. It flew directly on course. A broadside shot landing just behind the shoulder sent the deer limping off weakly into the woods.

"Where did ye learn that, Maggie?" Malcolm questioned.

She turned to him and winked. She couldn't say until recently she had been allowed to run free with her three brothers, as they might be able to figure out who she was.

Robbie chimed in, "That was incredible." His eyes were bright with appreciation and, for a moment, the overly serious lad looked like the boy he should have been. She wondered why he had been living with a priest.

"Maggie, lass, ye dinnae just touch a man's weapon like that. Ye might hurt his pride if ye are better with it than he is," Alan joked.

The Highlanders burst out laughing. She didn't get the

jest, but she smiled along until her gaze fell on Lachlan. Though he chuckled as well, his gaze appraised her as if she'd given too much away. Did the man no' miss anything? She berated her impulsive nature for making him think she might in some way be dangerous, or worse.

"Did I do something wrong?" Maggie asked, confused by his continued open assessment.

"Nae, Maggie. 'Twas verra impressive. I have never seen a lass make a shot like that," Lachlan replied as his gaze lingered. He made his way over and took the bow then handed it back to Malcolm. He pulled her down to sit so close to his side it was almost intimate.

"Alan. Ye want to go get dinner, or should I send the lass to do what ye couldnae?" he jested and then turned toward her. "Do ye ken how to dress them, too?"

She warmed under his scrutinizing gaze, and a blush crept up her cheeks. "Nae, I never did that part."

The cleaning had always been done close to home, and neither she nor her brothers would have risked her father seeing her involvement. She was a better shot than all of them, which was why they always brought her when they hunted. They took the credit, and she got what she needed out of the bargain—a reprieve from the confines of the stifling castle walls. She averted her eyes and wondered what she'd given away in her hasty decision to take down the deer.

Later, as they settled in for the night and she lay on her back staring up to the stars, she tried to imagine her life confined in a convent. Lachlan's pallet was spread sinfully close to hers, and he scooted in to bridge the distance between them, making it painfully hard to imagine a life of chastity. Even through the blanket wrapped around her, he lay so near she could feel the warmth of his skin. Without warning, he lifted the wool fabric and crawled under with her, and although she thought to protest, the part of her that ached to feel his touch kept her silent. Mayhap here was a man worthy of her trust, one who respected his sister enough to honor her request to leave Kentillie.

He inched closer and whispered in her ear, "Who taught ye how to use the bow?"

His close proximity shut down her defenses, and she could no longer lie. Despite his suspicions, he had kept her safe, and she owed him as much of the truth as possible. Hopefully he'd keep to his promise not to send her back or push her into more telling confessions.

She whispered back, "The only attention I got as a child was from my brothers. They would take me out. They taught me to hunt, to ride, to do a lot of things most girls are not taught."

Memories tugged at her heart, and she gave a sad smile. Her brothers and father weren't all bad—they just didn't listen to her when it came to matters that affected the clan.

"How did yer mother feel about that?" he asked.

Rolling over so she could gaze into his eyes, she swallowed, because their lips were only inches apart and hers craved the feeling of his being pressed against them.

It was somehow crucial that he understand she was being honest, that she was trusting him. She was almost secure in the knowledge that if she told him her father was Duke of Kirk he would find a way to help her, but she was not yet ready to take the risk. Still, she'd never tell anyone the whole truth.

"She was too busy yearning for my father's affections and cursing his infidelities. She hardly ever noticed me when I was around. That is, until I got older." Her eyes glazed over, and she looked away as she fought the old pain of not being enough to make her mother happy.

As a child, all Maggie had wanted was her ma's love and affection, but the only thing she ever received was indifference. She tried being the perfect daughter, sewing and cooking, but her mother had ignored her efforts. Then she'd gone through a rebellious spell when she'd even stolen from the kitchens and played pranks on her brothers, but nothing ever garnered a response other than a, "Mayhap yer father would still love me if I had not birthed all ye babes." That's when she quit trying.

"Why when ye were older?" He lightly stroked her cheek, and she turned in to the caress. Her eyes closed to savor the feel.

Her lids slowly rose. "Because when I was old enough to listen, she would tell me how much she loved my father with one breath, and how much she hated him in the next." A sigh escaped.

"She shouldnae have taken her grievances with him out on ye." His hand left her face.

"My father was never faithful, and it broke her heart. It is all history now, anyway." She pursed her lips and avoided his gaze.

"Did she leave him?"

Her heart ached as that day came back to haunt her like it had so many times before. She turned away from Lachlan and stared off into the distance. "She left us all."

Chapter Six

Lachlan came awake as Maggie turned onto her back on the pallet he'd made when they'd set up camp near a secluded copse of trees. 'Twas not yet light, so he closed the distance between them and wrapped his arm around her as he had the night before. She was a warm breeze blowing across the loch on a cool day, and having her in his arms somehow seemed right. He breathed her in and relaxed, knowing she was safe.

Although he was honor bound to see her home without further harm, there was something more to it than that. Her temperament and defiance ignited a burning in his chest he didn't want to explore, so he focused on how she smelled of heather and how his arm fit perfectly over the gentle curve of her waist. He ached to bury himself deep inside her.

For some strange reason, she had made up her mind she belonged in a convent, but the passion he had seen in her, the recklessness, the zest for life showed she was a lass with a spirit that couldn't be contained behind walls. Maggie would never be happy confined as a bride of God.

Tempting him with heated glances that made his cock

ache with need, she evoked in him a need only sinking into her warm and willing body would sate. He didn't want a wife, but he did want a bed partner. He wanted Maggie.

How he longed to see those dark blue eyes watching him with desire, and he yearned to watch her black curls bounce as she rode him astride. No one else would do.

After a few nights of bedsport, his obsession would fade, and he could escort her wherever she wanted to go. He would even keep his promise to send her to a convent if she wished.

Dougal should be back with news about her horse and mayhap her identity soon. Lachlan shifted his hips so his cock was nestled up against Maggie's arse. He yearned not only for her body, but the news it would be safe to take her to his bed.

The soft voices of Alan and Robbie drifted through the cool, dark air, so he did his best to concentrate on that and not the throbbing ache between his legs. His mission was to keep his focus on exposing Conall and protecting the boy, not savoring the feel of the small woman that fit so snugly into his arms. Och, but she was tempting.

It took some effort, but eventually his thoughts wandered back to his band weaving through the filthy, overcrowded streets of Edinburgh with Robbie. Lachlan had not wanted to stay long, so they dropped Fiona off and ensured she was in good hands then searched for lodgings in a nearby inn. He'd heard Argyll was in residence at the castle, and he thought best to keep well away from the leader of the Covenanter army. Tensions were running high as he feuded with James Graham, First Marquess of Montrose, and other Royalists over fundamental changes to the Scottish constitution and dissolving the Scottish monarchy. The last thing Lachlan wanted on this trip was a confrontation about religious rights.

Robbie had been skittish since they'd arrived in the city. His eyes darted around like a ball being tossed by children as he jumped at every loud noise. The lad watched everyone, as if he were a wanted man and someone would recognize him at any moment and string him up in the gallows. Odd that the boy had seemed so calm until they reached Edinburgh.

Seeming overly eager, he had rushed ahead of them to get to the inn and into a room.

When the lad froze as if he'd seen the ghost of the priest he'd just buried, Lachlan came up beside him, and Robbie latched onto his arm with a falcon-like grip. The boy had a bit of strength to him.

"That's him." His eyes were wide with fear, but his jaw ticked. Lachlan didn't have to ask what Robbie meant, but there were so many people in front of them, he wasn't sure who in the crowd was the Covenanter who had murdered his mentor.

"Which one?"

"The blond man. He's wearing my cross." His hand slipped from Lachlan's arm and formed a fist. Before Lachlan could stop him, he charged forward. Another man stepped in front and knocked Robbie to the ground to stop him from reaching his intended target.

Alan was there in an instant, standing between the beast and the boy. "Stand back," he ordered, ready to defend the lad.

"Tell yer boy to watch where he's going." The behemoth took a step closer.

Lachlan had full faith in his friend, so he turned his attention to the fair-haired man Robbie had identified and strolled over. The murderer smirked as if Robbie were a bug beneath his feet, then recognition flared and his features stiffened. His eyes turned cold with deadly menace.

Drawing attention away from Robbie before the man could make a move toward him, Lachlan spoke. "My friend seems to have a grievance with ye. Do ye ken why that would be the case?"

"I have done nothing to the boy." The man sneered. His eyes raked Lachlan, openly assessing the threat. "Whom am I speaking to?"

"Lachlan Cameron, the Lochiel, laird of the Cameron clan. And who are ye?"

"Conall Erskine." He puffed up his shoulders and returned Lachlan's icy gaze. "Son to the Earl of Lundin, governor of Edinburgh."

"Murderer," Robbie's voice broke in. "You murdered a priest, you bastard." Alan held him back while keeping a watchful gaze on the ox still threatening to squash him.

"You'd better have the boy watch his tongue, or I won't be responsible for what happens to him." Despite Conall's cold eyes, the fear of discovery glinted in the recesses of their depths.

"He tells the truth. Where did ye come by that cross around yer neck?"

Conall stiffened. "I don't have to defend myself to you."

"Give the boy his cross. 'Tis his only memento of the man of God ye took from him." The piece looked as if it were worth a small fortune. Why would a boy have such a possession? He waved away the thought—likely it belonged to the church.

Robbie broke free from Alan, grabbed the large jewel-encrusted cross from Conall's neck, and pulled. The chain snapped, and Conall's fist struck the boy with a barely discernible thud.

Lachlan shoved Conall, who fell on his arse. "Dinnae ever lay a hand on him again."

His eyes sparking with fury, Conall stood calmly, then he charged Lachlan, who dodged to the side. Lachlan spun, and his fist connected with the murderer's cheek.

Sounds of swords being drawn from their sheaths drew their attention to those around them, and he caught a glimpse of a group of frightened women nearby who covered the eyes of their children. He calmed and took a step back. "Ye will face justice for what ye have done." He caught Alan's gaze and tilted his head to indicate they should move from the street. "Here isnae the place."

"I have done nothing." Conall spit as Lachlan and his party continued on their way.

If Conall was to be believed, that his father was the governor of Edinburgh, Lachlan would have to seek justice for the priest some other way. He was inclined to believe it was the truth, because the blackguard lacked a Scottish brogue, which meant he'd probably had English tutors or been educated elsewhere. It was not likely the courts in this city would believe a young boy's word over an official's son, so until he could formulate a plan, he needed to get Robbie back to Kentillie, where he would be safe.

Maggie shifted and he returned his attention to the present. Focusing on the task ahead had succeeded in temporarily diverting his thoughts from the temptation in front of him, but Conall's revolting deeds kept him awake. Aye, he had bigger problems than the lass in his arms, but damn, she felt good.

. . .

Chirping birds sang in the thick pines above, but 'twas the feel of the man behind her that had heated her blood and pulled her from sleep. Lachlan's body pressed into hers, and he seemed to pull her closer as his hips rocked into her backside, eliciting a strange reaction from her body that called for her to turn over and sink farther into his strong embrace. She shimmied into the touch, and she thought she heard him groan, but only moments later, he released his hold and backed up as he stood and left her there alone.

Waiting for her body to calm from the strange reaction

to his, she wondered why he had slept so near her last night. The previous evening, it had made sense to share the bed, but last night when he'd climbed under the blanket with her, she'd stifled the protest of propriety and allowed him to hold her. It was a cool night, after all, and it felt surprisingly nice to have his body snuggled so close to hers.

Thinking about their conversation the evening before, another revelation came to her—by expressing her disappointment and hurt over her ma's actions, she had opened a part of herself to him that she hadn't shared with anyone in years, and she felt lighter for it. He had been a safe place to vent her frustrations, it had been so long since she'd felt as if she weren't judged by her thoughts, and he'd listened as if it weren't all her fault.

As she climbed from under the blanket, she pulled it over her shoulders, not wanting to lose his warmth or the masculine, earthy scent that still clung to the woolen fabric as she moved to join the others by a small fire. Lachlan slid from the only log and onto the ground. "Sit." He nodded toward the place he'd vacated and kept conversing with Seamus as he passed her the bowl of oats he'd just gotten for himself. His fingers touched hers and lingered a little too long, as if they, too, craved something more. As far as she could tell, he hadn't been watching her, but he seemed aware of every move she made. He was laird, but he was on a level with all his men and had given up his spot, something she was sure her father never would have done. Not for her mother or her or any other lass.

Before they left their camp, a light mist started to fall. It turned into sheets of rain as they traveled through the morning, and although she caught herself wishing she were cuddled up next to Lachlan as she had been the day before, she lifted her face to the cleansing droplets as they helped to clear her head. They meandered off the path they had been taking and onto a road; a small village came into view and the band guided their horses toward the little stable near a building with a sign that boasted TIMMY'S TAVERN.

Dismounting first, Lachlan said something to the other men she didn't hear then turned his attentions back to her and helping her down. Swinging her leg over, she slid down into his waiting arms and shivered as her soaked body skimmed across his and the combination of rubbing against his muscular frame and the heat from his body sent a visible shudder through her. She flushed as the fevered stirrings she fought to keep at bay returned with the simple action.

His arms stayed around her as her head tilted up; she expected to see his strong chin, but warmth pooled in her core as a heated gaze of the deepest blue met hers instead. "Ye are freezing."

Only she was smiling at him now because cold was the last thing she felt. He continued, "Ye should have said something."

"'Tis just a little rain, and it seems to be letting up." Noticing the quiet around them, she glanced around to see they were alone in the stable. Strong arms still wrapped around her, she turned back to him only to notice he was studying their surroundings as well. He backed to the wall and drew her along with him as his gaze seemed to take in everything.

She was about to ask where everyone had gone when his attention turned back to her, and suddenly, his head was dipping to hers, but his mouth didn't land on her lips. It was close to her ear, and he whispered, "Och, ye dinnae even ken what ye do to me, lass," before his lips closed over the lobe of her ear. Gasping as the soft, warm pressure sent chills spreading down to her core, she clenched her hands on his sides and held on. His breathing deepened, and his teeth nipped and pulled at the sensitive area as newly discovered sensations had her body arching into his.

It was as if her body had woken up for the first time, as one hand held her back and the other lowered to cup her rear and pull her up to give him better access. She was pinned to him as his mouth worshipped her skin, as if she were to be cherished and adored. Her body thrummed to know what else his touch could make her feel, and she knew at that moment she couldn't leave this man's side until she had experienced what his body had promised hers. She wanted to lie naked with this gentle man and experience what she knew would be a transcendent experience if just his touch made her feel like this.

Raising his head, he turned his attention back to the door, and then she thought he nodded at someone, but her limbs were weak and hummed with the desire that still pulsated through her. "'Tis safe, come." Lips curved into a satisfied smile, his gaze met hers and lingered as she shook her head so that the words would soak in, but she was having trouble processing what he said.

"Let's eat." One arm left her while the other kept her clutched to his side as he drew her from the stable into the tavern.

As they sat at a long table in the corner of the room, his hand resting on her thigh under the table, she tried to make sense of what he had made her feel. It had been as if her body had just woken from a long, dull sleep to discover sensation she'd not dreamed possible. What else could he do to her? She knew the basics from her mother and hadn't had friends who had educated her on what went on between a woman and a man, but she was going to let this man teach her. Just his touch drove her mad with thoughts she didn't understand, and if she made it to the convent and never experienced what he could show her, she knew she would always wonder and regret not taking the chance when she could.

In between bites of stew and bread, as the men talked

about the rest of the journey, she managed to catch that they should be at Kentillie in two more days. The rest of the conversation was a blur, because her thoughts were on what would happen when she made it to the convent, and for the first time, although she knew she would be safe there, she dreaded what she would be giving up—the intimacy between lovers.

She swallowed and peeked up at the rest of the table, glad they couldn't read her thoughts. Lachlan didn't look at her, but although he talked with his men, the lazy circles his fingers traced on her trews let her know he hadn't forgotten about her and sent shivers of want straight to a place that he'd roused in her. His eyes had warmed with lust as he pulled back from kissing her neck, and there was no hiding that he wanted her, too. Wanting to experience more of what he'd done, she came to the conclusion she would let this man take her to his bed before giving her vows.

When they emerged from the tavern, it was to clear skies. She was almost disappointed, because she had made up her mind that she would ask to ride with him for the heat. Now she had no such excuse to press her body into his and must be content to watch him while she puzzled out this strange desire that coursed through her body and how she was going to get him to sate the thirst he had stirred in the primitive part of her she'd kept locked away.

· · ·

Readjusting his position didn't help. The wench was driving him mad with lust. He'd not expected her to melt into him like a familiar lover instead of the innocent she was as he kissed her ear in the stable. If she could be that responsive with such a small show of affection, how would her body react when he gave her his undivided attention? He'd tasted her but kept his attention on the door as he sent the men in to assess the occupants of the tavern before they entered.

Then, while they had eaten, he hadn't been able to keep his hand from seeking her thigh, and once he had it, it had been a battle not to trail his hand up to touch other, more intimate parts of her as he watched her blush return from the corner of his eyes. Now she held her head up to soak in the rays of the sun, just as she'd done with the water droplets earlier, and her chest rose to inhale the fresh air left in the rain's wake.

As they passed the deep emeralds of the pines, the browns and glowing greens of the oaks, the purples from the heather, and the misty grays of the mountains, he was struck by how each one enhanced her beauty and how naturally they went together. She had unbound her long hair to let it dry, and it trailed behind her in lush waves as they trotted through his beloved Scotland. Just like the thistles growing wild in the sun, with their unpredictability, resilience, and beauty, she was born to be in the Highlands.

Any thought he'd had of denying himself a taste of her had evaporated with her reaction to his touch; a lass had never so easily turned him into a needy mess, but she made him act as if he were an untrained youth. 'Twas getting harder each evening to lie beside her and not take what he wanted, but thankfully, his honor and duty to the clan kept him grounded. Her reluctance to tell him who she was and well-spoken mannerisms led him to believe she might belong to a family that might not look too kindly upon him deflowering her, and that was a risk he couldn't take, so with each passing hour he kept vigilant to watch not only for Conall's men but also the return of his own to let him know whether or not he could act on all the fantasies he couldn't push from his mind.

As the sun started to descend and his thoughts turned to where they should camp for the night, Maggie pulled her horse to a halt and jumped down before he could stop her. His eyes immediately scanned the nearby woods for a threat, as did his men's and even Robbie's, he noticed.

Sliding down from his own steed, he walked over to where Maggie was bent over, studying something under the heather bushes. As he closed in, he saw her snapping branches from plants with small blue berries. He wanted to voice his frustration over her lack of judgment, but when she looked up, her eyes sparkled and her lips curved up in a smile that took his breath away.

"Blaeberries," she said innocently, as if that were the only explanation she needed to give. All he could do was return the smile and let her finish collecting her berries. Not only did she seem to belong to the land, she had a knowledge of it that only came from love and appreciation of what it offered.

"Do ye mind handing me my satchel?" Of course he didn't, — 'twould be an excuse to get close to her again, to possibly run his fingers across her soft skin and imagine what she would feel like beneath him.

He wouldn't allow her to say vows and become a nun. 'Twould be a life wasted if she did, because she would be confined to the grounds of the abbey. Maggie belonged out here in the wild, and she needed a man who could appreciate the sway of her lithe body as it leaned into his and he gently kissed her. She deserved a man who made her gasp and arch into him the way she had back in that stable, because her body was made not only to give a man pleasure but to experience it herself. Once he had taken her to his bed, she would see that.

He let his eyes stray from her long enough to see Malcolm had grabbed her bag. As he nodded, his brother tossed it to him, and he winced when vials clanked together inside. Returning his attention to her, he let out a breath as he saw she was back to picking the berries and hadn't heard.

"Thank ye." Her eyes lit when he gingerly placed the bag

next to her and knelt down to inspect her loot. "'Tis sometimes hard to spot, but ye seem to have more of it farther north."

"Do ye ken all the plants, then?"

"Aye, most, at least."

"What will ye do when the nuns dinnae let ye out to collect them?"

Her fingers paused and her eyes shut as if he'd dealt her a blow she'd not yet considered. Squaring her shoulders, she didn't meet his eyes but gazed longingly at the riches in her arms. "I'll do what is asked of me."

So she understood sacrifice for duty as well. He didn't want her to have to give up something she cared for. Not liking the far-off desperation that had taken over, he said, "Mayhap they will have need of yer talents." The corners of her lips turned back up, and he found himself wanting to keep the smile there. If Coira, the healer at Kentillie, needed help, he would talk her into taking the lass under her wing. It would keep her within his reach and out of the smothering solitude of a convent.

Pulling strips of cloth from her bag, Maggie lay them on the ground and spread her prize on them before rolling it into a bundle and placing it reverently back into the depths of the bag.

"Come, we need to find a place to camp tonight."

A short time later, they had made camp and settled in for the night. He had watch the first part of the night, so when he finally nestled into her warmth, he was instantly pulled into a deep sleep. Traveling all the next day, he attempted to ride ahead of her most of the journey, because just looking at her stirred desire so intense he ached with it, and he didn't wish to spend the rest of the journey pining for something he couldn't yet have.

The following evening, he wasn't so fortunate, because he lay next to her with his body on fire as he longed to bury himself inside her. He would have left her side, but he'd grown accustomed to her warmth and melding into her soft curves.

He wanted to beg her to tell him who she was so that he could alleviate the torturous longing in his cock, but even if she would tell him, the forest floor wasn't the place to take her innocence. So he settled for whispering to her all the things he wanted to do with her and pulling her arse into him so that he could nestle his swollen member into that sweet spot between her legs.

He'd thought her asleep, but as he spoke of tasting her with his tongue, she gasped and her head turned over her shoulder toward him. In the dim glow of the moon, it wasn't repulsion or fear he saw in her gaze — 'twas desire and surrender in the depths. She would have opened to him right then had he not the honor to hold back. "Dinnae look at me like that or I'll lose control." She nodded and turned her face away, but the image of her heated, needy eyes remained and had him painfully engorged.

Cursing to himself, he redirected his thoughts to the tasks that awaited tomorrow when they got home — getting Robbie to safety, meeting with his council, and then tupping the lass in his arms. Och, he wouldn't be getting any sleep tonight.

· · ·

Relishing the calm peace that washed over her when she woke, Maggie sighed, because her thoughts were clear and the pain had receded. Although the haze in her head had evaporated, thick air shrouded the camp in a wet mist. The eerie way the fog moved over and about them was unsettling, but she was rejuvenated and ready to start the day. She was closer to freedom, and the rest of her life would begin. They broke their fast with the remaining cheese and bread from their trip to the tavern and broke down the camp earlier this morning than usual.

"We will be there soon," Lachlan said as he lifted her up onto a horse.

Maggie smiled at the pride in his voice. The love and longing reverberating in his thick, husky brogue slid through his lips and lulled her soul like a soothing balm when he spoke of his home. She wanted to see it.

"What does Kentillie look like? I fear the mist may block my view."

"Kentillie itself is a bit stark and imposing with its gray stone walls and high turrets. But 'tis the landscape that pleases the eye. The mountains shield it from the north. The river empties into a loch with a beach where the children play. Heather grows on the moors and nearly glows when the sun sets."

She loved the way he spoke of it so fondly; she had no such affection for her home.

"'Tis large and comfortable."

She'd heard stories of raids and wondered if they happened here. Mostly, she'd known peace back home, so she thought nothing of asking, "Has it always kept yer clan safe?"

"'Tis a fortress, but also a home."

Alan's voice broke in. "The air is becoming thicker."

"Aye, the horses will be easily spooked," Lachlan said.

They continued to talk, but their voices faded as Maggie trailed behind, and her thoughts turned to her plans. As soon as they reached Kentillie, she would find maps and plot her journey to the nearest convent. Lachlan would most likely not let her set out on her own, and she would have to ask for an escort. More probably she'd be forced to sneak away, since his reaction had warned her that he was skeptical about her interest in taking vows.

Of course, she wouldn't leave until Lachlan showed her the pleasures she was certain awaited her in his bed. He'd held her these last couple of nights but not done more than talk, and she longed to feel that burning desire he had awoken with his kisses. She'd lain awake fighting the unfamiliar ache in her treacherous body that just the thought of his touch ignited.

While he'd thought her asleep, he'd whispered words of what he'd wanted to do with her, things that had made her skin flush and heart beat faster, promises of how he would make her feel once other matters were resolved. What those were, she didn't know. Thrumming now at the mere remembrance of his heated breath in her ear, her body yearned to experience what he spoke of as he had held her possessively.

Lachlan was suddenly at her side, grabbing her arm and whispering, "Halt." She did as a shiver ran down her spine.

A bird chirped, but 'twas the only sound she heard. Even their horses had gone silent. Ahead of them came a roar as a horde of men appeared from the mist, their weapons raised.

The fog shrouded a number of the attackers, but from the pounding of hooves and shouts that echoed a fierce battle cry, they seemed to be everywhere. Since Lachlan had sent away three of his men, they were down to five, plus Robbie and her. Her heart stuttered—the odds weren't in their favor.

She couldn't help—her brothers had taught her many things, but how to wield a sword was not one of them. If their father had seen her in the lists with them, he would have tanned their hides, so they'd never risked it.

"Ten at least, maybe more." Alan's voice penetrated through the vapor.

"We will have to split up. We ken this land better than they do," Lachlan returned. "Maggie, stay with me."

"Aye," she managed to eke out.

Alan's voice cut through from somewhere in the fog. "Robbie, stay close."

"Meet up at Kentillie," Lachlan called to the others then tugged at her reins. "This way. Stay close."

She didn't argue, just rode, thankful Lachlan knew where he was headed. The haze added to the disorientation of being on unfamiliar land.

Several men shouted, then the voices faded in different directions, likely to follow the dispersing Cameron men. Hooves followed them, almost as loud as her heart, but she couldn't tell how many. Her head started spinning from the jostling of the increased pace. She couldn't keep up and stay seated. "Lachlan," she cried out and pulled on the reins to slow.

"What the hell are ye doing, woman?" he fired at her.

"My head. I cannae go that fast. I willnae be able to stay seated." She wanted to cry in frustration.

He cursed, then said, "This way."

At least two men closed in on them fast. Lachlan led Maggie deeper into the woods and up a steep incline. They came to an area where they were forced to dismount—the fog was too thick, and they'd risk breaking their horses' legs otherwise.

Lachlan jumped down and grabbed her waist to pull her from the horse and set her on her feet. He pointed to a thicket of bushes and whispered, "Behind there. Stay low to the ground. Dinnae move until I come for ye." Then he rushed off in the direction they had come from, likely to put himself between her and their assailants.

Her heart beat so rapidly she was afraid she would faint for the second time in her life. How she wished she could do more than hide, but her head was pounding, and she'd be more hindrance than help, so she dashed into the greenery.

"Lachlan Cameron. Where's me brother?" a harsh voice rang out. She crouched down farther, hoping to remain unseen.

"I dinnae ken who ye are. Why would I know yer brother?" he boomed back.

"Because 'tis his horse there ye had a lass riding on. The air is no' so thick that I wouldnae recognize me own brother's steed." The venom in the man's voice was thicker than the air. "Glenn, here, his brother was with that party, too."

"What about the boy?" she heard another of the men say.

"He rode off with the other group. Dinnae worry. We'll get him." The sound of a sword sliding from its sheath pierced through the thick air, and she put her hand over her mouth to suppress a gasp. "Ewen, find the wench. She's around here somewhere."

Maggie stopped breathing. There were at least three men to Lachlan. She had seen him fight a huge ox days earlier and he'd handled himself well, but how many could he take on at one time?

No other words came, just the clang of swords and grunts. Unable to see much, she made herself as small as possible but snapped a twig in the process. She bit her lip and prayed the one coming for her had not heard.

"Come, lass. I willnae harm ye," a man crooned to her, and panic set in.

She'd heard the voice before. What had someone called him? Her heart sank as a name penetrated her hazy memory. *Ewen.* Conall's friend. The one who sneered at her every time they came to visit. The toad who had cornered her, groped her, and told her Conall sometimes let him watch. He'd said he would take pleasure in seeing him break her. Her head spun, and she was going to retch. She reached for her dagger, then remembered she'd lost it when she'd stitched up Malcolm.

Wood snapped, and boots clomping in the brush came nearer. Ewen was close. He was headed straight toward her, and she had nowhere to run. Cowering, she closed her eyes against the dizziness and prayed the thick bush was enough cover. A nearby sound caught her attention, and her eyes flew wide to see his face looming toward her as the mist cleared. A startled squeak escaped her lips.

He squinted, and the corners of his lips turned into a malicious smirk. She tried to bolt, but he caught her by the arm before she could even rise.

"Well, now, Margaret Murray. Conall has been looking for ye. Wonder what he'll do when he finds out ye were with Lachlan. Isnae going to be pretty, wench." He let go and kicked at her, striking her in the ribs.

She doubled over and drew a breath in sharply at the pain.

"Get up."

She attempted to creep farther into the brush, but branches and leaves scratched her hands and face.

Trapped.

The toad reached down, grabbed her again, and yanked her to her feet. He dragged her out of the bushes and into the clearing with a dirk to her neck.

Maggie was glad to see Lachlan had defeated one man and was about to go in for the kill on the second. He swung and struck the man on his left side, and dazed, the man dropped to the ground and rolled to his side.

Ewen yelled, "Look what I have here."

Lachlan froze.

"Put yer weapon down, or I'll slice her throat."

Lachlan turned to glare at the man holding her. Only one time before had she seen him look so deadly and menacing—when he thought she'd hurt his brother—and his furious gaze should have instilled horror in the man who gripped her. It terrified her.

Ewen boasted, "Do ye see this, Glenn? Look who I have here." Thankfully, Lachlan was facing them and missed the recognition flashing in Glenn's eyes as he writhed on the ground.

• • •

His blade grasped tightly at his side, Lachlan strutted casually toward Maggie and the bastard holding her. "Let her go," he commanded.

The man tightened his grip on her arm and twisted the point of the blade so it almost dug into her neck. It appeared as if the breath caught in her throat.

"Glenn, get up. We can take 'er with us. The Cameron wouldnae risk the lass getting hurt."

Lachlan spared a passing glance for the man he had just cut down with a killing blow from his claymore. Although he still squirmed, Glenn didn't appear as if he would be going anywhere.

"Ye are already dead. If ye harm her, I shall make it slow and excruciating. Let go of her now, and ye can die a swift, painless death." Tensed and ready to pounce, he tightened his grip on the hilt of his sword. His steady voice was deceptive; he was anything but calm. Maggie was under his protection, and no one would threaten her and live. A rage he had never experienced before coursed through him and threatened to unleash the primitive beast he kept buried deep inside.

The fool backed up as Lachlan stalked forward. He stumbled slightly with Maggie but recovered quickly. The dead man—for he was dead as soon as he'd laid a hand on her—jerked her along with him, and her feet dragged on the ground.

Maggie peered straight at him. "Dinnae worry with me, Lachlan. I had rather die than go with him."

His lip turned up at the brave words from his little lass. She was reckless, but he would get her out of this safely, and she would never be harmed again because of him. These men were here because they wanted Robbie and because of the piece of paper he had tucked in his sporran. She was an innocent.

"L-let go of me, ye brute," she stammered as she grappled with the arm encircling her waist.

The dead man only laughed at her, then whispered in her ear, but Lachlan couldn't hear what he'd said. The color drained from her face, and she went completely still. She stopped struggling and seemed resigned to whatever fate would come. Rage erupted anew.

"Ye willnae leave this land alive, ye ken that?" Lachlan shook his head at the man's ignorance. "Do ye ken how far north ye have come?" He let out a harsh chuckle as Ewen tensed and his eyes darted from side to side. "Ye are on my land now."

"If ye step closer, I will slit her throat. I'd rather take 'er alive, but I will kill 'er if I have to."

White-hot fury exploded in Lachlan's veins.

Just as he was readying to pounce, Maggie's hands darted up and grabbed the arm holding the dirk at her neck. She yanked the blade away from her as the heel of her boot came down on the scoundrel's foot. Despite her attempt, his filthy hands still held their grip on her. She struggled, but the other arm holding her did not budge.

As Lachlan dropped his sword, bolted forward, and latched onto the arm with the knife, Ewen yelped. Maggie ducked down, out of the man's reach, and won free. The dead man and he tumbled to the earth with Ewen pinned under Lachlan's much larger body. He raised the rogue's arm and forcefully thrust it back into a nearby rock, over and over until the man's fist unclenched and the weapon fell to the ground.

Lachlan struck the man in his face. Once, it felt good— he would never touch Maggie again. Twice—the man's hands had been on his woman. Three times—he would never touch what belonged to another man again. With each punch, some of the rage that had overwhelmed him was released. He didn't know how many times he hit the battered and bloody face before he heard Maggie's calming voice through his haze of fury.

A light touch on the small of his back roused him. "Lachlan, 'tis enough," she said.

He kept going.

"Lachlan, he cannae harm anyone."

She knelt down beside him as her hand moved to his shoulder and he stopped the relentless pounding. The bastard didn't move. He was motionless, and it appeared as if he wouldn't be going anywhere.

Maggie circled around to his front and took his bloody hand. She inspected it as he blinked her back into focus. "Are ye hurt?" she asked.

He wanted to laugh. She was asking if he was hurt—she was the one who had had a blade to her throat. Stretching his hand out for her, he tenderly took her chin and pushed it up so he could inspect the damage. There was a small pinprick where the tip of the blade had dug into her tender flesh.

"Are ye hurt?" he questioned as he rose and pulled her up with him. He wanted her away from this violence. A lass like her should never have to see anything like this.

The horses were still close by, so he gathered them quickly. He spared a thought for the fallen men, but his priority was getting Maggie to the castle and making sure the others had made it back. He would send someone to dispose of the bodies later. Glancing around to inspect the carnage before they left, he noticed one was missing.

The one he had fatally wounded was gone, and his horse was missing as well, although he wouldn't make it far. Lachlan would send a few Camerons out to look for him. In his weakened condition, he shouldn't be difficult to track.

"Come, we arenae far from Kentillie. We need to get ye to safety. I dinnae ken how many more men there are." In the back of his mind, he considered the missing man, although Maggie probably hadn't noticed and had no idea they were still in danger. Better he did not tell her.

Reaching up, she took his face in both of her hands. The gesture was so gentle it took him by surprise.

"Thank you, Lachlan." Her eyes watered, and she pushed up on her toes while drawing his face down to hers. Her lips brushed his and lingered. The kiss was tender and sincere and sent shock waves straight to that part of him that wanted to be buried deep inside her.

She pulled him in closer, and he groaned at the desire her sweet caress elicited.

As his hand slid to her nape, he groaned again then ended the kiss. It was not safe here, and if this continued, she wouldn't remain an innocent much longer. He wanted nothing more than to stake his claim on her, fill her, and make her cry out his name. But this was not the place, and he couldn't risk taking her until he knew who she was.

The sooner they moved, the quicker he would have her out of danger—he wanted her locked away behind the fortified walls of Kentillie.

"Maggie, I want ye, but no' here, lass. 'Tis no' safe." Reluctantly he pulled away, then remembered. "How is your head?"

"'Tis hard to concentrate and everything seems fuzzy, but 'tis settling down. It doesnae hurt."

"We will ride slowly to make sure we dinnae jostle ye anymore." He picked her up and put her on her horse, making sure she had her balance before he released his grip.

He glanced over his shoulder one last time and scanned for the missing man. A chill ran down his spine, but he turned and they were on their way.

Chapter Seven

When Ewen had the blade to her throat, he had threatened to take her directly to Conall; she would no longer have the protection of her family. Their wedding could take place immediately. Her stomach had turned, and she still wasn't sure how she had tamped down the nausea and panic. The recollection made her hands sweat and her heart race in fear, and she shuddered.

How had Conall's men found her? It was too quick, especially considering the meandering they had done to avoid the jagged peaks of the mountains. His men would have had to do the same thing, so how had they been able to track her? Her family should barely even realize she was gone, much less Conall, and there was no way they could have determined she'd ridden north with Lachlan and his men.

Could she be putting Lachlan and his people at risk? If Conall found her, he would let nothing stand in the way of retrieving her. Her betrothed was powerful, but so was Lachlan. She prayed she was not about to start a war.

Her time at Kentillie would have to be short.

The fog had cleared, and she didn't want to dwell on something she couldn't control, so she attempted to focus on the scenery as they rode. It was beautiful here. The terrain had changed along the journey, becoming harder to traverse, and the rolling hills of her home had turned to vast mountains. They were the largest she'd ever seen, and their majesty was mesmerizing.

Kentillie Castle came into view as they rounded a mountain and rode out into a glen.

"'Tis beautiful," Maggie said without even realizing it. Lachlan had been silent and on guard since the attack, but with his home in view he seemed to ease.

"Aye, 'tis. This is the River Arkaig. It runs behind the castle." He motioned to the fast-flowing water that had come into view. Pride resonated in his voice, and she could see why.

"Loch Arkaig is to the west and Loch Lochy to the east. Castle Kentillie is in the middle."

The land was lush and fertile—it was the most beautiful place she'd ever seen. Along with the green foliage, varying shades of purples from heather and thistle bushes dotted the landscape. Orange and yellow rowan trees were scattered about on the sides of mountains and streams, and hardy-looking, reddish-brown cows with long hair grazed in the open spaces and on the sides of the hills. She found herself looking at the vegetation as they passed, recognizing some herbs she could use and others she'd never seen before. This place was heaven.

As they rode through the gatehouse, a tall, willowy woman rushed up to greet them. Lachlan dismounted, and Finlay helped Maggie down from her horse as the lady drew Lachlan in and whispered something in his ear. Despite her height, she still looked small next to him. Her long golden hair, pulled back at the nape of her neck, had just started to gray. She had aged beautifully and had probably once been the most bonny lass in the area.

Easing back, she said, "Malcolm said ye were bringing a lass."

The woman beamed at him, then her gaze traveled to Maggie and perused her from head to toe. Her regard remained steady and unreadable as her focus returned to Lachlan. Maggie wasn't sure if the woman was taking her measure or had dismissed her.

"Malcolm is here, then." Lachlan's tense shoulders relaxed. "What of Alan and the lad with him?"

"Aye, they are all back, except for the three you sent south."

The lady smiled, and eyes the same shade of blue as Lachlan's turned from him and riveted on her. "Lachlan, boy, where are yer manners? Please introduce me to the lovely lass."

He actually flushed. "This is Maggie." His gaze shifted toward her shyly. She'd never seen him embarrassed, not thought him capable of such an emotion, the big brute of a man who cut down the ox and then three men at one time.

"Maggie, this is my mother, Elspeth." Was he ashamed to introduce her to his mother?

Oh, God, what would the woman think of her? She'd not considered how the rest of his family might react to a poorly dressed stranger he'd picked up on the side of the road. Days had passed since she'd changed into Robbie's old castoffs, and her boy's clothing suddenly seemed heavier. She probably smelled bad, too. Och, her hair—she'd not had the brush the rest of the journey and had resorted to finger combing and then pulling her tresses back to keep knots at bay.

The last thing on her mind after the attack today had been meeting his mother. Hers would have cringed at her appearance, but it was difficult to read Lachlan's mother. Where had the woman learned to hide her emotions?

I could use a lesson in it, she thought as Elspeth held out a hand. Maggie grasped it and said, "I am pleased to meet ye, Elspeth."

Despite Maggie's tattered appearance, the woman pulled her in for a tight embrace, which was warm and motherly. She seemed genuinely happy to meet Maggie. That surprised her, as she had expected Elspeth to distance herself instead of welcoming Maggie as if she were an old friend. Why would any of them trust her? Maybe Elspeth was still unaware of how she had come to be in Lachlan's company. What would Malcolm have said about her?

"Get cleaned up, Lachlan, ye are a mess. I will take this lovely lass and get her some proper attire."

Now Maggie couldn't hide the blush as Elspeth walked with her arm looped through hers and led her through the gates. A blessed calm washed over her as she realized this was what she had wanted.

She was free.

Maggie took a moment to enjoy the view of the mountains and river. Lachlan had described it perfectly, and she was already in love with the fortress in front of her. It loomed large but offered a sense of security she had never known. While she could, she would enjoy her time here, in this safe place, a sanctuary that would allow her to move on without fear to the next part of her journey.

"Malcolm tells me ye saved his life." Ah, this was why the woman was being so kind.

"I stitched his wound, but I think he would have mended well with some rest." She tried to minimize her role in the whole affair.

Maggie had never been good at receiving compliments, probably because she was not accustomed to being paid any. Her mother had ignored her accomplishments, while her father had always complained she was not feminine enough.

Retreating with her brothers had been a welcome respite from not living up to expectations, and she had spent all those years in the forest because she didn't want to be anything like the women her father and men of his ilk wanted. She would never be one to fawn over a man to the point her children no longer mattered.

Maggie sighed. She would probably never have children. The thought made her heart ache.

"He also tells me that my oldest has developed a fondness for ye." At Elspeth's statement, Maggie's steps faltered and her jaw dropped open, but no words came out.

What else had he told her?

As the woman drew her into the great hall, her embarrassment vanished. The beauty of the hall captivated her attention. Although she had imagined it would be large, because she had heard of the strength of the Cameron clan, she had not expected it to be so ornate.

Artfully woven tapestries hung from the walls depicting stories from the history of the clan. Elspeth pointed them out as they passed, telling her a brief history of each, and she beamed as she passed on the stories of the clan's home and heritage. Her enthusiasm was contagious—not that Maggie knew much of clan Cameron—it was the thought of someone taking interest in something other than her misplaced loyalties. A mother who loved her sons and her legacy.

She instantly felt a connection to this woman.

Elspeth turned and studied her. "Are ye going to tell me where ye are from?" Maggie froze, and Elspeth continued, "I dinnae ken if ye are aware of what Lachlan has had to deal with, but deception willnae be tolerated here."

Her chest rose and fell as she took a fortifying gulp and breathed in. "I dinnae intend to deceive anyone. I dinnae tell my surname to protect myself." Guilt assailed her for her selfish reasons. "I have nae intention of harming or misleading anyone. I plan to be out of yer way shortly. If ye are uncomfortable with me here, I can leave now if ye wish it."

The idea of leaving now left her cold, because she wanted to have a little time with Lachlan first. Yearned to feel his skin against hers, to know what it was like to have a man touch her in intimate ways, to give her a small handful of memories to cherish after she took her vows. But she would give that up if this woman asked her to go.

Elspeth scrutinized her for a few moments and then said, "Ye seem honest. I have a way of knowing good character, so for now, ye can stay."

"Thank ye for your kindness and welcome. I dinnae plan to stay long, and will need to be on my way soon. My presence here cannae be good for yer clan." She bit her bottom lip, privately scolding herself for revealing so much.

"I hope one day ye have the courage to tell me what ye are running from." Elspeth gave her a small smile. "But for now, let's find ye some appropriate clothes and get ye washed up." She looped her arm back through Maggie's and led her through the great hall, pausing only to issue orders for a bath to be brought to the room she would be putting Maggie in. They walked up some stairs and down a short hallway with a view overlooking the spacious room below.

Elspeth led Maggie into a chamber, saying, "I'll be back shortly," and left her to the peace of being alone for the first time since she'd left home. It wasn't long before a bath was brought in, the woman reappearing with a linen shift and a deep green woolen arisaid. Just after dropping the garments on the bed and a tray of pastries with a cup of ale on the small desk near the door, she said, "I'll let ye bathe in privacy," and was gone again.

After taking off her boy's shoes and garments, she folded and stacked them neatly by the door, where she noticed a pair of slippers matching the emerald hues of the plaid had been laid out for her. Returning to the bath, she dipped one finger in to test the water. 'Twas warm, so she climbed in and bathed with the soap that had been provided. Once done, she dried herself and walked over to the bed.

She picked up the soft shift and slid it over her head, then went to the desk and discovered a brush had been left for her as well. 'Twas refreshing to have her locks cleaned, and she set to work combing the long tresses, but let them fall loose when she couldn't find anything to tie them back with. After having the ale and pastries, she found herself becoming drowsy, so she sauntered back over to the bed and ran her fingers over the woolen fabric, noting the vibrant colors and fine craftsmanship.

The green would look nice on her. Men had always told her she was beautiful, but it had never been important to her before. On many occasions, she had purposely made herself look unattractive or had not tamed her hair because she didn't want men looking at her, but tonight was different.

She wanted Lachlan to notice her, and she wanted him to desire her—her only experience with a man should be a good one, and she had little time to tarry. Who knew when Conall would come for her, and she needed to be long gone before then. As her mother had ranted about her father's indiscretions, the woman told her about men and bedding; it could be a magical experience or it could go horribly wrong. Craving the intimacy he had promised as he held her the previous night, her body heated and a flush crept over her that made her knees wobble.

Pulling the covers back on the bed, she decided to lie down until Elspeth returned for her. Clean and sated, 'twasn't long before she drifted off into a deep sleep.

• • •

"Where is Maggie?" Lachlan's eyes narrowed as he looked around the great hall.

"When I made it back to her chamber, she was sleeping peacefully. I didnae wake her."

Rubbing his eyes, he sat. "I had to write some letters to some of the local clan chiefs." He looked to Malcolm and continued, "I've invited them here to see proof of Conall's betrayal. Robbie will testify before them, but reluctantly and only if he has to. The boy doesnae want the attention."

Hours of consulting with the council of Camerons had his head spinning with thoughts of Conall or his henchmen's imminent arrival. There was no doubt the bastard would be coming for Robbie and the letter, so they had talked defense. A rotation of guards would be on the lookout for the bastard, because he was sure the man was crazy enough to enter his land. But what worried him most was whether Conall would use his alliance with the Earl of Argyll himself and bring the Covenanter army swooping down on the Camerons.

Time would not be on their side, so it was crucial that they draft letters to the local Royalist lairds he could count on. By the time Conall discovered his latest group had been unsuccessful in capturing Robbie and retrieving the missive, Lachlan hoped to have the proof of his betrayal in the hands of other lairds. The fate of all the Royalist clans currently rested in his hands.

"Maggie may leave in the morn. Are ye sure ye should allow it? We're still unsure as to her loyalties or if she is as innocent as she appears," his mother said.

"We are likely better off if she does. Even if she is a spy, I dinnae think she has learned much that Conall doesnae already know." Lachlan put a forkful of roasted chicken in his mouth. The bonny lass abovestairs was not where his thoughts should be, but the thought of her leaving so soon soured his mood further.

"Ye dinnae mean that. She cannae be out there on her own." Elspeth waved her hand at nowhere in particular.

"I willnae let any harm befall her. We can see her to the convent." He scooped up another bite. 'Twas a shame she would suppress her spirit and give a body like hers to God, but he had to honor her wishes.

"She saved yer brother, and we could always use another healer. Cannae ye no' let her stay awhile?"

"Then a compromise. I willnae have her taken to the convent until we know who she is." *And until I've taken her to my bed.* He shook the thought from his head as quickly as it had appeared—his lustful yearning warned him he was making a mistake by allowing her to stay. He could not afford any distractions, especially as Conall and his men, and possibly some of the other Covenanters, could be plotting an invasion of Cameron lands, and a deceitful lass could be as deadly as Argyll himself. Still, he was in no mood to argue with his mother; he would just make sure the lass was watched at all times. "Does that please ye?"

"Aye, for now. Now, finish up, and ye get some rest as well." She turned her head to her youngest son. "Ye be careful with that wound tonight." With a nod, she rose and walked away.

"I like her, too," Malcolm started in.

Lachlan said nothing as he took another bite of the meat.

"She has a good heart. Do ye ken anyone else that would have jumped into a battle with men she didnae ken to help a stranger?"

"Nae. It's either that, or she's daft."

"She is no' daft. Ye saw her with the bow. She's a steady, clear thinker, if just a wee bit impulsive."

Lachlan questioned the "wee bit" part; the lass was too brash for her own good. He took a gulp of his ale. "Aye, ye get to bed, too. Let me eat in peace."

"I am just asking ye to no' be hasty in yer judgment."

"I will do what is right for the clan," he returned without any hint of amusement as Malcolm stood and turned to leave.

Finished with his meal, he made his way upstairs. His feet took him past his own chamber, and he found himself at the next, staring at the heavy wooden door to the room where Maggie would be. After hesitating only a moment to squash down his doubts, he eased the barrier open. This was his castle after all, and he was checking on her. Purely for safety reasons, of course. She was in bed. Quietly, he licked his lips, shut the door behind him, and padded toward the sleeping lass he hadn't been able to banish from his thoughts.

A spectral glow filled the room. He inched closer still and noted an ethereal quality to her moon-kissed face. She was even lovelier in peaceful slumber.

He had the urge to touch her cheek to see if it was as soft as it looked, but he held back, because if he did, his hand might drift to other places and linger too long. Until he had confirmation of who she was, he couldn't risk giving in to the urge to claim her, although he knew he would when the time was right. He had looked forward to seeing her at the evening meal, but the clan came first, and his priority was to them and their allies, not a lass who wouldn't even acknowledge hers.

A hammered silver cuff bracelet sat on the table beside the bed. He picked it up and rubbed it between his fingers. The cool, smooth metal was of good quality, and he walked to the moon-drenched window to inspect it.

A small cross was engraved on the elongated oval face. The craftsmanship was precise, and the value indicated she came from a family that had money to spare. It matched the one he had found in her medicine bag. Turning it over, he discovered something written on the inside. *A gift from God, M.M.* His shoulders drooped—maybe she did belong in a convent.

No, she would suffocate cloistered away. He walked back

over to the table and set it down harder than intended.

Maggie made a little mewling noise and shifted. He couldn't resist the temptation to touch the black locks strewn across the pillow and had the sudden urge to climb in with her and wrap her up in his arms as he had the previous nights.

Ye dinnae even ken who she is, he chided himself as he tamped down the foolish thoughts. He turned and left the room to climb into his own cold, empty bed.

Sleep refused to come as he tossed and turned all night. The urge to return to Maggie's room was like the call of a pastry left to cool on a window ledge to a hungry child. The desire to taste her consumed him.

Images of a black-haired temptress writhing beneath him and a painfully swollen cock woke him. With a groan, he crawled out bed. A bath in the cold loch might be in his future, so he dressed and made his way downstairs.

As he turned the corner, he spied Maggie and froze, because 'twas the first time he'd seen her in women's clothing. She wore a deep green plaid draped lovingly over her shoulders, and her dark curls were pulled back in a headpiece that made her look regal as she stood tall and conversed with the two most undisciplined Cameron children he knew. One had been crying, the other stood with arms crossed and face red, but Maggie held court over them as if she were the lady of the keep. The way she handled the children deserved praise. He'd seen their parents struggling to keep them from coming to blows, while Maggie practically had the children embracing.

Mesmerized by her beauty, he stood in the shadows, listening and watching.

Just as he moved to join them, Dougal came rushing through the door and gave a crooked grin. "I got back last night, but ye had already gone to bed."

"Did ye find anything?" He motioned for Dougal to

follow him farther into the shadows.

"Aye. The horse belongs to some man they call the Irish Priest."

"Are ye certain? Why would she have the horse of a priest?" Lachlan rubbed his head.

"I thought 'twas odd, too. He has a niece with dark wavy hair who stays with him." One hand made waving motions from his temple down to his shoulders.

"Did ye return the horse and meet the man?"

"Nae. I wasnae certain what ye would want me to do. I thought 'twas better if no one was aware we had been there, and the priest surely would have asked questions."

"Ye were right." Lachlan clasped him on the shoulder and tilted his head toward the great hall. "Get ye something to eat. I need fresh air and will be back soon."

As he walked out into the warmth of the morning, he couldn't help but smile. He'd found a woman who was the niece of a priest, and he could understand her misguided desire to take vows. His manhood hardened again with the knowledge it wouldn't be long before he was able to thrust into her and relieve the ache.

Maggie was no longer untouchable.

Chapter Eight

The first glow of morning's light filled the room when Maggie came awake to a cock crowing outside the window. Och, she'd fallen asleep and been an awful guest, not even joining them for the dinner meal. Elspeth must think her rude and unmannered. Hoping to make an early appearance and apologize for the slight, she quickly donned the plaid and slippers that had been left for her and rushed out of the room.

As she rounded the bottom of the stairs and entered the great hall, she came across two children arguing loudly. Introducing herself and gathering their names, she quickly learned they'd been squabbling over a mere apple. She'd had much larger problems to deal with as acting lady at the Murray castle, a duty she had assumed at an early age since her mother had lost interest in running the place without her father's attentions and had turned to making everyone as miserable as she could.

"Did ye hide his apple, Davina?" she questioned the little girl.

The angry girl's gaze shifted, and she bit her lip, but she

said, "Nae."

"She isnae telling the truth," the red-faced boy cried.

"Is that true?" Maggie asked the girl just as the apple in question fell from its hiding place in her arisaid. Sighing, she pursed her lips while Davina hid her face. Maggie sank to her knees in front of the little girl and took her hands. "Och, Davina, ye should never lie."

"But—but, he ate me roll." Davina pouted.

"That is another matter, and I'll talk with Alik about it." Her eyes darted to the other child then back to Davina. "Ye must never lie, lass. Once a trust is broken, it isnae easy to repair." Inwardly, she groaned as she realized 'twas exactly what she'd done when she met Lachlan.

Davina said nothing.

"Ye see that tapestry, the one with the beautiful reds?" Maggie pointed.

"Aye." The girl peeked through her lowered lashes.

"Imagine ye ripped it down the middle and ye only had yellow yarn to repair it with."

Davina's eyes narrowed, but Maggie kept going, "Ye could mend it, but 'twould never be the same. 'Tis what happens when ye lie. Ye have damaged a fragile trust, and no matter how hard ye try to mend it, 'twill never be as it was before. The person ye have lied to will always have doubts."

Was it possible to fix the tear between her and Lachlan? Not likely if she didn't tell him the truth, but if she did, she wasn't naive enough to think he would protect her as he did his clan. He owed her nothing.

A small tear ran down to the girl's chin. "I'm sorra. I willnae do it again."

Maggie wiped the tear from the little cheek. "Ye see then why 'tis so important to be honest?"

"Aye."

"I will forgive ye this time without the tear, but make sure to always be honest." Would Lachlan ever forgive her if he discovered the truth?

Maggie's eyes went back to Alik. "Do ye understand, too?"

He nodded.

"Now, did ye take her roll?"

"Aye," he said as his gaze avoided Maggie's.

"Well, then, Davina, ye may have my roll. Alik, I believe ye owe yer sister an apology."

"I'm sorry," he said.

"Let's get back to the table. I'll share my apple with both of ye."

Moments later, Elspeth greeted, "Good morn to ye," as the woman sat across from her and the children.

"Aye, 'tis a good morning. I have made some new friends." Maggie winked at Davina and Alik then smiled. For the first time in years it was safe to be happy, and she could have friends again without fear of Conall's rages.

Elspeth smiled at them then turned back to Maggie, "Since ye weren't able to take anything with ye, I am having my nieces bring some things to make ye more comfortable this morning."

She had brought something of her own. "My bag." She gasped, and her eyes widened. "It has my herbs in it. Did Lachlan say anything about it?"

Her medicinals were important. Some were hard to find, and many of the containers were from her grandmother and mother. They were irreplaceable.

"What kind of herbs?" Elspeth asked.

"For healing. My mother and grandmother taught me some about the art." Smiling, Maggie straightened. Her abilities were one of her only sources of pride.

"That is how ye saved my Malcolm." Elspeth beamed back. "'Tis a good skill to have."

Chairs scraped across the floor as two women sat next to Elspeth. She turned to see who had joined them. "These are my nieces, Lorna and Donella."

Maggie gave what she hoped was a welcoming smile, but she shook inside as an image of her friend Miranda flashed behind her eyes. The last few years, she'd kept to herself, intentionally avoiding interaction with girls her own age because of Conall. "Hi." She gulped. "I'm Maggie."

"We are happy ye are here, Maggie. Thank ye so much for bringing Malcolm back to us," Donella said. Slightly taller than Maggie, she had to be about four to five years older. Large with child and smelling of mint, she looked as if she would be bringing her babe into the world any day. Her rosy cheeks and warm greeting calmed Maggie's nerves fractionally, but the fear was so deep inside her, she wasn't sure she'd ever be able to shake it completely.

"I only sutured his wound and put some balm on the cut. I am sure he would have been fine."

"Malcolm insists you saved him," Lorna said. She looked to be Maggie's age. Flame-red, curly locks had been pulled back in a band, but some had fallen loose to frame her oval face.

"What would he know? He wasnae even awake." Maggie laughed.

"That sounds like Malcolm," Lorna agreed.

She smiled again. *Freedom and friends.* This was what it felt like to not live in fear. Since the incident, the day she'd become afraid, she had stayed away from all the other lasses back home. She had decided to never again put another lass at the risk of Conall's notice, but here, they were safe.

"We will be showing ye all about Kentillie today. This place can be a little daunting if ye dinnae ken yer way around," Lorna said.

After a morning touring the inside of the castle and a

light midday meal, she, Lorna, and Donella departed, and met up with Elspeth, who said, "Let's see what I can show ye outside the castle."

They ventured out to the stables. A familiar horse was outside grazing. "Freedom!" Maggie rushed toward him. "I'll be back in a few moments. I'd like to say hi," she called over her shoulder. "Ye have come back." She rubbed her hand down the horse's head. The steed sniffed and turned its head to look away. She whispered, "I am aware ye dinnae ken who I am, but ye can at least pretend to be happy to see me."

A shift in the air was the only indication she was no longer alone. Lachlan had joined her. A thrill shot through her and caught her unaware. She reached back up to stroke Freedom's nose and give her time to analyze her body's unexpected reaction.

"Would ye like to take him out for a ride? I'll show ye the loch. 'Tis always beautiful."

"Aye, it sounds nice." And she meant it. The landscape here was beautiful, and she wanted to enjoy it; the added boon was Lachlan would spend the time with her. "Och, but yer mother was going to take me out." She turned, but Elspeth had disappeared.

"She willnae mind if I take ye." He watched her intently as he grinned mischievously. Maggie smiled and then heated as his words took on another meaning. He collected his horse, and she took the time to catch her breath.

A few moments later, they were trotting away from Kentillie and toward the loch. "'Tis lovely here. I have never seen a mountain so high." She pointed to the largest.

"Aye, 'tis Ben Nevis. 'Tis said to be the largest in all of Scotland."

"I believe it." Tearing her gaze away from the scenery, she looked at him. *This suits him. He has to be one of the brawniest men in Scotland.*

"Ye look bonny."

She blushed but returned his suddenly heated gaze. The intensity startled her, but it was what she wanted. Something about him called to a primitive part of her that had lain dormant until he'd held her naked body in the river. Now she thrummed anytime he was near.

"Thank ye. Ye are pleasing to look at as well." She cringed after the words spilled from her lips. It was a feeble attempt at flirtation, but he grinned anyway.

They came to a beach, and Lachlan dismounted. He took her hand to help her down and seemed to scan the area before settling the horses at a nearby tree.

Children laughed and splashed around in the water. She had only been around a few younger cousins on occasion but loved to join in the innocent play when given a chance. It was liberating to give in to the moment, as she had so rarely been able to truly be herself.

"Come," he said. Although he didn't take her hand, he walked so near her they could have almost touched.

"Ye have so many bairns here."

"We tend to be as fertile as the valley is."

Maggie bit her lip as her face warmed. "Do ye miss yer sister?"

"Aye. Ye remind me of her. She speaks and follows her mind no matter how much trouble it will get her in."

"Does it bother ye that a woman may want things different from a man?"

"Nae. How are ye to understand others with a different point of view if ye never listen?" They were at the edge of the water.

She sat on the nearest boulder and removed her slippers and stockings. Children continued to laugh and splash in all directions. "There are no' many men who would bother for a woman's opinion."

"I have discovered that most women are capable of logical thought. Sometimes more so than some men."

Maggie rose, pulled her skirts up, and waded into the water while Lachlan remained close on the beach, but she noticed he stayed watchful of their surroundings. The cool water was refreshing. She sighed then turned to take in the full view of him. "Would ye force a woman to do something she doesnae wish, if it got ye something ye wanted?"

His gaze returned to her. "Not unless it was for the good of the clan."

An image of Conall flashed in her head, and she shuddered as dread washed over her. It was the answer all men in his position would give.

"But I would listen to her reasons," he continued. "Sometimes women see things we dinnae."

She breathed out. Even though her reservations about revealing her identity lingered, it was nice to know he was willing to listen. Would her reasons be sufficient to appeal to him as a man? She thought he might listen, because he didnae seem the type to force his sister into an abusive marriage. He'd let her go out on her own.

As squealing children ran by, cold droplets speckled Maggie's legs, and she made a small shriek as the liquid sent chills through her. One of the boys heard her and turned then splashed her again. Suppressing a giggle, she reached down to cup a handful of water and toss it back. She dropped her skirt, and it fell into the water.

The lad laughed, and they continued back and forth. A stream of water hit her headpiece. She scooped up and aimed, but he ran just out of reach and took off to join the friends who were calling to him. Pulling the wet headpiece off, she ran her fingers through her hair, and when she looked back at Lachlan, he had a boyish sideways grin on his face. Well, it wasn't that innocent. He suddenly looked as if he wanted to devour her.

Her chest tightened, and her core clenched. Something about the way he looked at her made her want to taste him, too, and she didn't even know what that meant.

"Come here, lass." His deep voice washed over her and sent waves of excitement coursing through her.

Swallowing, she sauntered toward him. His arms snaked around her waist and pulled her flush to his chest as his lips crashed down on hers, causing tingles to erupt on her skin and need to ignite in her core. The kiss was warm and slow, strong and possessive. She melted into it.

When his tongue delved into her mouth, she returned the caress and rose up on her toes to get closer and her arms grasped onto his hips. Being in his arms held a strange appeal she wanted to spend more time exploring, learning why her body turned into a wobbly mess when any part of her brushed up against him.

Water spattered her cheek, and the kiss broke. The boy and his friends laughed, and she looked at Lachlan. He had not been spared, either. Drops of liquid streamed down the side of his face.

He looked dazed. She would have expected him to be annoyed with the boys, but he continued to study her as if she were the only person in Scotland. Fighting back the blush this time, she licked her lips. She wouldn't be ashamed of wanting him.

"Ye know I want ye, lass."

"Aye." She wanted him, too.

His hand rose and caressed her cheek. It trailed down until one finger was left tracing her lips. She gasped. She started to quiver with anticipation, then he backed away. "Tonight," he said.

• • •

This is absolute torture, Lachlan thought as he watched Maggie's sinful lips close around a spoon of cooked apples in cream sauce. Her eyes had lit then her tongue darted out to lick the smudge left behind on the utensil. His loins tightened as he imagined several other ways for her to use that beautiful mouth.

The last few days had been sheer torment. He had lain awake last night thinking of the things he wanted to do with her. The previous nights had been no better. It had been torment holding her in his arms, the whole time his body craving to do more. He ached thinking of her pliant body beneath his and longed to hear the soft feminine moans she would make as he slowly delved in and out of her.

Lachlan wanted to please her. One time with her wouldn't be enough, and somehow it was important to him she would want more. As he took her, he wanted to hear her screaming his name. He wanted—no, needed—to see those blue eyes filled with pleasure, her head tilting back as she accepted his body into hers. The thought of her thrashing in ecstasy below him nearly drove him mad. This dinner would not end soon enough, and he nearly growled with frustration.

She was perched in the seat next to him, so close her arm kept brushing against his and shivers of awareness rushed through his already fevered nerves. He'd thought her bonny in her rags, but now, he could not keep his eyes off her. The green plaid had slipped loose from one shoulder and her low-hanging shirt offered an enticing view of the pale skin just above her breast. Her black hair curled in perfect spirals, and his fingers itched to delve into its mass and pull her lips to his.

The candlelight from the hall reflected in her deep blue eyes, and they sparkled as if they mirrored the stars of the sky. She looked both shy and confident, with rosy cheeks presenting the perfect picture of a priest's innocent niece with the carefree spirit of a tavern maid. Why would she be running from her uncle's protection? But then he remembered what had befallen Robbie's guardian, and he let the doubt slip from his thoughts. Maggie was full of contradictions he wanted to puzzle out, but he would not fall under her spell.

A delightful shade of red crept onto her face when she caught him watching her. He wanted to see more of that blush—he would not mind seeing it forever. Damn, where had that come from?

Maggie would be his.

No one had ever had the privilege of touching her; he'd work to keep that in mind and not go too fast with her. That would be hard, considering his perpetually aroused state.

Already, he had waited an eternity—she belonged in his bed. He wanted her there so he could touch her whenever the mood struck, because it seemed to strike every time he glanced at her. The thought of having her at his beck and call heated his blood.

As she laughed at something his mother said, her dark locks bounced. How he wanted to run his fingers through her thick tresses, to feel the silky strands as they tickled his chest. He thought of those curls cascading down around her face as she rode astride him. But he had to stop this, or he wouldn't make it through dinner. Thankfully, Alan broke into his thoughts.

"Yer mother seems to like her." He tilted his head toward Maggie and Elspeth, and his eyes twinkled with mischief.

"Aye," he said as he eyed the pair with a crooked grin.

"I dinnae remember her ever talking with Aileen that way." Alan's smile broadened, showing straight, white teeth.

"Nae, she didnae approve of her." Still trying to get his wayward thoughts under control, Lachlan gulped his ale.

"Ye should give her a chance, get to ken who she is. She might make a good wife." Alan's tone and impassive expression meant he was serious. It was a tenor he only used when they discussed serious matters.

Lachlan froze and inspected Alan through squinted eyes. "Have ye gone daft, man? Ye ken how I feel about that." Taking another swallow, he realized the normal conviction behind his protest was missing.

He didn't want to analyze how those words that only days earlier were granite in his heart now seemed hollow to his own ears. He slammed down his cup in a vain attempt to show his friend he still meant it, but all he succeeded in doing was spilling his drink.

"I think she may be the one to change yer mind," Alan continued, ignoring the scene Lachlan was making for his benefit. "Kirstie would like her." His eyes glazed as he spoke of Lachlan's sister. He looked off in silent contemplation, then his hopeful eyes returned to Lachlan's, not knowing how much he revealed on his face. "She might come home for the wedding."

"There will be no wedding." Lachlan ground out as he leaned in toward Alan. He glanced back to make sure no one had heard, because the last thing he wanted was to embarrass Maggie in front of everyone at the table before he could get her up to his room. If she wished, she could feel distressed tomorrow after they'd spent the night together, but now was not the time to jeopardize the evening he had planned by soothing her sensibilities over an ill-timed comment.

Alan laughed. "I cannae wait to see how this turns out. It is going to be a pleasure watching ye fall." With a mock salute and a twinkle in his eye, he lifted his glass.

The scary thing was his friend had always been able to read him. That's why they worked well together in battle— they knew each other so well they were able to anticipate the other's next move.

He wanted to laugh, too, but somewhere deep inside, he already knew he might be waging a war he couldn't win. That he was losing his resolve scared him. Maggie spoke to the part of his heart he had believed dead; she made him feel whole again, giving him back what Aileen had taken.

At the same time, were the mysteries she concealed as deadly as Aileen's had been? He prayed not. He couldn't give his heart to another only to be betrayed again.

His gaze slid back to her. It was worth the risk. She was worth it.

Och, this was madness, and he had to get her out of his system.

The crowd gathered for dinner tonight was small, and he was thankful it went quickly. Finally, the meal was complete, and his pulse sped as he took Maggie's arm in his and guided her up the stairs. She trembled but came willingly.

At the top of the landing, he spun her to face him and looked into her frightened doe eyes. "Do ye know what will happen if ye walk through that door with me tonight, lass?"

He had to make certain she was willing. Blushing, she looked up at him through lowered lashes.

"Aye, I do." Her voice had taken on a husky quality. It hummed through him and heated his blood.

"Do ye want to be with me, then, Maggie? I willnae take ye against yer will."

Her quivering hand rose to his cheek, caressing it tenderly. Dazed, dilated eyes gazed directly into his own. "Aye, Lachlan Cameron, I want ye to take me to yer bed."

His staff hardened, and a primitive growl rose from somewhere deep inside. A sudden urgency swept through him—he had to get her in his chamber before she changed her mind. Too afraid to talk, not wanting to break the spell, he took her hand and guided her down the hall to his room. Once inside, Lachlan bolted the door shut.

Finally, I have her to myself.

Chapter Nine

Lachlan's room took away Maggie's breath. It could be compared to the size of her father's, but his had woolen tapestries covering each wall, where her father's seemed relatively bare. They were probably as much for function as decoration. It must get cold up here, farther north in the Highlands.

Holding her hand, Lachlan walked in behind her. The sound of metal scraping against metal let her know he had latched the heavy wooden door. She could not back out now, but she did not want to.

Her eyes landed on the massive canopy bed, and her heart started to race. She would be splayed across those thick woolen blankets on the mattress soon and would no longer be a maiden. It was terrifying, but at the same time a shudder of excitement thrilled through her veins, because she would learn what the maids only whispered about and experience the sinful pleasures Lachlan had murmured in her ear. Afterward, she would be able to move to the final phase of her freedom and take her vows, but tonight was about being a woman. Before she had time to form another thought, Lachlan spun her in his arms, and they were face to chest. She looked up to meet his wolfish gaze, which looked hungry, as if he were about to devour her.

With one arm he held her, while his other reached to gently glide his fingertips across her cheek. The room was suddenly hot, her breathing becoming shallow and her skin flushing at his caress. Although she had been looking forward to this all evening, now she had become the shy innocent she had hoped not to portray.

She swallowed and licked her dry lips. "I have never been with a man." Her body trembled.

"I ken, Maggie. I will be gentle with ye." He worked to unpin the headpiece from her hair. Her scalp tingled and shivers ran down her spine as his fingers danced in her hair. Dark ringlets fell like a cascade down her cheeks, and she had to peek through them to see him.

The headpiece was tossed away and quickly forgotten. His hands returned to splay through her hair and massage her crown. She moaned as his tender ministrations released the tension she had unknowingly kept locked inside. Her chest tightened and breasts swelled at the heated exploration of his gaze trailing slowly down her body, then back to her eyes.

"I am going to undress ye now, Maggie." The words sent electric pulses coursing through her to culminate in her most private, feminine areas. "Do ye want me? Do ye want me like I want ye?" His eyes didn't leave hers as she nodded. "I want to hear it. Tell me ye want me. I need to see it in yer eyes." She gulped as desire surged through her at the husky tenor of his voice.

Her gaze locked with his. "Aye, I do, Lachlan. I want ye to teach me how to please ye." A need took hold of her, a powerful longing she'd never before experienced as she struggled to control her breathing.

A primitive groan sounded deep in his throat, and he leaned down and connected his lips to hers. It was a gentle kiss, slow and seductive, but she sensed him holding back and realized he was trying not to push her too hard. But she wanted to see him lose control, desired to see him mad for her and her alone. She needed for this night to be everything she had dared ever dream, because she might never get another.

Gazing up into concerned eyes, Maggie pulled back, and as she carefully removed the intricately carved silver pin holding her arisaid, she watched him intently. His pupils dilated at her attempt to become a temptress, and his breathing turned shallow. The power she wielded over him emboldened her.

Maggie sashayed over to an ornately carved wooden table, where she set down the pin and then turned back to Lachlan. Seductively, she pulled the overlay off one shoulder, then the other, and placed it reverently on the nearby chair. He looked like a wolf ready to pounce on its prey.

She sat on the chair and bent to remove her slippers. As her hair fell over her face, she glanced through the curtain to see Lachlan devouring the sight of her. He was still, focused on her alone. Only his fingers moved, rubbing up against each other, as if itching to touch her.

Stockings and shoes removed, she rose and walked toward him in only her shift and stays. Her heart beat fast and out of time like a drum she couldn't control, nor did she want to. Their gazes met again, and she froze. Fear and excitement warred inside her at the fevered intent of his stare.

In a blur, his plaid was unbelted and fell to the floor. As it was pulled up and over his head, his shirt ripped, and he threw it to the floor without inspecting it.

His nakedness shocked her. Although she had seen her brothers when they were younger, Lachlan was larger in stature, and his manhood stood straight up. She had never seen a cock so considerable in size. She gasped. He would rip her apart.

"'Twill be all right, Maggie, I willnae hurt ye." Amusement danced in his blue depths.

Taking her cheeks in his hands, he kissed her. Their tongues mated, swirled, and tasted. She forgot all else but that kiss until he reached down and deftly untied her stays and tossed them to the ground.

His eyes returned to linger on her in the nearly transparent garment. The heat in his gaze frightened and excited her with its intensity while his hands ran down the length of her body and reverently traced her curves. Then, in one swift movement, he grabbed and brought her shift over her head. The whoosh of cool air and lack of clothing left her bare and exposed.

Involuntarily, Maggie's hands flew up to cover her naked breasts.

"Nae, I want to look at ye." Lachlan's hands cradled hers and lowered them to her sides. "Stay," he ordered as one finger touched her chest lightly. His finger circled then crept lower to the apex of her breast, where her engorged nipple stood poised, erect and sensitive. His touch gave her skin goose bumps, but made her blood hot at the same time.

His other fingers extended to grasp the globe, then his heated stare returned to hers. "I am going to taste ye now." Her core heated. She could feel a strange need taking root deep within her.

With his head lowered, his tongue laved the tip of her breast, and the peak hardened almost painfully full. He had one hand on each now. He nipped at her breast, and she gasped. Withdrawing, he looked up at her with a devilish grin, then his mouth returned to the inflamed peak, causing sparks to ignite in unfamiliar areas of her body as he sucked.

One hand trailed to the apex at her legs, and his fingers massaged the curls then delved farther. Slowly, one slid over the nub at her core, sending a shock wave pulsating through her entire being. The finger went deeper and slid easily back and forth over the entrance to her passage.

"Oh, God, ye are wet for me." He growled.

She had trouble keeping her breath steady and controlling her hips when he touched her there. "Wet?" she questioned. "Is something wrong?"

An amused laugh escaped, and his heated gaze returned to her face. "Nae, it means ye are ready for me." In one move, he scooped her up and carried her toward the bed.

After he set her down, she sank into the soft worsted-wool blankets as he backed up to study her. Tempted to climb under the warm material and hide what no man had ever seen, she blushed and squirmed under his scrutiny. His eyes were hot and dilated as they took in every curve, and his gaze promised her there was nowhere left to hide.

Lachlan climbed on, and the mattress shifted with his weight. Her bare skin rubbed his flesh, and her heart began to pound with trepidation and anticipation. His coarse, callused hand was gentle as he eased her legs apart and seated himself between them. She squeezed her eyes shut and turned to the side.

"Look at me, Maggie, 'twill only hurt for a moment. I'll go slow."

Positioned at her entrance, he braced himself on one arm, and with the other cupped her face. The pressure at her core ignited a flame so intense her body instinctively pushed up into his shaft as it sought to alleviate the growing desire consuming her. He grinned at her eagerness and teased her by sliding the head of his erection up and down her engorged, slick passage.

An intense pressure filled her as he slowly slid into her channel. She felt full and complete, but somehow it wasn't enough to soothe the ache that coursed through her.

Stormy blue eyes pinned her with a possessive glance,

and he stopped as the head of his penis came up against her maidenhead. He drove forward. Her back arched up, and her fingers dug into his sides as she gasped with the force of the invasion. As her body accepted him completely and stretched to take his long, thick member, she trembled and her eyes watered. He stilled to give her time to adjust, and when her gaze returned to his, his stare had turned primal, with a hungry glint that begged to be sated.

"Mine," he ground out as his eyes bored into her. "Ye are mine." All she could do was nod and hold on.

As if she would argue; she'd give him anything he wanted. He surveyed her as if he revered her, leaving her feeling desired and cherished, like she was a woman, not a token for men to barter and scheme with, but someone to be treasured and respected.

He slowly pulled back, and she tightened her grip to keep him where he was. One side of his lip curled up with approval, and he thrust forward again, but this time more gently. It didn't hurt as much. She relaxed, and the pleasure of his touch returned, along with a new pressure that built and made her long for more.

Lachlan's thumb on her cheek lowered to her chin, pushing it up and forcing Maggie to look into his lust-filled eyes. He continued to pump in and out of her, the friction with each thrust becoming more intense as it threatened to overwhelm her. A slow, pleasurable torture over and over until tremors assailed her as a dam inside her gave way and waves of ecstasy engulfed her.

The currents of her release pulled her under, and everything outside this room ceased to exist. She couldn't control or comprehend the ripples of sensations that coursed through her as thousands of tiny tingles burst all over her body. She whimpered uncontrollably, and her gaze locked with Lachlan's, not understanding what was happening. His face had tightened, and his intent eyes stared directly into her soul.

He moaned as his eyes widened, and his thrusts deepened. One, two, three more times and he exploded inside her. His hips still moved up and down as the contractions still throbbing in her passage walls milked his seed.

It took several moments for their beating hearts to calm and for Maggie to contemplate what had just happened. He switched arms and continued to brace himself over her as he peppered her with kisses on her mouth and cheek and forehead as if he worshipped her.

When he pulled back, she whispered breathlessly, "I think I see stars." She blinked and tried to come back to earth. He chuckled, deep and hearty as his member still pulsated inside her.

"That would be one way to say it." He laughed again and then rolled over to her side and drew her in close against his hard, sinewy chest. She was boneless and couldn't move, could barely think. *So that is why women fall in love.*

• • •

Lachlan studied the sleeping lass in his arms as he lazily trailed his fingers over the sensitive flesh of her collarbone. She was small and delicate, and he had been careful not to let the full weight of his body rest on her, too scared he would crush her.

He had never allowed a female in his room before. Something just did not seem right about having a string of women passing through the laird's bedroom, and he admired how his father had always been faithful to his mother.

Maggie was different. She was an innocent, and bedding her and leaving her in some room in one of the towers was not palatable, so he had brought her here. He had never slept with a woman in the same bed, either, but having her beside him seemed natural.

He was her first, and he would be her only. He never wanted another man to see that look she'd given him as she'd climaxed beneath him. It had shattered his defenses and he'd lost all control, even spilling his seed inside her. From the moment he'd touched her in the river, he had become strangely possessive, and now he knew why—she was made for him.

The stares and appreciative looks she received all night had driven him mad with a jealousy he had not known he was capable of. All the men tripped over themselves to get a look at her, and he'd been sorely tempted to pummel several of them. If he hadn't taken her to his bed, he was sure someone else would have, but now he had staked his claim, and no one else would dare touch her.

The slow rise and fall of her chest fascinated him as he studied her pale, milky skin and breasts, which just fit in his hand. He cupped the gentle weight of one then trailed his fingers down her flat belly.

When she squirmed closer into his chest, his cock jerked. He was hard again. If this hadn't just been her first time, he would wake her and take her once more, and that probably still wouldn't be enough. He had to restrain his desire and be careful not to push too far.

She had enjoyed lying with him. Aileen had treated it like a duty, while the others seemed to try too hard, because they all wanted to be in line to be the laird's lady wife, but that was something no one would ever have. He had never been himself around the other lasses. It was hard when he knew they were just looking to him to raise their lot in life.

Maggie was different—she wasn't looking to stake a claim on him. Maybe that's why he had this comfortable and simple ease with her that had not been possible with any of the Cameron lasses. It lifted all the pressure and relaxed him.

There was still the matter of her deception, and he didn't like secrets. No form of dishonesty was acceptable, but with time she would open up to him. His little lass didn't appear to be afraid of anything except what she had left behind. He wouldn't push too hard, because he didn't want her to flee again. He'd had her, and now he was certain he wouldn't tire of her anytime soon, because she belonged here, in his bed.

It no longer mattered what she was running from—she was his and he could not imagine sending her away. She would not be going anywhere until he was ready to say she could leave.

Chapter Ten

Maggie woke to a delicious warmth and weight blanketing her. She sighed and peeked over to see Lachlan's arm was draped over her waist; she was amazed at how much she liked it there. Not wanting to wake him, she studied him quietly. He looked peaceful and relaxed with his golden locks falling over his forehead and cheek. He was irresistibly handsome. His dimple was missing, but she liked that it only appeared when he graced her with the smile that made her insides tighten. Och, her perusal of his fine form was heating her right now.

Seeing him in this state, so relaxed, with her in his arms, when he was always on guard around her, gave her hope that despite her secrets, he would give her more of those coveted smiles.

On the journey, he had been wary of their surroundings at every turn. Now he was home, and she was sure he would turn his attention to discovering her identity. Maybe she would be lucky enough to have a few more nights like the previous one before he pushed her for the truth and she left for the convent.

Since their arrival at Kentillie, he had been as tense as a

bowstring about to pop every time she had been near him. At dinner last night, he had worn a pained expression she couldn't read. When they'd finally reached his bedchamber, it all changed. His only concern had seemed to be to bed her, and he had been so distracted by having her, he had forgotten to keep her at a distance. Or maybe that was his plan—keep her close since he couldn't be sure of her.

She took a deep breath and expelled it slowly to let the worries go. Whatever his reason, she would enjoy this time with him, and last night had been more than she had ever hoped for. Her mother had told her the experience would shake her to her core and leave her always wanting. She didn't want to admit it, but her mother had been right. Wanting a few extra days of bliss, she decided, 'twould be all right if she didn't rush to take her vows. He would be done with her soon anyway—why not enjoy his touch while she could?

Maggie stretched, and Lachlan's eyes opened. She continued to gaze at him but said nothing. What was said the morning after? A sated, sleepy grin curved his lips, and she found herself melting into him. A deep male hum reverberated from his chest, and he turned to face her as he threw his leg over her possessively. He wanted to bed her again, she realized as his hips rocked into her.

Her body thrummed with a thirst she only now understood, but she returned his gaze shyly. Already, she was heated and willing to take him into her body again, so she reached up to fork her hand into his thick, wayward hair. Maggie bit her lip then drew him toward her, and her mouth crashed down on his. The kiss was needy, a prelude to what had happened the night before, and oh, how she wanted that again.

The kiss deepened, and the evidence of his arousal hardened and jerked on her thigh. She sighed and tried to get closer, but he groaned and then pulled back, pushing her to arm's length. The abrupt coolness between them shocked her, and tears stung the backs of her eyes at the denial. She'd not been expecting him to reject her. Was he done with her?

"'Tis too soon. If ye keep doing this I willnae be able to control myself. I dinnae want to hurt ye, lass." His hand skimmed her face tenderly.

Without giving her a chance to speak, he threw the covers back and jumped up. His gaze lingered on her body, then he pulled the woolen blankets over her. "My mother will finish showing ye around today," he said as he dressed. "I have been gone too long and have matters to see to. I will see ye at the evening meal tonight." And he was dressed and out the door.

He had just run out on her. She had no idea where to clean herself. She had envisioned lovers would talk to each other, yet he was gone with hardly a word.

Sitting up, she stared openmouthed at the back of the door. Apparently nothing was said the morning after, and you just parted ways. It felt wrong. Last night, she'd been so close to him, and now she wasn't even sure if she knew him.

A light knock sounded, followed by the door inching forward slowly to reveal a maid who had helped her bathe the day before. She smiled at the lass and quickly let the hurt go. Everything would be all right, and it truly didn't matter if he was done with her, because she was free.

Most of the morning, Maggie toured the castle grounds with Elspeth, Lorna, and Donella. At some point they came upon a small redheaded girl staring up into a tree and calling, "Dina, Dina, come here."

The child was probably all of eight summers but had the bonniest freckled cheeks, as if she'd spent all of those years out of doors. Images of her own youth spent out of the keep and away from her parents' eyes flooded her mind.

Maggie looked up to see who could be in the tree but didn't see anything, so she walked up to the wee lass and asked, "Who are ye calling, little one?"

"Me kitten." The girl looked up at her with iridescent green eyes so sad that her heart almost broke. With eyes like that, she would have all the boys clamoring for her attention when she grew into a woman.

Maggie inspected the tree to find the little rascal and measure how high up it had gotten. "What's yer name? I am Maggie."

"My name is Agnes." Her front teeth were missing, and her name came out with a slight slur that made Maggie want to smile.

"Well, now, Agnes, looks like we have work to do. I am going to help ye get Dina down. What we need is a rope and a basket big enough for Dina to fit in."

The child beamed, and those sad little eyes brightened. "Aye, I ken where to find that." The little girl ran off.

Panicked mews came from the kitten that had made it to about the eighth branch. The first was just about shoulder height, just low enough to get a grasp and swing up on. The rest would be an easy climb.

Followed by a group of friends, Agnes was back with the basket and rope so quickly Maggie had barely had time to plan the climb. The ladies slipped away as she went to work, but she hardly noticed. Securing one end of the rope to the handle, she pulled tightly to check the strength of her knot.

"Hold the basket now," she ordered Agnes.

Maggie removed the brooch holding her arisaid, folded the fabric, and placed it gently on the ground with the pin. After tying the free end of the rope around her waist, she grabbed hold of the tree branch and pushed up quickly with all the force her feet could give her while pulling up with her arms. Her midsection landed square on the branch, and she was able to shimmy full on. Slowly, she stood and balanced by holding on to the trunk. Claps and cheers greeted her from below.

It was easy to follow the branches around and up, almost like a ladder. When she got to the seventh one, she called out to the little gray-and-white-striped fluff ball, careful not to spook the wee thing. Once she'd pulled the basket up, she reached over for the kitten and grasped it behind the neck. Leaning against the tree, she turned and reached for the basket.

"Maggie," Lachlan's voice boomed from below, startling both her and the cat. It dug its sharp claws into her shoulder, and she flinched but concentrated on keeping her balance. "What the devil are ye doing, woman? Have ye lost yer head?" Maggie winced at his tone, which hurt more than little Dina's nails. "Get down here before ye get hurt."

She held tight but spared a glance down to see Lachlan, hands braced on hips as he glared at her. The climb had been farther up than she thought, but not so bad—she had always been good at climbing and had been much higher than this on many occasions. She hadn't answered him yet, afraid to do so, because she thought they had made progress in their relationship, and now with his demands, they had taken a step back.

"Do ye hear me, Maggie? Get down here." His voice crackled with irritation, probably due to her continued silence.

"Almost done." She smiled at the little kitten. "Ye are going to be just fine. Dinnae let him scare ye."

The little cat fought going into the basket for a brief moment, then hunkered down and mewed in the bottom. Maggie slowly lowered the basket until Agnes grabbed it.

Dina was safe, however she was not sure if she would be. Staying put seemed like a good idea, but she started the descent anyway.

Out of an abundance of caution and trepidation at facing the fuming laird at the bottom, the trip down the tree took a considerably longer time than the climb up had. Lachlan's face was impassive, but as she got closer, she could see his jaw twitching.

When she got to the bottom branch, she stretched out and moved sideways then leaped and landed with her back to Lachlan. Arms swiftly locked around her waist and swung her around, and she almost lost her balance. "Are ye mad, lass? What did ye think ye were about?"

Disappointed at his reaction, she squared her shoulders and faced him. "I was helping little Agnes get her kitten."

"Ye could have been hurt."

"Nae," she said dismissively, "'twas an easy climb."

"Dinnae ever do that again." Had he actually ordered her to never climb a tree again? How absurd.

"What is wrong with climbing a tree?" Irritation sparked as her brow crinkled. He was treating her like a little child.

"Ye are in nothing more than a shift. If there had been men down here, do ye ken what they would have seen while ye were moving about up there? I got a good view," he ground out.

She blushed. Och, she seemed to be doing a lot of that lately. The children stared wide-eyed as their laird berated her.

"'Twill be all right," Maggie reassured them when Agnes hung her head to study the ground. "Make sure Dina gets home safely. Go play." The group ran off, following Agnes with Dina in the basket.

She turned back to Lachlan. "Ye didnae have to scold me like that in front of them," she said, defiantly crossing her arms, but she wanted to stamp her foot in frustration. She was doing her damnedest to make friends while she was here.

"What am I going to do with ye?"

"I am not sure I ken yer question. What do ye want to do with me?" she asked with a hint of sarcasm and tilted her chin up to meet his eyes.

He groaned, and his eyes grew dark. He stalked toward

her, and she shivered as his large hands coiled around her small wrists and pulled them up. He backed her against the tree and pinned her arms above her head. His eyes raked her with a hot stare that had nothing to do with his anger but was filled with the desire she'd seen in him as they'd lain together the night before.

The bark was rough and solid, but his steel-forged body was even harder, and her core heated at the pressure. With intense, needy eyes, he continued a slow perusal of her body. He smelled of musk and the woods and all things forbidden, and the scent ignited a fire in her womb.

He closed in and growled in her ear, "What I want is to take ye here and now. I want to be inside ye again."

She melted at the words, and if he'd not been holding her up, her knees might have buckled. A triumphant smile turned up the corners of her lips.

"I want to feel yer body in mine again, too." The words flew out unbidden, and this time she didn't blush. She couldn't deny how her body reacted to his.

His mouth claimed hers, devouring her eager response and driving her senseless with need. She groaned as his heated, velvet touch fanned the flames churning inside her, and he ground the evidence of his arousal into her belly. The proof of his desire called to a primal part of her.

All rational thought escaped her, and she thought, *then take me*. But the words were lost as his tongue delved and tangled with her own.

"Lachlan." Elspeth's voice cut through. Not harsh, almost in jest. "This is no' the place for that." Maggie opened her eyes to find his mother, a wry smile and knowing eyes, with Donella and Lorna at her side giggling like little lasses and not trying to hide it. "Maggie has more of our kin to meet."

He ground his teeth and whispered in her ear, "Tonight. I will have ye tonight."

After releasing her arms, he stomped off without acknowledging his mother. Color stole across her cheeks as she turned to face the ladies and realized they didn't seem to disapprove of the display they had just witnessed. Did that mean they approved, or that 'twas common for Lachlan to so brazenly kiss a lass in public? Not certain she wanted the answer to that question, she swallowed her doubt and asked, "Where to next?"

While touring the buildings and grounds outside the keep, they stopped at the textile mill, where she was introduced to Arabella, another girl close in age to Donella, Lorna, and her. The woman latched onto Maggie as if they had always known each other, and something about her overly friendly manner set warning bells ringing in Maggie's head.

Arabella guided her to a back room filled to overflowing with bright colors of woven fabrics. Bright midday sun shone through the windows and illuminated the lovely material, but the air was stifling, and she had the urge to run over and fling open a window. When the woman motioned for her to sit on a bundle of the warm woolen material, she did so, not wanting to offend her. Sweat prickled at the base of her neck, and she fought the urge to fan herself. Pacing, Arabella peppered her with questions, first about her home, then about Lachlan.

"Ye need to be wary of the man. He doesnae give his heart to anyone." Mayhap she was trying to be helpful.

"I heard he had a bad experience, and he never wants to marry." So far, no one had given her much insight into Lachlan's past, and she found herself leaning in to hear Arabella's reply.

Although she would never love a man, a strange curiosity had overcome her, as if the balance of her new freedom hinged on what she could learn. Maggie had to admit she cared for Lachlan. He was a good leader, and she'd seen nothing but high regard for his men; they had laughed and joked most of the trip as if they were friends, while her father and brothers didn't have that kind of relationship with the men who worked for them.

Most of all, he seemed to hold an admiration for what women thought.

"Aye, she broke his heart." Arabella placed both hands over her breast, pursed her lips, and shook her head sympathetically. The exaggerated gesture seemed practiced and lacked any real emotion.

"He seems more distrustful than hurt. Did he love her?" Maggie held her breath and found it a little disconcerting that she cared what the answer was.

"Oh, aye, they were inseparable from early on. He definitely loved her." An odd twinge of disappointment took root in her belly. "He never looked at another lass while she was here."

Maggie perked up. "Has that changed?"

"Aye, it has. He looks at all the lasses now."

As she suspected, he was a rogue. Her heart sank, and she chided herself for feeling anything.

Arabella continued, "They all love him, too. I think he has a different one every month. I fear he will never settle down."

"Oh," was the only response Maggie could muster as she fought the tightening in her chest.

"He even chose me for a time, longer than most. He threw me away, just like all the other lasses." Arabella's lips thinned and her voice had an edge, but her calm, friendly exterior remained. "There is always hope that he will come to his senses. He says he willnae marry, but he is the laird. He has to have heirs."

"Did ye wish to marry him?" Maggie pulled at her arisaid; she might disrobe soon if she couldn't get to some cooler air.

Would it bother her if this woman wanted Lachlan? It shouldn't, but it did. She did not want a man. Or did she? She could still want a man and not have to love him. Something stabbed at her heart, and she recognized it for what it was: jealousy.

After last night, she wanted Lachlan. Aye, every fiber of her being wanted him. Even before that, she had come to enjoy his company and respect him. "Respect"—it was a word she'd never imagined she could use in the same sentence as "man." He made her feel things she didn't understand, and the thought of his eyes straying toward another woman made her hands tremble with fear or rage or a combination of both.

"Aye, I did, along with every other single woman here. Everyone wants him, and that is why he has his pick of bedmates. He goes through them faster than a summer storm. Then he leaves them heartbroken to pick up the pieces."

'Tis too much. She had to get some fresh air. Maggie stood and started toward the door, but Arabella's hand clamped around her arm.

"I like ye." She coiled her arm around Maggie's shoulders and squeezed a little too tightly. "I think 'tis important ye ken he willnae keep ye. I am trying to protect ye from the heartbreak." Arabella released her grip, but moved to stand in front of Maggie and gazed directly into her eyes with what appeared to be real sincerity. The gesture was meant to be reassuring, but it made her uncomfortable.

"Maggie, there ye are, lass. We didnae ken where ye had gotten off te." Elspeth burst into the room like a ray of sunshine. Arabella turned to smile innocently at Lachlan's mother.

Doubt and inadequacy engulfed Maggie. She didn't plan to stay at Kentillie for long, but she couldn't shake the disappointment that Lachlan would never care for her. It was the same feeling Maggie had experienced around her own mother, that no matter how she tried, she wouldn't be able to earn the love she craved.

'Twas for the best. Although he had seemed to worship her the night before, mayhap the emotion that had been elicited by their bedplay was common, but she could see herself getting lost in those feelings. Before his attentions snared her, she would need to be gone.

. . .

Music floated through the air of the hall, but it did nothing to soothe the frayed nerves that had plagued him all day. Normally, Lachlan enjoyed the revelry of a good celebration, but tonight he wanted nothing but to be alone in his bed with Maggie. The day had been unusually stressful and long—very, very long. He wanted to forget everything from the day and sink into his siren's welcoming warmth.

He had made his rounds, seen to the farmers who were concerned about recent cattle raids, and worked to make sure all was in preparation to welcome the lairds he expected to arrive soon. But thoughts of Maggie or glimpses of her had driven him to distraction.

She plagued his every moment like a cold he could not shake. He was having trouble concentrating on his duties, and his lack of focus was detrimental for a man in his position. He had to get this woman out of his system so he could sever ties with her and return to being the leader his clan deserved.

Minstrels played from the balcony and the notes drifted down to the gathered crowd, and when they raised their voices, och, it was loud. Ale was served tonight as usual, but as with other special occasions, whisky flowed unchecked, and inhibitions fell like men on a battlefield.

His mother had ordered a welcome home dinner, and judging by the spread on the tables, she was happy indeed to have Malcolm and him home. Yet she seemed more intrigued and happy about the lass he'd brought with him than about their journey. Some part of him wondered if his mother had gone through all the fuss for Maggie and not her sons.

Elspeth had cornered him this morning. "I like her."

"Aye. For now she can abide here. But she willnae tell me about her home, her family, or where she is from. I must protect the clan, and I'm no' sure how far we can trust her. I will decide if she is to stay or go."

"Use yer head, son. A woman wouldnae leave her home if she felt safe there. She doesnae want to go back. Something scared her, and yer arrival was good timing. She used ye to escape whatever she is running from."

"She doesnae trust me, so I willnae trust her." The conversation over, he stalked away.

In the early afternoon, he'd been able to finally get Maggie off his mind and make some progress on his work with his brother when his mother, Lorna, and Donella walked into the hall grinning as if they had beaten him to the pastries and there were none left for him. His gut had tightened as he realized Maggie wasn't with them, although he had instructed his mother one of them should be with her at all times. She was a flight risk, and she didn't know her way around. He didn't tell her the other fear he was grappling with—Maggie was too bonny and not everyone knew yet she belonged to him. He didn't want any other man going near her.

His mother had had the nerve to walk by, smile, and wink at him to let him know Maggie was out there on her own without an escort. Did she know he wouldn't be able to concentrate on his work with the lass outside the keep and not guarded?

"Where is Maggie?" Lachlan ground out between clenched teeth.

"She is fine. We will go back to her in a moment, I just couldnae watch."

Watch what? His insides twisted as she smiled and raised

one challenging eyebrow but kept walking. Lorna snickered as they passed.

"Lorna, where is she?" he commanded.

"She is helping little Agnes." Lorna was trying to keep an impassive expression, but she was failing miserably.

"Doing what?" The tenor of his voice became strained in frustration.

"I believe Maggie was about to climb the big oak in the yard to retrieve a kitten. She sent Agnes for a rope and basket."

"Maggie looked as if she kenned what she was doing."

A prickle of unease ran down his back.

"The lass is quite brave—the kitten is verra high up. I would never climb that high." Lorna shook her head.

"And ye three didnae talk her out of it? She is recovering from a head injury. What if she falls?" he barked with frustration. A sick feeling churned in the pit of his stomach.

"Malcolm, take over." Lachlan stood so quickly his chair almost toppled over, but he hardly noticed as he strode briskly out the door. He didn't want anyone to see how concerned he was, but damn, what if she hurt herself. He was going to tan her hide.

When he got to the base of the tree, his eyes roved up the thick trunk until he found her. His heart sank. She was so far up, if he had not been looking for her, he never would have seen her. He glared up at the lass who had plagued his every thought and kept him from his duties.

Was she right in the head? What would possess a woman to do such a foolish thing? The cat would have come down eventually. He wanted to shake her, he wanted to throttle her, but as soon as she made it down and his hands were on her, all he wanted to do was touch her.

He had intended to scold her. But she'd been so bonny, with her cheeks flushed from the exertion, breathless, and only in her shift, that his rational thoughts had fled and another part of his body had taken over. His groin had tightened, and all he wanted at that moment was to taste her.

She had said she wanted him, too, and he'd been tempted to throw her over his shoulder and carry her back to his bedchamber, until his mother came up behind them. He had wanted to growl with frustration.

He would have her again tonight, though. Lachlan shifted in his seat to adjust the position of the evidence of his arousal. His hands itched to touch Maggie, to feel her thigh under the table and remind her that she would be in his bed again tonight.

Alan broke into his reflections as he pulled out the chair beside him. "We've searched everywhere, but there is no sign of the man—Glenn. He isnae on our land." His worried tone was not lost on Lachlan.

Lachlan grunted. Not the news he wanted to hear. He didn't like loose ends, especially if Conall Erskine was part of the equation. "Did ye ask the MacDonalds if they had seen him?"

"His tracks led to their land, but no sign of him there, either. We lost him in the stream."

Unease as thick as the mist on the moors spread through Lachlan. How far could the man have made it? He had a mortal wound, Lachlan was certain of it, but still the man had been able to make it off his land, and his whereabouts were cause for if not apprehension, then at least caution. He cursed himself for not being thorough, but he'd been so concerned with getting Maggie away from the skirmish that he'd been careless. Clearly, being around Maggie was clouding his judgment.

"He was wounded and shouldnae have made it far. Let's hope he doesnae make it home," Lachlan said more to reassure himself than Alan.

"Aye," Alan agreed.

"Whether he did or no', Conall will come. There hasnae been a sighting yet, but we need to keep alert."

"Do ye think Argyll will come with him?"

"Nae, but we should be prepared. Has any word come from the other lairds yet?"

"A reply arrived from the MacDonalds today. They will be here." Alan had spoken with the MacDonald's brother when he'd taken Robbie to their lands, so it made sense they'd be the first to respond.

"Robbie is with Art and Magaidh MacDonald?"

"He is. 'Twill be safe there, too. Conall will expect him to be here in the keep and willnae think to look there."

"Ye instructed all their nearby men to be on watch?"

"The MacDonald clan was happy to protect the lad. What do ye think Conall will do when he gets here?"

"The bastard is insane, so there is no way to ken." His gaze drifted to his mother and Maggie. "Best we guard the women in the keep until the danger is gone."

Alan nodded.

The music became livelier as tables were pushed to the sides to make room for dancing, and he was about to get up and grab Maggie to indulge his need to touch her, but his mother stopped him. In that instant, Malcolm took Maggie's hand and led her out to the floor. Lachlan frowned.

Elspeth smiled brightly at him as the pair walked away. "Her grandmother is from Ireland. I was also able to find out she has three brothers and no sisters."

Maggie had mentioned brothers. Why had they not taken her in when she was orphaned? Mayhap they were too young or their uncle, the priest, was better suited to care for her. He fought down the apprehension that threatened as he remembered she'd talked about her father as if he were alive, as well, but still the unease lingered.

Could Dougal have been wrong about who she was? If so, it was too late—he'd had her and would have to shoulder any consequences. He shook the thought away.

His attention returned to Maggie as Malcolm spun her around with ease, as if he'd never had an injury. She was smiling at something he'd said, and Lachlan caught himself smiling. She was quick to laugh and found pleasure in the smallest things. He liked that about her.

Maggie seemed to belong here. Despite only being at Kentillie for a short time, she had charmed everyone, but Aileen's betrayal had left him cynical. Was the hurt worth opening himself up to any lass again? He wanted to believe he could have that with Maggie, but there were too many unanswered questions.

The song ended, and Malcolm bowed to Maggie as she giggled and curtsied, cheeks red from her exertion. Alan caught his eye, gave a crooked smirk, then walked up to Maggie to take her in the next dance. He glanced back over his shoulder at Lachlan and had the nerve to stick his tongue out.

"Excuse me. 'Tis my turn for a dance." Lachlan stood and stalked across the floor toward Maggie. He almost cursed aloud when Arabella cut him off. He attempted to skirt around her, but she placed one hand on his chest and then the other, feigning hurt at his possible rejection.

"Lachlan, dance with me." Her large, pouty lips insisted, but it was the last thing he wanted to do. He wished desperately to turn her down and go to Maggie. He had bedded Arabella only once and had come to regret it—she was looking for a husband and had apparently decided he would do. She was an attractive lass and some man would want her, but he had tasted Maggie's sweet lips, and no other would satisfy the thirst she had awoken in him.

Arabella kept trying to seduce him, though, and with each

rebuff, she would come back stronger and more determined. Recently, she had tried to lure him into the stables, but he had spurned her advances. With cold eyes, she had turned on him and threatened to do harm to him and then to herself.

Arabella's mental instability was why he found himself blowing off his concerns and once again dancing with her. He didn't want to deal with her hysterics, and now was not the time and place to have a confrontation that would lead to verbal blows and possibly a physical assault from her. As they moved across the floor, he mentally made plans to send Arabella to live with her cousins near Dundee.

This one dance would hopefully placate her. Then he would make his way to Maggie. He could survive another moment of torture knowing he would be next in line to touch her.

Chapter Eleven

Tight jawed, Maggie glared from the table at Arabella dancing—no, almost gyrating against Lachlan. The auburn-haired beauty was so close to him it wasn't decent, and her hips moved as if the two of them were alone and unclothed. It was obvious she still wanted him, and she wanted the whole keep to know it.

What heated her blood was he didn't even try to put distance between them, and offered no hint of restraint as she inched closer and rubbed her breasts into his chest. Arabella laughed in his ear and threw back her head as she gazed at him seductively. Still, the man continued to dance with her.

Maggie reached for the untouched goblet near Alan's plate. It was a generous dram of whisky he had pushed away as soon as it had been poured. She had never been allowed to have it before, as it was one of those things her father had considered unladylike, and she had stayed clear of it in order not to incur his wrath.

Well, now seemed as if the perfect time to try the drink, men be damned. She peered into the glass, then swirled the amber liquid. It looked harmless. It even looked as if it might be good, so she raised the cup to her nose and sniffed. Not so bad, mayhap a little stronger than ale. Her nose twitched.

What the hell. She lifted the cup toward Lachlan in mock salute and took a big gulp, only to hold the liquid in her mouth, afraid to swallow right away. Her eyes watered and she squared her shoulders to fortify herself before she was tempted to spit it out.

Then she let the liquid glide smoothly down. The whisky was warm, her nose stung, and then her insides started to burn, all the way down to her stomach. A slight aftertaste lingered in her mouth, although it tasted like some of her medicinals. She'd even used whisky for that purpose.

The burning gave way to a warm sensation that was not altogether unpleasant. *'Twas no' so bad.* Without hesitation, she gulped the rest. Her tongue burned a little, but it went down more smoothly. This time she liked it—why had she waited so long to try it?

Briefly taking her thoughts from the witch with her claws around Lachlan, an unbidden image of her father and brothers drinking was a welcome intrusion. They were not such a bad a sort. Her father didn't value her opinion—he merely had an antiquated view of women. And her brothers had kept her sane after what Conall had done with Miranda, when she had been forced to turn her back on her friends.

Otherwise, she wouldn't have made it through those terrible years, her mother's death, the betrothal to that arse, and her father's determination to use her to further his ambitions.

The whisky was growing on her, and it had gotten her mind off Lachlan for a few moments, but then Arabella stroked Lachlan's arm with her hand. He was facing the other way, so she couldn't see his reaction, but still, he did nothing to stop her. The witch laughed and flashed her big, brown, seductive eyes at him. Maggie's stomach churned, but it was the thought of losing Lachlan so quickly, not the whisky making her sick.

The amber liquid was quite good. Maggie peered into the empty goblet and smiled at her little act of defiance. Her irrational feelings of jealousy had started to fade until Arabella pulled Lachlan out the door. Her breath caught, and her eyes started to water.

So Lachlan was done with her already. She'd known it was coming, but after only one night? She reached for the cup by Lachlan's trencher. His portion was even larger. After gulping it, she slammed the goblet back down on the table with a little more force than she'd intended. Luckily no one had noticed.

"Good eve, fair lass." The words were purred seductively by a dark-haired man who bowed and took her hand. "I am Brodie, Lachlan's cousin."

He held her hand just a little too long. There was a resemblance—his smile was similar to Lachlan's, except he had two dimples and chocolate-colored eyes that twinkled with a playful glint.

Brodie was devastatingly handsome, but his practiced pleasantries were almost too much of a good thing. He didn't have the rugged quality Lachlan possessed or the command of a born leader or that overly serious glare, which hinted of a need to keep her safe. Yet, the man in front of her would make any lass swoon just for a few moments of his time. But she felt nothing. Lachlan had ruined her for life.

"Will ye let me have the privilege of escorting ye in the next dance?" His eyes sparkled merrily like he was impersonating an English lord at court instead of a rough Highlander from the wild free lands of Scotland. A momentary flash revealed a deep sadness hidden beneath his skillfully crafted words. She barely picked up on the emotion before it was gone.

"I would love to, sir." Rising, she giggled at his overly flagrant formality and returned a perfectly overdone curtsy as she banished her melancholy.

This was a celebration, after all, and she was determined to have a good time. She had been to so few in her life that Maggie wouldn't let irrational jealousy ruin her fun. Surely there were no parties at a convent, which was still her final destination.

As they glided to the center of the room, she offered her arm to Brodie and he threaded his through hers. She smiled and turned to face him with the intention of letting the music and dance sweep her into another world, one where she would forget the man she'd given herself to, who had left the hall with a viperous trollop. Damned if she was going to let his roguish ways ruin her good time.

It was easy to believe they were kin. Brodie's darker eyes weren't as piercing as Lachlan's; they were softer and warmer, despite the pain that flitted through the depths, yet he almost had her bent over with laughter.

"If my cousin werenae so enamored with ye, I would compare yer eyes to the stars in the heavens and your curves to the gently rolling hills of bonny Scotland."

They moved swiftly and smoothly around the floor. He had one hand on her waist and held her other as the beat picked up in the lively tune.

"Ye are a heartless rogue, but I would love to hear ye tell me how fair I am." Before long, his amusing banter coaxed her back into good humor. Her cheeks warmed from the exertion and quite possibly from the effects of the whisky.

Brodie spun her around, and she almost lost her footing. He pulled her in close to keep her from falling over. "Och. Steady, lass. Lachlan willnae forgive me if ye are injured in my care."

"'Tis the spirits. I am usually all grace." She rolled her eyes.

Maggie almost lost her footing again when Brodie's

sinewy form lurched backward and disappeared from her grasp. As he had let her go abruptly, she flailed to keep her balance, the motion a blur that sent the room spinning around her. The music stopped.

The loud thud of Lachlan's fist hitting the flesh of Brodie's cheek reverberated in the hall, and everything went silent. Maggie gasped at the fury in Lachlan's eyes.

Her hands flew unbidden to her throat. It was the same look he had given her when he had held her up against that tree.

. . .

Lachlan stalked back into the hall shaking his head. Arabella had had the audacity to try to kiss him. Too many times he had told her they were through, but she was hardheaded. The last thing he needed was Maggie seeing the wench behaving like she owned him. He was done with Arabella's antics.

The hall was crowded tonight, but he didn't feel like celebrating. He was determined to collect Maggie and take her to his bed. Elbowing through the crowd, he made his way toward the table. She wasn't there. He caught a glimpse of her dancing and laughing with Brodie, of all people, and he cursed under his breath.

Brodie was an insatiable rogue, able to woo any lass; there was something about him they couldn't resist. He had a silver tongue skilled in the art of persuading wenches into his bed and he was well-known in the Highlands as a heartbreaker. But Maggie wouldn't know of his reputation.

Flushed and smiling, Maggie looked up at his cousin with those deep blue eyes he wanted focused on him alone. His knuckles whitened as his hands clenched the back of his seat. The couple shifted, and Brodie pulled her into his body, which was when Lachlan saw red. In one leap, he bounded over the table and stalked toward them, intent to kill. He was out of control, but his only concern was getting his woman out of the worm's lecherous hands.

Lachlan reached them, latched onto his cousin's shoulder, and swung him around. Someone grabbed Lachlan's arm just as his fist flew toward Brodie's face.

Brodie had been slightly off balance from being spun, so when Lachlan hit his cheek, the blow slid off without causing much damage. As he tried to go for him again, a set of arms coiled around him and Malcolm jumped between the two, yelling, "Calm down."

"What have I done, cousin?" the rogue asked as he rubbed his cheek.

"Ye had yer hands all over my woman." His breath was ragged as he fumed through clenched teeth. Maggie's head was quirked to the side, and she blinked as if she was trying to bring him into focus, and her hand went to her throat. Hell, he'd not meant to scare her.

"Maggie tripped. I caught her. Would ye rather I let her fall?" Brodie clipped back.

Lachlan looked to her for confirmation. She nodded, and he saw the truth in her eyes, which calmed him some.

"Ye got yer senses back, Lachlan?" He recognized Alan's voice from behind. He was one of the men holding him back. "Maggie may need some fresh air. She looks flushed."

Once Brodie backed farther away from Maggie, Lachlan's tension loosened and his fists unclenched. Alan, and whoever else held him, slowly let him go. Taking Maggie's hand, he pulled her toward the door. He could use some space to cool his temper as well, and he wanted an explanation as to why she had been gazing up at his cousin with flirtatious, welcoming eyes.

She stumbled as he pulled her through the door and out into the crisp night air. He wasn't sure if it was because he dragged her along or because she could not handle her ale, but when he realized her small frame couldn't keep up with his much longer legs, he slowed. An invigorating breeze cleared his senses and eased the muscles that had tightened like a bowstring, but he was still far from calm. Because she followed him without protest, he slackened his pace.

Unfamiliar emotions swirling in his head drove him mad. In that moment, he could have killed his favorite cousin. Had she wanted Brodie to hold her like that? The thought reignited his fury, and he tightened his grip on her again.

"Och, ye brute. That hurts." Her delicate fingers squirmed to be freed. He grunted in return and loosened his hold slightly.

Finally, when they had come to the base of the old oak where he'd found Maggie earlier, he stopped. Even through his fevered haze he was struck by how beautiful she was in the moonlight and how her pale skin contrasted with her dark hair.

It was a dark night, but the moon and stars played a game of peekaboo through the clouds and teased him with their reflections in her sapphire eyes. Up close, he could see a pink flush on her cheeks. He wanted to stay angry, but as he studied her bewildered gaze and took in how her fingers trembled in his, he lost his resolve.

"What was that with Brodie?" His jaw ticked.

She pursed her lips and didn't reply right away. Now he wished he had taken her somewhere better lit—he could usually tell if she was lying, but in this light, could he trust his senses? Thankfully, the clouds rolled away and he had a clear view into her eyes, her soul.

She blinked. "We were dancing. Ye were off with Arabella." She had the audacity to roll her eyes and tug her hand free from his. Was that jealousy in her bitter reply? "Why do ye even care?" she finally bit out, then turned back toward the keep.

Catching her wrist, he twirled her to face him and said tersely, "Ye are mine. Ye willnae let another touch ye."

"I belong to no one. I amnae wed," she retorted as she pulled out of his grasp and crossed her arms. She stamped her foot. It was strangely amusing until the words registered.

Aye, her view had merit, but he wouldn't accept it. "Ye are on my land." It was weak, but she couldn't argue with it.

"I will leave if ye wish," she countered as her eyes narrowed into slits and her lips tightened.

How could she consider leaving him after last night? Could he make her stay? "Nae, ye willnae."

"Why? Ye have Arabella." Her lip quavered.

He saw it for certain now—she was jealous. His chest swelled, and a primal pride eclipsed his anger. He had left the hall with Arabella to tell the woman to leave him be, and she had gotten the wrong impression. His heart leaped. Maggie was jealous, just as he had been, and he couldn't help when one side of his mouth curved up in satisfaction.

"Nae," he said softly, and he reached up to touch her cheek then push back a stray curl. "I dinnae want her. I want ye." His fingers traced her lips. She shivered and closed her eyes, then swayed. He snaked his other hand around her waist to catch her. "How much ale did ye have, lass?"

Opening her eyes, she gazed directly into his. Hidden just below the surface were her secrets, there for the asking. Would she let them out? Maybe the drink would get her to open up to him. "Just the one cup with dinner, but someone put whisky on the table."

She smiled an impish grin that lifted her flushed cheeks as if she were a child who had gotten away with something she shouldn't have done.

"'Twasnae so bad after it stopped burning." Then she hiccuped, and it was the most adorable thing he'd ever seen.

"What made ye drink that, lass? 'Tis potent stuff." He laughed at her innocence.

As sincere as she could be, she peeked up at him through lowered lids. With a sadness that had crept into their depths, her bonny eyes cut to his bones like a cold night on Ben Nevis. "Ye were dancing with her." She pouted.

Oh, heaven help him, she was even beautiful when she was sulking.

He lowered his head and kissed the rosy lips he'd been craving all day. They were soft like French silk, but when she opened to him and her tongue met his, he was reminded that her heart was as free and wild as Scotland herself. Lachlan deepened the kiss, and his length began to waken and strain beneath his plaid. She tasted of whisky, warm and bold and full of life.

He wanted to continue, wanted to forget about the world and get lost in her, but he pulled back. This was not the place; his Maggie deserved better than this. Swaying into him, she giggled. Dipping his head, he lightly kissed her forehead then coiled his arm around her and slowly started back toward the keep.

As she leaned into him for support, another hiccup escaped. If she would open up to him, she just might be the one lass in all of Scotland that he could fall for. He didn't like the thought of plying her with drink for answers, but since she had done this to herself, he wouldn't let the opportunity slip through his fingers.

It was better to leave any angry feelings outside—he didn't want to invite them back to the bedchamber—so he guided her to a bench and pulled her down beside him.

A cool breeze blew the rebellious ringlets of her dark hair back into her face. He took it between his fingers and brought it up to his nose to sniff. She smelled of smoke and whisky mingled with the fresh night air.

"Maggie, why will ye no tell me where yer home is, and what it is ye are running from?" His other men would be back soon, and he didn't want to hear the truth from someone else.

"I cannae." She sighed. But she didn't immediately jump up and run; she shook her head and maintained eye contact. A glimmer of tears misted her eyes and swirled around her fear-laced pupils, but he couldn't be sure, as the moon went back behind a cloud. "I cannae go back."

"Trust me. Ye belong here with the Camerons."

"That is what ye say now, but ye are a man of power and position. I ken what is truly important in yer world. Yer clan, yer people, and I amnae one of them. Ye would have no choice." She looked away. "Please, let's enjoy the time we have together while we can."

His talk had not gone as planned, and a new worry niggled at the back of his mind and took root. Had Dougal been wrong? Her words didn't indicate she was the mere orphaned niece of a priest, but that she had ties to a family of some consequence in the Highlands.

She took his face in her hands and pleaded, "Take me to bed, Lachlan. I want to ken ye are real. I want to feel ye inside me again. I dinnae want to dwell on what we cannae control."

He wanted that, too, had wanted it from the moment he had woken with her in his arms. She did things to him no woman ever had. He stood and looped his arm around her waist to lift her to his chest. His feet returned them to the hall and toward his chamber as his head told him, *'Tis too late to give her back what ye have taken.*

She truly believed him capable of tossing her aside for political gain, but she was wrong, so wrong. He would not be sending her anywhere.

Chapter Twelve

Several nights had passed, and with each one, Maggie and Lachlan had slept wrapped in each other's arms. But he had started spending more time behind closed doors with his men on some secret clan business he didn't speak of, and he came to bed later each night. Although he continued to lavish her with attention during the night, he seemed more distracted with each day, which fed a creeping apprehension that warned her all was not well.

Even this morning as she'd been on her way to meet Lorna at the stables, she'd been walking through the great hall and had overheard Conall's name and then Glenn's. Her complacency had shattered and her insides had trembled as the false sense of security she'd erected came tumbling down. Lachlan was a strong leader, but if Conall came for her, there would be nothing he could do to save her.

She climbed onto the steed she'd chosen from the stable and moved her horse over to Lorna's, the thrill she felt at having a companion again bubbling inside her chest. She loved having friends and Lachlan's affections, but as her time at Kentillie passed, her conviction that Conall might find her had become stronger.

Throat tightening, she looked to her new friend. What had she done? The clan could all be in danger because of her. First thing tomorrow morning, she would find a map and be on her way before it was too late.

"Lorna, this is a wonderful idea. I havenae ridden with a friend in ages." She forced a smile, determined to enjoy her last day here as she attempted to let thoughts of the danger and what she'd be leaving slip away.

Wallace, the stable master, had tried to steer her toward Freedom, but she had wanted to feel the wind rush across her face, and she needed a horse bred for speed. Mayhap some distance from her growing fondness for Lachlan would force her to make the right decision.

As they rode through the gatehouse and the purpled heather and majestic mountains came into view, Maggie couldn't contain her smile. The scenery and the company seemed surreal and magical, like a dream to have friends again, to wake and have hope for the future, and to be free to ride as she pleased. But her pleasure had been ripped away with just the mention of the snake's name.

Lorna had become important to her in such a short time, and while the days here had gone by fast, the seeds of friendship had taken root. Lachlan had been busy during the days, and if Lorna and Elspeth hadn't been there, she would have gone insane with boredom. She had formed an unbreakable connection with these ladies and dreaded the thought of going to the convent, where she would spend her days poring over books and living a life of silent solitude.

"Oh, I have lots to show ye. Since Donella is with child, her husband willnae let her go and I have missed riding." Lorna's infectious smile cut into her thoughts.

Maggie hadn't ridden since the day Lachlan had taken

her to the loch.

She gladly let Lorna lead the way. It was sunny, a welcome break from the seemingly endless drizzle and being stuck inside with sick and unhappy people. The days had not been so bad—she'd helped deliver a child, her first. Maggie had met many people, and Coira, the midwife, had knowledge of herbs and remedies she had not known. Coira had listened with real interest to Maggie, valuing her advice and skills, which felt good. No one had ever appreciated that part of her life. Her training had almost been a secret she was never allowed to use back home. Putting it into practical experience was rewarding.

The fresh air and sun lightened her spirits, and despite the lingering concerns over being discovered, she had not been this carefree since she had been a child. Mayhap if she told him the truth, Lachlan would let her remain at Kentillie. Och, she wanted to stay—she would be useful and would not have to spend the rest of her life locked away in a stuffy convent. But with the way his men spoke in hushed tones about Glenn and Conall, she feared Lachlan would never endanger his family for her. Her father concerned himself only with the greater good for his clan, and Lachlan would be compelled to do the same.

As they trotted through an empty field, she imagined this could be her new home, her new people. They were all accepting of her despite not knowing where she came from. Maggie could forget the person she had been and be whom she wanted without the daily fear of her father's condemnation or of being sold to that monster. Her thoughts continued to meander back and forth as she struggled with what she should do.

Confiding in a friend for the first time in years, she asked, "Do ye think Lachlan would protect me from danger if it meant putting the clan at risk?"

Lorna drew her horse to a stop, and she was forced to come to a halt alongside her friend. "Aye, can ye no' see how he feels about ye? And 'twould be the whole clan defending ye if need be."

"I have been told he will be done with me before the month is out," she said, hoping to squash the silly ray of hope that had blossomed somewhere deep in her belly. She didn't want to acknowledge the emotion.

"Who would tell ye something like that?"

"Arabella." Just saying the woman's name grated on her nerves.

"Och, she is jealous. Our laird is smitten with ye." Lorna waved her hand in the air dismissively.

The confidence of her friend was reassuring, but doubts remained. Despite all the blissful nights she had shared his bed, Lachlan hadn't promised her a future, and he still didn't know she might bring war to his clan if she stayed. But mayhap, if Lachlan wanted her, she could convince her father the match was good and he would break the contract with Conall. Even so, how could she attach herself to a man who didn't love her? She was left with a poor choice—leave or tell Lachlan the truth and hope he would let her stay on Cameron lands with her tortured heart.

"My mother killed herself because she gave her heart to a man who didnae return her love. I couldnae abide that situation." It was odd how easily the words flew out and how they relieved the burden that had pressed on her chest since her mother's passing. If she'd known how it would free her, she would have spoken of it earlier, but then she hadn't had people she could confide in until now.

"Ye arenae her."

"Nae, I would never leave my children."

They continued to ride and talk until, around noon, Lorna suggested they get back for a meal. Not quite ready to return,

Maggie allowed her horse a burst of speed as they entered the meadow closest to the keep. Riding hard and fast, she relished the thrill of the ride, jumping a few obstacles and flying like she was part wind. It was exhilarating as the pace pushed the fears from her head.

Lost in the moment and the beautiful land with its deep greens and mountains in the distance, she reveled in having a true friend, a man she cared for, and the possibility of freedom. Lorna had remained at the edge of the field and she pulled up next to her, out of breath and energized.

"Where did ye learn to ride like that, Maggie?" Her mouth was ajar.

"I have three brothers. My mother never cared what I was doing, so I ran wild with them." The words came in gasps as she fought to control her breathing. Her eyes still watered from the sting of the wind.

"Ye arenae afraid? I dinnae think I could ever ride like that." Lorna sounded both astonished and admonishing at the same time.

"Nae, it makes me feel free." She laughed.

The beat of horse's hooves coming toward them diverted their attention. *Lachlan.* Maggie was reminded of the first time she had seen him on his horse by her home and how he had looked like a god. He still did.

Knowing him now only drew her closer to him. So far he showed no signs of tiring of her, but she was out of time and had decisions to make—tell him the truth, or gather her few things and leave before first morning's light.

Lachlan had saved her, and she would always be grateful, but 'twas time she left to ensure the clan's safety. She could no longer put the Camerons in danger, and she couldn't risk him acting as a noble laird and sending her home.

Today would have been her wedding day.

• • •

Lachlan pulled up beside them and with a deceptive calm he didn't feel said, "Lorna, go on back. I need to speak with Maggie."

Once they were alone, his tranquil facade imploded, although he tried to keep his tone even when he said, "What the devil were ye doing, woman? Ye could have broken yer neck."

Or been captured or killed by my enemies. He'd been looking for her and Lorna for what felt like hours. Ice had been churning through his veins from the moment he'd been alerted that they had left the fortified walls of the keep.

She just stared at him, which only fanned the flames of his worry. "Can I trust ye to do anything without putting yerself in danger?" He tried to hide the critical tone in his voice, but he knew it came across as more than annoyed.

"'Twas just a couple of jumps." She sat up straight and returned his icy glare.

Although he wanted to scream at her lack of caution, he had sworn as he galloped out to meet her he wouldn't scold her too hard, because he'd not told her of the true danger that could be lurking in the woods. The idea of bending her over his knee and swatting her came to mind, but if he touched that sweet ass, it wouldn't be long before he was undressing her, and here did not seem like the proper place.

"Ye dinnae ken that horse. What if he has a bad temperament?" Lachlan tried to coax her out of her stubborn response. But, damn, what was he supposed to do? She drove him mad with all the reckless things she was doing and it was imperative he find a way to talk her out of her foolish behavior without causing her to turn stubborn and rebel.

It had been over a week since Conall's man disappeared, and there had been no sighting of him or the bastard on his land, but chills ran down his back when he thought of Maggie out there without protection. Christ, he still didn't even know how many men Conall would bring with him.

"He seems fine to me." She patted the horse and rubbed behind his ears.

He couldn't help but notice her reddened cheeks and still labored breathing, and images of her, naked and panting beneath him, floated through his mind. He was going mad for sure.

"Last time ye rode like that ye nearly fell off." He chastised himself for not heeding his own advice to watch his temper, but he couldn't help the retort.

Her back stiffened. "My head is better now. I will be fine. I am accustomed to horses," she protested.

"Mayhap I would trust ye if ye told me where ye came from. Why ye are so accomplished with both bow and horse." The old betrayal and distrust returned, and suddenly he was wondering if Maggie had been riding out to find Conall, and if she was the spy he'd first thought her to be.

Lachlan again pushed the subject to the back of his mind because he still had that niggling feeling he wasn't going to like the answer. Maybe tonight he would ply her with whisky until she couldn't hold her tongue. He was so frustrated at this point he was truly considering it. "Let's go back to the keep."

At the stables, Lachlan climbed down, then helped Maggie from the horse she'd chosen to ride. He was glad to have her off the beast, even more so that it was Brodie's prized steed, and it had only been in the stables because his cousin was off somewhere with a lass. It was almost as large as his warhorse, and she had no business being on it. Now that she was off the massive creature, he had to acknowledge that she had probably picked the best stallion in the stables. Like its master, it was steady and reliable.

Lachlan had apologized to his cousin, but he still felt bad

for attacking him. Despite the lecherous way Brodie chose to live these days, he was one of the best men Lachlan knew, and he could depend on his cousin with his life.

"Go on back to the keep, I will get them settled." He had something he wanted to take care of but didn't want her to know.

Once she left, he tracked down Wallace. The beefy man was as big as a mountain but as gentle as the rolling hills, and because he had several daughters Maggie's age, Lachlan was confident the man would understand.

"Dinnae let Maggie take out a horse unless ye have talked to me first."

The man gave him a blank stare, then his brows shot up, and he dipped his head.

"She is wild and careless, and I cannae have her putting herself in harm's way."

"She willnae like it." Wallace pursed his lips and shook his head disapprovingly.

"I ken that, but 'tis for her own safety. Ye are aware the Covenanters are a threat right now as well." Wallace had been instrumental in developing a plan should they all come under attack.

"Aye, I am, but ye should let her ken the truth." He laughed. "Ye've never dealt with a determined lass, have ye?"

Lachlan had no response. He'd never been overly concerned with Aileen's nor any other lass's comings and goings. But this wench, Maggie, was different.

"I will keep her off the horses unless ye say, but ye will be the one she blames. 'Twill no' be pretty when she finds out." The stable master took the steed Maggie had been on and directed him into the stables.

Lachlan would rather deal with Maggie's wrath than another injury or worse. Mayhap her head was no longer giving her trouble, but he couldn't help the image that had played through his head as he watched her ride wild in the field or the strange need he felt to keep her safe.

Conall's men, likely Conall himself, would be here soon, and the last thing he wanted was for them to find Maggie. Some of the other local lairds would soon arrive to review the letter, and he didn't want her out on display for them, either.

As Maggie's hips swayed while she strolled back toward the keep, his thoughts drifted back to Edinburgh. The night Finlay had commandeered the letter from Nathair.

With the first rays of morning light disappearing behind him, Finlay had limped into the inn and closed the door, but not before peering over his shoulder as if someone were trailing him. The rest of their group was sharing the corner table in the common room for breakfast, planning to make a hasty exit from Edinburgh before Conall could find his father and have them arrested after yesterday's altercation. Lachlan had just started to become concerned that his man hadn't returned.

The quiet, unassuming one, Finlay had a knack for moving around people without being noticed, which was the reason Lachlan had sent him to Edinburgh Castle to keep an eye on Conall.

"Och, what happened to ye?" Dougal said as he approached the table.

Finlay sank onto the bench by Alan. He said nothing, but opened his sporran and pulled out a folded piece of paper then tossed it onto the table in front of Lachlan. Then he leaned in and said quietly enough for only their band to hear, "I amnae certain what is in that letter, but 'tis sealed with the mark of the governor of Edinburgh and is directed to Archibald Campbell, Earl of Argyll. I overheard Conall telling his man that the deal was almost done before he handed it to him. I kenned anything going to Argyll wouldnae be good."

Lachlan picked up the intricately folded paper and studied the red wax seal, then broke it and read the contents.

"We need to leave now. He plots his father's murder and pledges the Erskine men to Argyll. They will come looking for it." Conall had used his father's seal to ally himself with the monster who was prosecuting men and women for standing behind their kin and beliefs.

The crafty bastard was a dangerous man, and what he'd read in that letter, combined with testimony from Robbie, would either put the blackguard in jail for the rest of his life or send him to the gallows.

Aye, Conall would be out for blood.

"I'll take 'em now." Wallace returned and interrupted his thoughts. He nodded as he passed the second horse to the man and turned toward the keep just in time to see Maggie disappear inside.

She would stay in the gates until this business was over. If Conall found out how much she meant to him, the bastard would take her. He didn't want the man to know she existed, and that meant keeping her within the castle walls and out of sight.

• • •

That next afternoon, Finlay and Gillies returned. Loaded with food from the kitchen, they met with Lachlan in the library. News of their arrival had him hurrying into the room to see his typically exuberant men sour faced and quiet. They lounged in chairs and threw each other furtive glances as he entered. Dread assailed him, and he briefly considered walking back out.

Finlay spoke up. "We have news." He averted his gaze. "We were asking about the wrong lass. At least we were using the wrong name."

"Her name isnae Maggie?" Lachlan pinched the bridge of his nose then rubbed his hand up to his temple and back down again.

"She does go by Maggie to her family, but most everyone knows her as Margaret." Finlay gulped. "Margaret Murray, the Duke of Kirk's only daughter."

It was like a physical blow, as if the wind had been knocked out of him, and for a moment he couldn't breathe. The Duke of Kirk was a powerful laird, a Royalist and an ally.

"This cannae be true. Dougal tracked her horse. She is the daughter of a priest's sister." Lachlan shook his head, but the denial he'd refused to analyze before rose up, and he knew they had uncovered the truth.

"The day she went missing, there was a priest visiting her family. His horse disappeared as well," Gillies said.

Lachlan gulped. He had bedded her. A duke's daughter. Silence filled the air while he let the news sink in.

"She's a Murray, then. That isnae so bad." He sighed as he let go of the tension. He would just have to wed her. Sure, the man was of higher status, but Lachlan was laird of one of the most powerful clans in all of Scotland. Many titled lairds had tried to get him to form an alliance.

It surprised him how easily he gave in to the idea of making Maggie his wife.

His shoulders relaxed, and he gave Finlay a smile. It was not until then he noticed neither man was smiling back, and in fact, they looked downcast, as if the worst was yet to come.

Finlay looked to Gillies, likely for some kind of reassurance, but he avoided Finlay's gaze as well. "That isnae the disturbing part." Finlay swallowed, and he shifted in his seat. "She is betrothed. Well, *was*. The wedding was to be yesterday. 'Tis why the priest was at her home."

Lachlan's breath became shallow. His insides twisted, and his gut hurt as if it had been repeatedly punched. He had to sit because his legs had turned to mush, and he was afraid they would not hold his weight, so he skirted the corner of his desk to collapse into his chair.

He wasn't ready to lose her—he'd just gotten started with her. He could feel the color drain from his face as he contemplated handing her over to another man, then his disbelief turned to anger. How could she have kept something like that from him? She belonged to another, and she had led him to believe there could be more between them.

"Who?" Lachlan growled, slamming his fist down on the desk.

Finlay gulped. Lachlan did not recall ever seeing the man frightened before. How could this get worse?

"Who?" he barked and stood to stare daggers at the messenger.

"Ye arenae gonna like it." Finlay's voice dropped to a whisper. He shook his head as if he did not believe the words coming from his own lips. "Conall Erskine."

Lachlan's heart stopped beating.

Conall. His worst enemy. The man who had betrayed their country and was forcing his religion on others. The man who had murdered a priest and had tried to kill Robbie and him was Maggie's betrothed. It would have been better had she been betrothed to a Sassenach.

"Ye didnae just say Conall Erskine?" he asked with barely disguised fury. A scalding rage clawed at him and threatened to destroy whatever was in his path. Finlay nodded, and Lachlan's hands shook. He was going to kill someone.

Was she a spy? She had not asked him any questions of a political nature, had even said at one point she didn't care for the politics of men. Had she been lying to gain his confidence? He was a fool.

All along, she had been right. Had he known who she was, he would have sent her home the moment he found out, or he would have left her there in the woods. Her presence at Kentillie could cause a war. Hell, he'd slept with her.

She had put his people in danger, and he had been

blinded by her looks, just like with Aileen. But this was worse. At least Aileen had cared about his people — Maggie didn't even know them.

Although he didn't want to believe it, the pieces started to click together. The Duke of Kirk had three sons, but he had not known of a daughter. That wasn't uncommon, though.

Lachlan kept up with news from the other clans and recalled the man's wife had died several years ago. Maggie had confided to him only last night she'd found her mother dead after she had taken too many of her own herbs. He had not heard the duke's wife had taken her life, but the family would have hidden the stigma of a suicide in the laird's home.

She was near Murray land when they found her. What a lucky coincidence to insert herself into their midst.

He didn't believe in coincidence.

The whole affair had probably been planned, some scheme orchestrated by Conall to find out what Lachlan knew. How gullible he had been to put his faith in another woman. He wanted to scream, but despite his rage over Maggie's betrayal, the thought of Conall putting his hands on her soft skin still made bile rise in his throat.

His men looking on, he paced the room, clenching his fists and shaking with the anger consuming him. It ate at him, a fury he had never known, not even in battle.

"What do we do, Lachlan? If she is found here, it could be war." Gillies only told him what he already knew.

"We will have to get her back to her family, but I need time to think. I slept with her, thinking she was the orphaned niece of a priest. I willnae be returning her in the same condition she came to my bed."

Maggie's father had probably been scouring the countryside looking for her, and the Murrays would be out for blood, thinking they had kidnapped and compromised her. He couldn't blame them; were she his daughter or sister, he would do the same.

Chapter Thirteen

The sick room door flung open and banged against the wall with a heavy thud. Maggie jumped at the intrusion and almost dropped the salve in her hands. Two men took up the doorway scouring the room, but with the late-day sun shining through, she couldn't make them out.

The dark, ominous shadows seemed to swarm the room hunting for a victim. As they marched in, their faces took form, and Maggie recognized them as men she met the first night she had left her family's lands.

The silhouette of an even more deadly form, more formidable in size and stature, took their place in the doorframe. They scanned the room until their gazes stopped on her and knives of unease stabbed her when they glared at her as if she were Satan himself.

The third shadow lingered in the door a moment longer; she couldn't tell what he was thinking, but she knew it was Lachlan as he marched in behind the other men. He was stiff, his brows pinched together and teeth bared. Looming closer, his menacing stare came into view and sent shivers racing straight to her heart.

Villagers and farmers crowded the room seeking medical attention, but as he glowered at her with rage through the narrowed slits of his eyes all movement ceased.

The balm fell from her hands to the floor, her heart sank, and her entire body went numb.

He knew who she was.

He hated her for her deception and was taking it worse than she had ever imagined. Waves of fury emanated from him like currents hammering a lonely vessel trapped on the sea in a squall.

And she was that little boat that was about to sink.

His eyes were so cold hers started to blur, but she held back the tears, because she'd brought this upon herself. A small crack formed in her heart.

He was going to send her away, was rejecting her, and would return her to Conall.

Her breath caught. No, she couldn't breathe at all and was on the verge of collapsing and tumbling into an endless abyss. She teetered. It was a good thing she was sitting, because her shaky knees wouldn't have held her up, and he was so angry he would probably not believe it if she fainted.

But defending herself would only make him angrier, so she opted to remain quiet. She had no excuse to justify putting him and his people at risk, and she should have left long before now. It had been a mistake to take time to enjoy herself, to think she could be wanted here and he would keep her safe. Now she would pay.

What hurt worse was the set of his jaw and the angry gaze that warned her he wouldn't give her a chance to justify herself. If she'd sought out the map this morning like she had planned, she would be gone, but Coira had sent a maid to fetch her early because a man had been injured and the Cameron healer had wanted her help to set a bone. There hadn't been another opportunity to leave the sick room, because it had been overflowing with others in need of assistance.

"Margaret Murray, ye were right. I am going to send ye home, but as far as I care, ye can go to the devil." The icy-cold words pierced her heart, and it felt as if the world had disappeared from under her.

Too numb to do anything but breathe, she rose on trembling legs and stood tall. It took all her willpower. Anxious to be away from all the stunned faces, she walked toward the men and kept her face as emotionless as possible. She was so mortified and hurt, her only focus was to get away.

Lachlan looked to one of the men—she couldn't remember his name. "Take her." And he disappeared.

A wretchedness like she had never known assailed her.

She was vaguely aware of Lorna jumping in front of the men in what would have been a vain attempt to stop them. She didn't want her friend to be punished for trying to help her, so she placed her hand on Lorna's arm, she said, "I will go. Dinnae worry."

She nodded to the men—Finlay and Gillies—she remembered now. They had been so nice to her that first day, but now they glared at her as if she were Satan's spawn. A strange numbness washed over her as she placed one foot in front of the other and followed them from the room.

Her thoughts turned to what would happen when they sent her back to Conall. Bile rose up and threatened to consume her. The fiend would punish her. He was not the kind of man to brush off a slight like that without stiff penalty.

Surely, Lachlan didn't know what kind of man he was. If he had cared for her even the smallest bit, he would never turn her over to the likes of that beast.

Numbly, she walked between the two men, her head straight and posture erect, as they marched to a side of the keep Elspeth had told her was not in use. They proceeded past the shocked faces of people she had met and come to care about. Curiosity, pity, or anger filled their eyes.

They would all hate her now. What had ever made her think she could have friends? That she would be anything other than a pawn in the games men played?

After ascending two flights of stairs, she was taken to a tower, left in a room that had only a bed and chamber pot. Heavy scrapes reminded her that she was bolted in like a common criminal, a caged bird, a game piece yet to be played. Her freedom was gone, and she collapsed on the cold stones. Only then did she break down and let the tears flow.

. . .

The moment Lachlan opened the door to the garderobe, Elspeth burst into the library. "Get her out of there right now. What are ye thinking, lad?" She only called him *lad* in private and when she disagreed with a decision he had made. It was morning. It had rained all night, and he had barricaded himself in the room and drowned himself in whisky.

"Do ye ken who she is?"

She blasted past him, forcing him to turn back into the room. His head pounded and there was a shooting pain in his neck, because he had fallen asleep on his desk in the wee hours of the night. While his mother continued her verbal assault, he massaged the back of it with his hand.

"Aye, I heard who she was born to and who she was pledged to, but ye ken that isnae who she is. She is a lass, the daughter of a duke, and has no choice in those matters."

Her words rang true, but they didn't change the facts. She was betrothed to the man who had tried to have him killed twice, a man who would slit a boy's neck without even flinching. Oh, Christ, had the second group of Conall's men been after him or her? Thinking back, that man with the dirk had acted as if he knew her.

But if she were here spying, why would they take her away? His thoughts swirled with unanswered questions and too much whisky. In a vain attempt to clear the fogginess, he shook his head then stomped over to his chair and plopped down.

"She lied to me. She may have brought our clan into a war." He jammed his elbows on his knees and buried his aching head in his hands.

"She didnae lie to ye. She told ye the truth. If she had told ye who she was, ye would have sent her back. And she was right, now wasnae she?" She poked a finger into his chest.

Lachlan groaned, reached for his whisky and gulped, but he didn't even taste it anymore. He wanted to drink Maggie into oblivion.

"Give me that. Ye have had enough." She snatched the bottle from his hand, walked across the room, and poured the whisky out the window, then turned to cross her arms, daring him to challenge her. "Have ye even given her a chance to explain?"

"Explain?" He growled. "What? That she is to be wed to my greatest enemy? I dinnae think she can explain it away." He rolled his eyes, and his brow knit together as the fury overtook him again.

"Let me talk to her, then," Elspeth pleaded. "Dougal willnae let me in to see her."

"No one will see her. She willnae get the chance to poison another's mind. She will go home tomorrow and with all speed, and I pray the Murrays and the Erskines dinnae swoop down on us the next."

"She has been in there all night with no food or drink."

"She can starve."

Elspeth gasped. He said it, but he did not mean it—he still felt so betrayed. He reached for the flask she'd put down on the desk and tipped it back, but it was empty.

"Ye willnae mistreat her. Aileen poisoned yer mind, and ye let it cloud yer vision." His mother stamped her foot. "I see the way Maggie looks at ye. The lass is in love with ye. She would never do anything to harm ye or our people."

Did the lass care for him? A dim ray of hope attempted to burst into his frozen heart. Even if she did care for him, though, what could he do about it? She was pledged to Conall Erskine.

"Ye owe it to yerself to get an explanation, and ye owe it to yer brother, whose life she saved, to let her defend her actions."

. . .

Lachlan unbolted the door to the tower room and strode in confidently. He didn't want to show any signs of weakness. He expected her to be on guard and ready to hurl angry words at him, but the bed was empty.

Scanning the small chamber, he found her huddled on the floor, leaning into the curved stone wall. Her arisaid was unclipped and wrapped around her like a blanket. She was a small lass, but now she looked more like a child. Maggie didn't move or acknowledge him.

His steps echoed in the almost empty room, and her gaze lifted to stare at him blankly. She didn't say a word; he knelt down beside her, and she flinched away. Her tearstained face was dry, but trails of salt had been left in their wake.

She was sallow, not her usual glowing pale, but a drained, dull shade of white. Guilt gnawed at him. He had not expected to find her so broken. She wasn't the fiery, reckless girl he had come to know.

"Finlay," he called out to the man guarding the door, "she needs some food and drink. Have Lorna bring her something.

Some whisky, too. She needs a little color."

Crouching down, he reached out to touch her cheek where the salty trails lingered. Her skin was cold to the touch, and he looked around to find there were no coverings on the walls to keep the chill at bay and the fireplace looked as if it hadn't been used in years. It had been unusually cold for September last night — the wind and rain had pounded through the night as well.

She didn't move but followed him with her sad eyes. Lachlan hated seeing her like this; he was used to the fearless lass who matched his verbal quips.

He stood and scooped her up in his arms. Although she tried feebly to pull away, he held on and carried her to the bed. She shook, refusing to meet his eyes.

He'd missed having her next to him last night. When he'd woken up on his desk, it was because he had reached out for her warmth. Sitting on the pallet, he cradled her body against his and rocked with her until he could speak. "Why, Maggie? Why did ye not tell me?"

She continued to look down and away from him. Her voice scratchy and weak, she said, "Because I kenned this would happen. I kenned ye would send me back." Her breath caught, and he thought she would sob. "I dinnae want to go back. I dinnae want to be wed to that monster."

He stiffened. "Conall?"

She nodded and finally gave him a tentative glance. He caught her chin in his hand so she couldn't look away. "Aye. Have ye heard of him?" Her eyes were wide with surprise. "I have been dreading it for years, and then ye came and I thought I was safe. I thought ye would save me." A single tear fell down her face. "I never should have believed ye would be different." A spark of defiance lit the watery depths of her eyes.

"Are ye aware of Conall's treachery, then, lass?"

Everything hinged on her answer. He studied her carefully, because if she was being less than honest, he would pick up on it instantly.

"I only ken he is a monster, and I would rather be in the cloisters than tied to him."

Lorna entered with a tray and smiled at Maggie. "Dinnae worry, Maggie, ye belong here." She huffed at Lachlan, "If he tries to send ye away, Elspeth will castrate him." She set the tray on the bed beside them.

"Out with ye, Lorna," Lachlan said.

She ignored him. "Are ye all right, Maggie? Elspeth will want to ken he is treating ye fairly."

Maggie nodded but didn't meet Lorna's gaze.

"Lachlan, she is one of us now." Realizing all the women were rising up against him, he snorted, raised his eyebrows, and pointed toward the door. She smiled at Maggie and turned to go.

Rising, he set Maggie down on the bed, grabbed a glass, and poured her a generous dram of whisky. "Ye need some color. Drink," he ordered as he placed the cup in her cold, trembling hand and molded her fingers around it. She obeyed and shuddered as the warm liquid went down.

"Now, tell me what ye have against Conall."

She flinched at the mention of his name. Obviously struggling to say whatever she had kept hidden, she peeked up at him through her long, dark lashes.

Maggie took another swallow and whispered so quietly he could barely hear her. "It started on the day the betrothal contract was signed." After another gulp she continued, "He cornered me in one of the stairwells at home. It was dark. He said he wanted a taste of what he would be getting." She shivered. "I refused him, and he got angry." Maggie looked down at her glass and watched the amber liquid swirl around as she rotated the cup.

Seconds ticked by before she added, "He punched me several times in my midsection. Afterward, I told my father. He either didnae believe me or didnae care. He told me I would have to get used to the man's gruff manner, since we were to be husband and wife."

His anger returning, Lachlan ground his teeth at what had been done to her. A tic in his jaw twitched fiercely.

"'Tis not all. That night, a light rapping on the door woke me. It was Miranda. We had been friends since we were babes." Maggie stopped to inhale sharply; she blew it out and closed her eyes. When she opened them again, he sat next to her and took her empty hand in his much warmer one. "She had been beaten. Bruises and blood all over her face. He had raped her. I will never forget the way she looked."

As she stared blankly at the wall, she continued, "Broken. It was like she was a broken doll. 'Tis the only way I can describe it. She could barely hold herself up. And she blamed me. Miranda never spoke to me again."

Finally, Maggie looked at him. Tears filled her tired eyes. "She said if I told anyone he would kill her, so I never said a word."

Maggie lifted the glass and gulped the rest of the whisky. "He told her to come show me what was going to happen to me when he got me home. He said he was going to enjoy breaking me in."

Lachlan remained silent, but he secretly swore he would kill Conall if he ever laid a hand on Maggie.

Her body trembling, she stared down into her cup and swirled the now empty vessel nervously. "Conall kept coming to visit. He threatened me every time. I closed myself off and stayed away from people. I was afraid he would hurt someone else."

As the truth rolled in his head, Lachlan went still. He couldn't send her back, not knowing what Conall was capable of. He had heard stories of the man's cruelty on the battlefield and had seen what he had done to the priest and the church, but he'd had no idea the bastard could be so cruel to an innocent lass. The thought of Maggie in his hands made Lachlan's blood run cold.

"Please dinnae send me back to him." A hiccup escaped as she pleaded. She looked lost and helpless. His fearless Maggie, who had braved a skirmish to save his brother, dived naked into a river, climbed the tallest tree to save a wee kitten, and rode a horse as if she was chased by the devil himself, was terrified of Conall.

"I can go to the convent. I can join them. He doesnae have to know I was here." Maggie put her cup down on the tray and went to her knees before him on the bed. She gripped both his hands so tightly he was sure there would be marks, but at the same time, the vise that had been strangling his heart since the moment he'd found out who she was lessened and he finally felt as if he could breathe again.

"Please, please dinnae send me back."

The lass had no idea he even knew Conall. How had he ever thought she might be plotting against him?

He put a hand on her cheek. "I willnae send ye back, Maggie. I willnae let the man touch ye ever again." He meant it. His Maggie would not be going anywhere.

"Will ye send me to the nuns, then?"

"Nae, Maggie, ye belong here. I'll write to yer father. He and I will come to some agreement."

"He willnae back out on the contract with Conall. He is a man of honor." She shook her head, eyes wide again with fear.

"Let me worry with that. I can persuade yer father. I have proof Conall is not what he appears to be."

Still, Maggie looked frightened.

She didn't know what he had in his possession, so he told her about the letter to Argyll pledging the support of Erskine men to the Covenanter cause and that Conall had vowed to kill his own father and become governor of Edinburgh. How Conall would be an outcast after Lachlan and his allies were done with the bastard.

She was still on her knees, nestled between his legs. He pulled her in for a tight embrace, thrilled she had no part in Conall's deceit. Her cold cheek brushed against his warm face. Guilt stabbed at his heart, and he hugged her closer.

He had been cruel, had locked her in this dank, cold room since before dinner the previous evening. Scanning the sparse surroundings, he cursed. She was Maggie, not some prisoner.

"I am sorra for denying ye the chance to explain yesterday. I was so angry. I shouldnae have locked ye in here. I should have listened." While he had been warm with drink in his study, she had huddled on the floor of this prison. Why had he not believed in her innocence? But something still bothered him—he'd just said he had proof of her betrothed's treachery, and she didn't flinch, didn't even ask about it.

Doubts remained, but he shook them aside as he loosened his grip and slid his hands down to her hips to pull her off her knees and onto the bed beside him. Mayhap she was just distraught.

"I couldnae blame ye for being angry. I didnae tell ye the truth." Her gaze cut to a corner of the room and stayed there. "The day ye found me in the woods, I was running away. Freedom isnae my horse. I gave him that name after I stole him. I didnae have a plan except to run. I needed to get somewhere safe and far away." He took in the shattered look, the one that said she had been desperate and had no one to turn to but a stranger. "Ye said ye would bring me to yer home, but I thought if I told ye who I was ye would insist I return to my father. If I had, I'd be married to him right now."

"Eat," he instructed. "We can rest after. I didnae get enough sleep last night, and I cannae imagine ye did, either."

She was weary, and he just wanted her in his arms.

She had not plotted against him. Her only crime had been trying to save herself from life with a monster.

He'd do whatever it took to make sure that didn't happen.

· · ·

Lachlan guided Maggie down the steps. Despite her weak and wobbly legs, she had become light and unencumbered by the secrets that had weighed her down for years. Her mind still reeled. He wasn't going to send her home, was not even going to send her to the nearest abbey—he wanted her to stay.

A slight mist still swirled as they walked hand in hand out into the morning air, where they were met by a crowd of people. Lorna ran up and nearly tackled her as her friend hugged her fiercely.

"Whoa, slow down, Lorna. Ye dinnae want to hurt her," Lachlan chided.

Maggie was glad to see Lorna had been on her side. It was nice to have a true friend, one who believed the best about you without question. At one point, Miranda had been that person, but it had been so long since she'd had someone to trust, a person she could count on, that she almost broke out into tears again.

"Ye should take better care of her, and I willnae have to worry so," Lorna huffed.

Pinning Lachlan with imploring eyes, Elspeth asked, "Is all well with ye now?"

"Aye, ye were right."

Elspeth let out a sigh, and her eyes became bright. "Ye look pale, Maggie. Are ye sure ye are well?"

"I am a little tired." It was an understatement. She was exhausted with fatigue all the way to her bones, because sleep had eluded her during the night, and she'd cried until her tears were dry.

"She needs rest." Elspeth glared at him, and Maggie wished, not for the first time, her mother had been like this woman. She was a fierce woman who would do anything to take care of her babe.

"I am taking her to rest," he bit out defensively. "Malcolm. Ye take over for the day?"

"Of course," he replied. Maggie heard him say something else, but Donella pushed Lorna out of the way and latched onto Maggie in a sideways embrace so her swollen belly would not push into her.

"Thank God ye willnae be going anywhere. I like ye here, and I think Coira needs yer help to bring my babe into the world."

Alan appeared at their side and tilted his head down toward Lachlan, crinkling his brow up at the same time. Lachlan leaned over and whispered something in his ear.

"The thought of marrying Conall would scare the hell out of me, too," Alan burst out. Maggie laughed. She couldn't help it—maybe it was from the fatigue. He grinned at her response.

"He may come for her." Lachlan broke the mood, and her insides twisted.

If he knew she was here, he would come; he was not a man to easily relinquish what he thought to be his property. "Mayhap he doesnae ken I am here."

"We cannae go on that assumption. One of the men who attacked us outside Kentillie has disappeared. They seemed to recognize ye. Did ye ken who they were?"

Her steps faltered, and she gulped as the implications washed over her. "Glenn."

"Aye, were they after ye then? I thought they were after Robbie and the letter."

"Nae, they were just as surprised to see me as I was them. Why would they be after Robbie?" A cold breeze skidded across her skin and dotted it with rain that had started to fall harder, and Maggie shivered.

"He witnessed Conall murder the priest."

A vision of the charred remains of the church and Robbie standing over a newly dug grave invaded her memory, and she gasped. "That man will go to hell for all the horrible things he has done." She turned her head into Lachlan's shoulder as the watery assault increased.

"I need to get ye in out of the rain." Lachlan picked up the pace and pulled her along with him.

Behind her Elspeth called out, "I'll send up some water to bathe and then get some rest." She'd almost forgotten about the trail of family and friends in their wake as the fear of Conall's imminent arrival chilled her.

Practically dragging her up the stairs and to the bedchamber, he said, "I thought they would keep us out there all day." Exasperated, he let go of Maggie's hand to turn and bolt the door.

"They made me feel wanted."

He touched her cheek tenderly, and she turned her head into his palm. "Why would ye not feel wanted?"

"After yesterday, I thought everyone would hate me." The remembered stares of the Camerons as she was escorted to the tower made her shudder. Focusing on his gaze, she saw something there she'd never seen before, something sad and haunting, mayhap regret.

His hand combed her hair, but his thumb lightly rubbed back and forth on her cheek. Resting his other hand on her waist, he said softly, "I shouldnae have done what I did yesterday. If I could do it over, I would."

His head tilted down and almost imperceptibly shook as raw emotions swirled in the depths of the eyes focused on her. "I will make certain the entire clan kens ye belong here."

His head dipped, and his lips gently, reverently caressed

hers. It made her feel precious; she melted into him. Pulling back, his gaze penetrated to her soul. "Everyone will ken ye belong here at Kentillie. In my arms, in my bed, by my side."

She believed him and knew he thought his own words to be true, even though she was aware that in time he would move on to another.

Those words went straight to her heart, and the walls she had built for years crumbled down and disappeared. He would hurt her, but it no longer mattered because she would give anything to stay by his side. She was falling hard into a place she'd never wanted to be, and as much as she had tried to fight it, it was there, stark and vivid. A truth she could no longer deny. She loved him.

His mouth eagerly closed over hers in a scorching kiss, and her thoughts scattered, leaving her senseless and needing. She knew it was too much to hope for, but it was as if he was telling her with that gesture that she was his whole world. That he was as lost to her as she was to him.

Chapter Fourteen

His mother had set up yet another feast with music, likely sensing how tense Lachlan was over the imminent meeting with the lairds who would arrive any day, the threat of Conall and Argyll on the offensive on his land, and the lack of reply from Maggie's father. Almost a week had passed since he'd sent his proposal to the Duke of Kirk, and until he received a response he was in no mood to celebrate.

The men he'd sent to deliver the message that she was safe and in his care still hadn't returned. Had he put too much information in the missive? Had it not been enough? What would be the duke's answer? Was Maggie's father in league with Conall? The questions ate at him.

Elspeth had ordered some of Maggie's and his favorite dishes prepared: meat stewed with carrots and potatoes for him, while Maggie enjoyed the roasted mushrooms. He hand fed her a few just so he could watch her close her eyes and savor the morsels. The sight of her in the candlelight relishing the small bits tempted him to haul her upstairs and end the night early.

As before, tables were moved aside and the volume of the music intensified as Maggie pulled him onto the floor. 'Twas the bonniest sight he'd ever seen as her dark curls bobbed playfully while they twirled to lively fiddle music, and he reluctantly admitted that his spirits were slightly lighter. She captivated him. Hell, she captivated everyone with her full lips and easy smile.

Several times over the last few days, there had been one calamity or another to deal with, but her unhampered zest for life had pulled him through. He would be exhausted at the end of the day, but just seeing her face light up when he came into the room filled him with a hope he had never expected to feel again, and he was able to put away feelings of frustration and enjoy life himself.

That was what she did for him. She brought back the joy he'd not felt since his father's passing, since he had become the man in charge of his clan. There had been no peace, only duty and responsibility. Now though, he had Maggie, and every day was worth it. He could deal with whatever the day brought as long as he had her at the end of it.

The song ended, and Malcolm claimed her for the next dance. Although Lachlan skirted back along the wall to avoid Arabella, she found her way to his side and attempted to pull him out to dance. Her infatuation had gone too far, and he snapped at her insistence, "Since ye havenae been able to accept that there is nothing between us, I have contacted yer Fraser cousins and ye will be leaving tomorrow to live with them."

"Ye will regret taking that spy to yer bed. She isnae a Cameron and cannae look after ye like I can."

"Nae. 'Tis done. Ye are no longer welcome on Cameron lands."

Her eyes turned cold, and he caught her wrist just before the palm of her hand connected with the side of his cheek.

"Ye bastard," she screeched, "she'll betray ye just as Aileen did."

"Leave. I'll send Dougal to take ye to yer new home tomorrow." She scowled then pivoted and ran from the room. Instead of regret, Lachlan was relieved.

He walked back to his table, and Alan greeted him as he took a swig of ale. "Any word from Maggie's father?"

"Nae, nothing yet. They should have been back by now."

"I ken," Alan said grimly.

"If they arenae back soon, we will have to go looking for them." As he watched Malcolm twirl Maggie around the floor, he took another gulp.

"'Twas a good idea to put Robbie with the MacDonalds. If anyone will keep him safe from the Covenanters, 'twill be them." Despite the Campbell clan's continued attacks on MacDonald lands, the MacDonalds never failed to beat them back.

"Aye, the Campbells are a miserable sort. Murdering innocent women because they are Catholic. 'Twill be war if they ever come near a Cameron lass." Lachlan's chest tightened along with his fists.

"Duncan Campbell is heartless and bloodthirsty. Ye ken his mother is an Erskine. Probably how Conall got involved with them." Alan's jaw clenched. "Ye should have Kirstie come home. I dinnae like the Campbells are between us and the Macnabs. If there is war, we may nae be able to reach her."

"I will write to her again, but the Macnabs have sworn they will keep her safe."

"Can they promise ye that if Argyll comes down on them with all his Campbells she will still be safe? She belongs here." Desperation flashed in Alan's eyes, the same anxiety Lachlan felt at keeping Maggie safe with the possible approach of Conall. There was no better man to care for his sister, but until the threat here was dissolved, Kirstie would remain where she was.

At some point, he would have to force them back together and let them sort out whatever had gone wrong between them. A pleased smile crossed his lips at the thought. He glanced over to check on Maggie, and Alan mistook his grin, because he said, "I kenned ye wouldnae be able to resist her after that first day she spent with us at camp. Ye ken she fell for ye right away, too."

"Ye wouldnae be insisting I wed the lass." He tried to sound angry.

"She is the one for ye, Lachlan. When are ye going to admit it?"

"Aye, ye were right. She is."

Alan's jaw dropped open. It was worth telling him the truth just for the response.

"I didnae expect to hear ye admit it." His friend put his hand over his heart and held his other up as if he were in shock.

"I want her as my wife. 'Tis why I am so anxious to hear back from her father. I let him ken as much in my missive."

Alan whistled.

"I asked him if we could discuss terms and let him ken I had proof Conall was a traitor to his own family and no' fit to be her husband."

The music ended, and Lorna rushed to take Maggie's hand.

"Ye shouldnae have to wait much longer. Any man in Scotland would be proud to have ye for a husband to his daughter."

"I hope you're right."

"Does she ken ye want her?"

"Nae. I dinnae want to promise her anything before I ken how it will go. We still have Conall to deal with." His eyes cut back to Maggie as his thoughts turned to the task ahead.

"With the letter, though, Conall shouldnae be a problem for long. His own father will have to put him in jail."

"Let's hope it works. Robbie is reluctant to testify against him."

"If we can get enough to send him away without using the boy, we should," Alan agreed.

"I get the impression he is hiding from someone himself." Lachlan reflected on Robbie's reclusive behavior. He was intelligent and skilled with a weapon, but he hid his face when they were in public and nervously rubbed at his shirt where the cross they had retrieved from Conall lay hidden beneath. If all went well, within a few days' time, Conall would no longer be a concern, and Maggie would be his wife. He left Alan's side and walked toward her but couldn't shake the dread.

Nothing was ever as easy as it should be.

• • •

During the night, Maggie woke to a delicious sensation of warmth that flooded her senses with longing. Lachlan's hand curled around her waist, and he rose up on the other elbow, leaning his powerful, taut body into hers. His hungry blue gaze scorched her right to the center of her heart.

Although she wanted to beg him to touch her, to claim her, the words did not come, but her eyes must have reflected her desire, because he groaned and lowered his head to her neck. He trailed kisses down the tender curve to her shoulder, then back to the sensitive area just below her ear. She shivered as his teeth gently nipped at the lobe of her ear.

His warm breath sent yearning spiraling through her, and her hand clenched on the covers as need exploded in her. Shock waves pulsated through her veins right to her core. Gasping, she flung her head back to give him better access.

As she nestled closer into his body, he groaned, and his

cock was hard with yearning as it bulged into her hip. The evidence of his desire thrilled her. Her core was hot and eager, and wetness pooled at the apex of her thighs, which spread and rose in a primal response, involuntarily seeking the fullness of his staff.

Craving to taste him in return, Maggie turned into him to reach his lips. Gentle at first, her lips touched his. Seeking, her tongue delved into his mouth, and his covered hers in a hunger that matched her own, taking from her as she gave.

His hand slid up and caressed her breast, reverently kneading the soft flesh and sending involuntary shudders pulsating through every part of her body. His thumb and forefinger clamped down on her erect nipple and pulled. She drew back from his mouth and gasped with the pleasure. The intensity in his eyes shocked her. It was raw and tangible, a searing desire only matched by her own heated yearning.

In the moonlight, his golden hair appeared brown and his eyes had darkened as well, predatory and ravenous. He watched her with a primitive appetite that spoke to her soul.

This was how she wanted to spend every night for the rest of her life. Never would she get enough of him, so she surrendered to the emotions she had been fighting the last few weeks. He had become her whole world, and consequences be damned, she loved this man with all her heart.

Lachlan shifted onto his back and pulled her into the warm length of his body. "Straddle me, Maggie." The strangled order was more like a plea. There was desperation in his voice he was only barely able to control. He was on the edge, waiting to be pushed over a cliff into the pleasurable abyss. "I want to be inside ye."

Not sure what she was doing but trusting him, she flung one leg over his body and came into a sitting position over him.

"Raise up your hips." His hands were on her, and he

guided her up.

Her sheath ached to take in his cock.

Reaching down with one hand, he guided himself to her entrance and slid the head of his shaft back and forth over her slick folds. He groaned and then inserted the tip. Slowly, he guided her down onto him, impaling her, the walls of her passage stretching to accommodate the engorged length of him. She was full and complete.

His hands spanned her hips and held her still. "Dinnae move, Maggie. I want to look at ye on top of me." His gravelly voice was harsh and strangled. She wasn't sure if she wanted to cry out in frustration, pleasure, or the realization she had given her heart to this Highland warrior.

"Please, Lachlan." It was too much. She was dizzy with longing and an all-consuming need to reach her climax, but he held her there, a sweet, unbearable torture.

"Ye look so bonny," he said as one hand held her in place and the other trailed over her belly. His gaze traveled from where they were joined up to meet her eyes, and the desire she saw there heated her more than she thought possible.

Just as she thought she would go mad, he guided her hips up. Her gaze riveted on him as the length of his shaft became visible and then disappeared again into her waiting sheath. He was enthralled at the sight, and she was transfixed by him. He was beautiful.

Moving her slowly until she got a rhythm of her own, his hands traveled back to palm the globes of her backside. He squeezed hard, and she gasped at the pain. Or was it pleasure? The wicked smile he flashed at her sent tremors through her, and the pace he'd set faltered, but she found her own. Her hips ground into his, and she rotated in delicious circles as his cock hit places in her channel that made her feel complete.

"I willnae outlast ye with ye moving like that," he growled between clenched teeth. "I want to watch ye climax above me."

She nearly reached her peak at his words, but he put his hands back on her hips, stilled her, and took away her control. He fixated on her face as he slowly lifted her up and then pulled her back down. She gasped at the intensity. He did it again and again, each time his length thrusting inside her; he was so deep, the tip of his erection slammed into her womb.

One of his thumbs lowered to the sensitized nub between her legs and flicked back and forth as he continued to raise and lower her on and off his manhood. It was too much sensation. Flames ignited and beat a rapid pulse deep in her core, spreading out and encompassing her whole being.

When the explosion came, the waves overtook her and pulled her into a vortex of drowning feelings and emotions. Strangled gasps, somewhere between a scream and a pant, came from her throat as the pleasure shattered in her again and again and again. Her clenching muscles pulled Lachlan under with her.

He shouted her name as his pelvis rose into her, quicker and harder, no longer in control. Their shared climax drew out the ecstasy, making it go on and on as her clenching muscles milked the seed from him. It filled her to bursting.

Maggie collapsed on top of Lachlan, spent and exhausted, her legs shaking, their bodies slick with sweat and the evidence of their lovemaking. He trailed his fingers reverently over her as they lay there sated.

Sprawled on his chest, she realized nothing else mattered but being with Lachlan. This Highland laird who cared enough to go against alliances to protect her. The one who knew what her favorite food was, the one who worshipped her body in the night. He was the man who cut right to the essence of her being and spoke to the part of her she'd denied all these years. There would never be another. She loved him, and nothing else mattered.

• • •

Beams of light from the moon softly filtered in the window as Lachlan lay with his arm draped around Maggie's naked waist and his hand cupping her breast. Her back was against his chest, skin to skin, and he was drifting in between that place where reality and dreams melded together and peace seemed attainable.

It felt right. The way it should be. He could no longer imagine sleeping in his bed alone—it was now their bed. She had just made him feel like the luckiest man in Scotland, because never had he had such a mind-blowing experience or felt such contentment.

She gave him faith again. That there was a woman for him, and she was here.

Maggie spoke so softly he thought he had imagined it at first. "I love ye, Lachlan Cameron. I tried so hard not to. 'Twill break my heart when ye are done with me. But I can no longer deny it. I love ye."

He remained still, almost not breathing. She had thought him asleep and had not wanted him to hear her declaration. He couldn't help but smile.

The lass was the complete opposite of Aileen—Maggie would never try to manipulate him. She loved him but did not want him to know and thought he would be done with her soon. Silly woman.

But he pretended not to hear her, because he couldn't say the words back. They bubbled up to the top of his heart and threatened to spill over, but he wasn't ready to let her know how much power she had over him.

After breaking his fast, Lachlan strutted to his chamber to

retrieve his claymore. He'd been so distracted with thoughts of Maggie this morning, he'd forgotten he was going to practice in the yard with his men today.

Maggie had told him she loved him. The lass had become the air he breathed, his reason for waking, and why he smiled again. She had restored his faith, and there was no way he could ever repay what she gave to him so selflessly. He looked forward to seeing her every eve when coming in from the fields or after meeting with his men, and he lived to wake beside her in the morn.

His reckless Maggie, his miracle. He would tell her he loved her, but it would wait until he'd spoken with her father.

When the door to his chamber clicked shut behind him, his nose twitched at the unfamiliar, sickly sweet smell that greeted him. Scanning the room to see where the offensive odor was coming from, his gaze landed on the bed and copper-colored hair that should not be there. Arabella. Oh, Christ, what was the crazy woman doing here? This lass had him ready to tear his hair out. He gritted his teeth and prepared for battle.

"What the hell are ye doing here, woman?" he asked, rubbing his head with his hands.

"I've come to please ye, Lachlan," she replied shyly but determinedly. He was stunned, although he did not know why anything this trollop did surprised him. She peered at him with an provocative grin and cocked her head while raising an eyebrow suggestively.

"I dinnae want ye, woman. Get up and get out of my bed. Ye dinnae belong there." The audacity of her presence in Maggie's and his chamber frustrated him. He'd only one other time been tempted to strike a woman. His hands clenched as he prayed for the same restraint now.

She pulled back the covers and rose seductively. The woman had nothing on. Instead of piquing his interests, it infuriated him further, and he spun away to avoid the show.

"Arabella, put clothes on now," he continued as he pounded the wall with the ball of his fist to release some of his anger. "Ye ken I'm with Maggie. We had bedplay once, and I never called on ye again." He was done with trying to spare her feelings. She had crossed a line.

Lachlan risked a peek over his shoulder. She was partially clothed, so he turned to lecture her. She wasn't crying, merely put out at his rejection.

"You shouldnae have slept with me if ye didnae want me," she yelled as she stooped to retrieve her boots.

"Ye kenned it would only be one time. Ye knew I didnae want anyone." He did not feel the need to defend himself—he'd told her the truth from the beginning.

"Then what are ye doing with Maggie?" Her breath rushed out while glaring at him.

What would he say to her without driving the lass to violence? She looked as if she would tear his eyeballs out or at least throw a shoe at him.

He ticked off the reasons in his head. She was not as bonny as Maggie; she didnae make his heart sing like Maggie did; she did not lighten up a room when she walked in it.

He settled for simple. "She found her way into my heart."

"I am one of yer clan. I am better for ye than she is." Half dressed, she slunk over to him and reached up to touch his cheek. But Lachlan flinched and backed toward the door. "She will betray ye. She will betray our clan. She plots yer demise with that earl's son."

Chills ran down his back at the mention of Maggie and Conall linked together in such a way and scheming against him. He pushed down the distrust he'd buried when he'd decided to take Maggie as his wife.

Maggie isnae Aileen—she wouldnae do that to me. But even as he thought the words, Aileen's betrayal clouded his thoughts.

He opened the door with all haste and slid through. But as he reached the hall, he braced himself on the jamb. He was not going to cower from the lass even if she'd lost her mind.

The low, menacing growl he gave her would have terrified any of his men. "Ye are done here, Arabella. I want ye out of Kentillie. I am sending ye to the Frasers. Ye can live there with yer cousins. Ye have overstepped yer bounds and are no longer welcome here."

He stormed down the hall but stopped and turned. "I want ye off Cameron lands today. Go pack up yer things now."

Fuming at the audacity of the lass, and the fact that she'd driven him to the point he had to send her away, he pounded down the steps.

Why did she think Maggie would betray him? As he strode down the hall, his heart beat rapidly, and he cursed how easy it had been for Arabella to opened up the old wound so easily. The one that told him he couldn't trust any lass, not even Maggie.

Chapter Fifteen

Donella had given birth to a squalling boy. The mother and baby were doing well, and Maggie had finally met Donella's husband, Gawen. The way he'd looked at Donella and the new babe endeared him to Maggie right away. He doted on her, and it was easy to see they loved each other. He'd proudly taken the babe from Coira and gently placed a kiss on its wee head.

Maggie had been paralyzed by a momentary jealousy for something she would never have. She would give anything to have Lachlan look at her with such tenderness as she brought their children into the world, but he'd never professed any feelings for her other than lust. She sighed.

At least she would never have to give birth to one of Conall's bairns. She hummed a tune from the night before as she pranced back to the keep.

Bounding into the great hall, she bypassed the stairs to greet Alan and give him Donella's happy news. Just as she was about to reach him, a movement from the balcony that overlooked the great hall caught her eye. Lachlan. He was leaving their chamber.

Maggie smiled. She wouldn't have to track him down to tell him the babe was here. He was leaning on the doorframe, one hand on his hip and the other braced on the jamb itself. His head was turned down facing someone. Lachlan stood back, and she was shocked to see a woman. Maggie sucked in at the air that wouldn't fill her lungs, and the joy from moments earlier melted away, replaced by a gut-wrenching pain.

Arabella stood in the doorway to the chamber Maggie had come to think of as her haven. Her own special doorway to heaven. There was the woman who would replace her, scantily clad in a chemise while she held her arisaid draped over her arm.

His back to Maggie, Lachlan leaned over Arabella like he was ready to devour her. Her hair was a tumbled mess as if they had already been together. His broad shoulders towered over the harlot as he pinned her to the wall. That rotten bastard. How stupid she had been. How utterly naive to have hoped she meant something more to him than the lasses of his past.

As her heart broke into a million pieces, the words her mother spoke to her long ago haunted her. *My heart doesnae matter to yer father. The member between his legs leads him where he wants to go.* That was hours before her mother had taken her own life. Maggie choked back a sob at the memory and the sight of Lachlan with another woman. This is what her mother had experienced all those years—the all-encompassing deluge of loss and despair.

It was the reason she had sworn never to love. She was a fool.

Her hand rose to cover her mouth, her body shaking with the pain as the first wave of nausea assaulted her.

"Oh my God, I have become my mother." The words were

almost inaudible, but Alan offered Maggie a sad, remorseful gaze, as if he was apologizing for Lachlan's behavior or lack of discretion. Tears filled her eyes, and his face blurred. Just as well—she could not look at him, would not listen to the excuses.

Alan started to speak, but she would not hear. Her feet were already moving.

Maggie dashed from the hall, stumbled and fell to her knees when she reached the outside. Her belly churned as a wave of agony assaulted her like a physical blow. She crawled, heedless of her surroundings, to the side of the stone building and crumpled.

When she was capable of standing, she rose and sprinted for the stables. She had to get away. She didn't belong here. Her life would not be spent pining over a man who did not return her love. Mayhap she had been stupid enough to give her heart to the man, but she would not sit by while he crushed it over and over again.

By the time she reached the stables, tears fell unchecked. The stable master met her at the door. "What has happened, lass?" His forehead crinkled.

"I need Freedom. I just need to go for ride to clear my head."

"I cannae let ye take him, lass. I have been instructed to speak with Lachlan before ye can ride." He pursed his lips in a sad smile. "He was concerned about yer rough riding last time ye went out."

He did what? Frozen, Maggie stood there, stunned for a moment. This fired her blood and made her want to scream, because there was no way she was going to ask that treacherous man for his permission.

Maggie backed away and sprinted for the gatehouse. She had planned to plot a route to the abbey, but now she fumed at her stupidity. She had been so content and sure Lachlan would protect her now that he knew her identity that she had never made it to the map room—she didn't even know what direction to go in.

"Damn," she cursed aloud. Once she got away, someone would tell her how to get there, but she could not ask anyone here—it was impossible to look them in the eyes, knowing she'd meant so little to their laird that he'd replaced her without even telling her.

She ran toward the sparsest field, away from the villagers, away from the man who had shattered her heart and hopes.

When she heard the hoofbeats behind her, she was more than halfway to the other side of the field. They closed in fast, and she turned, praying no one had come looking for her. She was wrong. It was Lorna.

"What has happened?" her friend asked as she drew up beside her and frowned. Maggie slowed but continued to move away from the keep, bracing her hands on her hips. She couldn't speak until she'd claimed the breath that had fled with her.

Lorna walked the horse beside her. Apparently, Maggie was the only one with restrictions on her riding. "Did Wallace let ye take out yer horse?"

"I was just riding her around the castle grounds. He told me no' to leave the gates, but when I saw ye run out, I followed ye anyway. Now, tell me what's wrong."

"He was with Arabella. In our bedchamber." The tears started falling again as her words pierced her heart. "I willnae stay with a man who cannae be faithful."

"There must be a mistake. He wouldnae do that to ye. Lachlan hasnae had eyes for another lass since he laid them on ye. He doesnae even like her," Lorna insisted.

"I ken what I saw. He was with her, or he was about to be." She hiccuped in a large gulp of air.

Looking past her, Lorna lifted a hand above her brow to

look at something in the distance. "I dinnae ken those men. Do ye?"

When she turned, icy dread spread through her veins as a familiar frame rode into view. "Conall."

She gasped as several men on horseback galloped toward them, and though they were still a good distance away, they were approaching quickly. She would recognize the monster in the middle of the group anywhere.

Her breath caught, and she backed up, almost tripping over her own feet. Her head shook in denial until Lorna's horse snorted and reminded her what was at stake. Images of Miranda's broken and battered face loomed in her thoughts. She would not let that happen to Lorna. He was too close, there was no chance for Maggie to escape, but this time she could save her friend.

"Go. Ye have to go now. He's an animal. Go."

"Climb up. Come with me." Lorna reached out to pull her up.

"There isnae time. 'Twill slow ye down." Maggie straightened her shoulders and slapped the horse's backside as hard as she could. The beast whinnied and bolted. Her palm stung from the impact, but it worked. She said a quick prayer the horse would be swift, and Lorna would have time to get to safety.

She turned to face Conall and hoped he and the three men with him would be satisfied with her and not pursue her friend. The evil smirk on his face terrified her as he pulled up short right in front of her. Thankfully, the other men stopped as well.

Conall jumped down, and it felt as if the earth beneath her feet shifted, but that could have been because her whole body shook. He stalked toward her like the calm before a winter storm about to unleash its fury with a vengeance.

His face remained expressionless, but his voice crackled

with venom. "Margaret."

He clucked his tongue as he paced back and forth in front of her like a feral beast ready to strike. She was trembling inside but steady on the outside, because she refused to let him know how he affected her.

"Imagine finding my missing bride in a place like this." He stopped pacing and glared, his long fingers making a circle in the air to signal the Cameron lands. "Why is it I find you so far up in the Highlands?" She couldn't help the involuntary shudder as his malevolent gaze pierced her like fangs attacking prey.

She couldn't speak, she couldn't even breathe as she stared at the man not much smaller than Lachlan, a golden-haired man with malice and promises of destruction in his cold gray gaze. What would he do? He'd been cruel and unpredictable when he seemed calm. Now, he was coiled and ready to strike.

On top of what he had done to Miranda, she had heard countless stories of his cruelty when he felt slighted. She had given him the biggest slight of his life. Silently, she prayed for a quick death. Nothing he did to her would be any kinder.

"How is it you come to be on Cameron land so far from home, love?" Rage slipped through his tranquil facade before he tamped it down to wear the impassive mask he used best. His words sounded tender, concerned, but it was for show, and she was certain his anger was spiraling inside him like the venomous snake he was, waiting for the right moment to strike.

"Do you know the Lochiel?" he asked gently.

She blinked, because she wasn't used to the formal title afforded to Lachlan as the Cameron laird.

This time when she did not respond, he screamed. "Do you know him?" Spittle flew from his tightened, angry lips.

She jumped at the verbal assault then slowly nodded in acknowledgment.

He smiled an evil grin that screwed his face in a maniacal, twisted mien. "Now we are getting somewhere. Have you slept with him?"

He was not going to like the answer and would make her suffer. She attempted to maneuver the conversation in a different direction. "I was on my way to the abbey to take vows. I want to devote my life to God. I amnae wife material."

"I am only going to ask you one last time, Margaret." She hated her given name when he spoke it. "Did you sleep with Lachlan Cameron?"

Aye, there would be retribution, but if she didn't answer him, it could be worse later. She slowly nodded and waited for the worst.

His eyes bulged and face reddened for just a moment, then he calmed, as if he had already been thinking on the matter and had come to terms with it. He walked up to her, seeming in control of his emotions, and she looked down to avoid his gaze.

The crack of his fist striking her cheek blindsided her. The blow stung, the most intense pain she had ever experienced. Conall's face started to blur, and she collapsed in a heap on the ground.

• • •

Lachlan cursed as he stomped down the steps and rounded the corner into the hall. He had regretted bedding the wench several years ago when he was trying to wash Aileen from his mind and had tried to apologize for his drunken error. One time had been all, but Arabella had never let it go.

He wasn't prepared for the fist that collided with his face as he stepped onto the ground floor. A loud thud reverberated through the hall, and he stumbled backward. He caught himself on the cool stone wall, scraping his palm as he did.

Alan?

"What the hell?" In the years they had known each other, his best friend had never raised a hand to him, not even in jest.

"That is fer Maggie." His friend spit as he took up a fighting stance and glared at him.

"I am only going to ask ye one more time before I beat the shit out of ye. What is going on?"

"What were ye doing in yer chamber with Arabella?" he retorted, shoulders up and back bowed for a fight.

"I found her in there and told her to leave." That his friend would think such a thing offended him. The day kept getting worse.

"'Tis no' the way it appeared from down here. Maggie saw ye hovering over an almost naked Arabella. It didnae present a pretty picture." Alan shook his head.

"I swear the crazy wench sought me out and I rebuffed her. Ye ken there is nothing there." Many times he had told Alan about his inability to shake the woman and they had laughed it off, but now it wasn't so funny.

"Aye, I ken, but it looked bad, Lachlan. 'Tis what Maggie thought, too."

"Where is Maggie, then?" He scanned the hall but saw no sign of her.

"I dinnae ken. She ran from the hall mumbling something about being a fool like her ma." Alan shook his head. "She looked verra distressed."

Lachlan's blood froze. Last night, as he held her close, Maggie had told him what had happened to her mother, and about the sorrow and the heartache she had suffered over her mother's infatuation with her father. She would not do what her mother did—Maggie had more sense than that. Didn't she?

"I have to find her. Which way?"

"She went out the front. I dinnae ken which way from

there. I waited down here to confront ye."

Where would she go? What would she do? Lachlan bolted for the door. Reaching the yard, he looked around. Several people were milling about. "Where's Maggie?" His heart stopped when they pointed toward the stables, and he sprinted in the same direction.

When he found her, he would have to talk some sense into her. She couldn't pick up her skirts and take off every time she was frightened or angry. She had to learn to communicate with him.

He slowed only when he got to the door of the stables. Wallace was walking out, and Lachlan almost ran the man over. "Where is she?" he panted as he struggled to catch his breath.

The man held his hands up. "I didnae let her take a horse. Ye told me not to let her have one."

"Do ye ken where she went?" His shoulders relaxed as relief washed over him; she could not have gotten far.

"She took off in that direction." He pointed to the gatehouse. "Lorna went after her. She seemed pretty torn up. I hope Lorna can talk the lass down."

Not bothering to saddle up, he dashed into the stall, jumped on his horse, and galloped off. Just as he got to the edge of the field, he saw Lorna speeding toward him. Alone. Had she not found Maggie? Maybe she had not been able to convince her to stop.

"Where is she?" Lachlan called as Lorna got close enough to hear him.

"At the other end of the pasture. There was a group of men I'd never seen before, but Maggie kenned them. She was scared and told me I wasnae safe, to come back. She hit me horse."

His eyes trained on the small images too far away to make out. "She kenned them?"

"Aye, and she was shaking and said 'twas Conall."

His heart stopped. The bastard was here, and he was going to get Maggie.

"Tell Alan. I need him and more men." Lorna paled. "Now," he ordered over his shoulder as he took off toward Maggie. "She's in danger."

As he got near enough to make out what was playing out before him, Conall looked up at him but continued to march back and forth in front of Maggie. They had her surrounded, and Lachlan was too far away to be of any use. She looked even smaller than normal, but she kept her shoulders squared back and posture defiant. He stopped at a safe distance away and reached to his side, only to discover he had again left his sword in his chamber. He cursed. Three men flanked Conall, all armed, and he could make out a few more in the woods. Until his men arrived, he would be sorely outnumbered, especially with only the dirk he kept on him.

The bastard turned and smirked at him. Then the arse hauled back and struck Maggie full on the face with his clenched fist. She stumbled and caught her balance, then crumpled to the ground.

A guttural battle cry wrenched from some deep chasm roared from Lachlan. He jumped down from his horse and started toward Conall, but the bastard snatched up Maggie's limp body and snaked one arm around her waist while the other gripped under her delicate jaw. Her head lolled onto his shoulder.

"Halt. Come closer and I'll snap her pretty little neck."

The Erskine men all drew their swords and stepped in front of Conall. Despite the obstacles, his palm itched to grab the dirk at his side and lunge at the arse, but somehow he was able to restrain the urge to charge in.

"It seems you have taken some items that belong to me. I came to retrieve my letter, and look at what I have found. My missing bride." The murderer looked down at the woman in his arms. "Margaret is mine."

Inside, a primal part of him screamed and begged to attack, but outside, except for the tic that started in his jaw, Lachlan kept a calm facade.

"She is to be my wife, but I can see you have a desire for her, too. While I do want her"—the bastard turned her head to the side and licked from her mouth to her temple in an obscene gesture—"I have no emotional attachment to her. I am, however, willing to consider a trade."

His fists clenched, and his body was so tight it thrummed with barely contained fury.

"I want my letter." Conall let the words hang in the air.

"What letter?" Lachlan was usually good at bluffing, but the stakes were too high. Maggie was worth so much more to him than that damned letter. She stirred in Conall's arms.

Lachlan didn't want Conall to know how much she meant to him and tried to avoid looking at her—the bastard would use that knowledge to his advantage. It was bad enough he'd yelled when the brute had struck her.

"Don't play with me. I know you have it."

If Alan arrived with more Camerons, they would be able to get her back, so he stalled.

Conall must have taken his silence as a dismissal. "Ah, Margaret dear, the Lochiel must have decided he doesn't want you after all." He forced her head up to meet his gaze, but her body continued to sag.

Damn. The bastard had reinjured her head. Lachlan wanted to bellow, but he forced himself to remain calm.

"He is not willing to trade a simple piece of paper for you. Guess that means you will be coming home with me, where you belong." Conall started to pull Maggie toward his men.

Lachlan's heart pounded so loudly he thought it would burst out of chest. "Stay. I will get the letter."

Conall smirked, but he said, "No, tomorrow. If you want her, bring it tomorrow at noon, and if you come for her before then, my blade will find her heart. Tomorrow, or I will take her with me." He forced Maggie's face toward his, and she stiffened. She must have regained consciousness. "We can even stop on the way home to say our vows."

The thought of the bastard touching Maggie infuriated him. "I can send for it now, and then ye can leave." Why was Conall stalling? Why not take the letter and ride off today?

Alan and Brodie rode up and flanked him. Fortunately, they had their claymores but there were still too many men against them.

"Tomorrow at noon. Bring me the missive or Margaret goes with me." Maggie struggled violently in his arms and tried to dig in her feet, but he tugged her along, laughing at her feeble efforts. "Settle down now, love. If he brings me the letter, you can have the laird."

Conall pinned him with a glare. "If you or any Cameron man enters our camp, I will kill her. I have nothing to lose."

A shiver spread through his veins—the bastard would do it.

"If ye harm one hair on her head, I swear I will gut ye, Conall," Lachlan growled and his fist clenched at his side where his missing sword should have been. Emotion had overcome his attempt to conceal his feelings for Maggie.

Conall released Maggie's neck and pulled a dirk from his side. He let go of her long enough to grab her by the hair. He cut one long ringlet off and dropped it, challenging him. "To remember what you'll lose if I don't get what I want." He snorted, then turned and dragged Maggie into the woods.

Lachlan started to charge, but men stepped in front of the bastard and cut off his path.

Chapter Sixteen

"How did he get onto my land?" Lachlan roared as he turned over the table in the great hall. Cups and plates clattered to the floor. He cursed as despair ate at him. Curses that would probably earn him a place in hell, but he didn't care—hell was a world without Maggie.

"There were men patrolling, but his group is small and the area so vast, somehow they slipped past our guards."

He didn't see who answered, didn't care as he picked up a chair and threw it at the stone wall. The mangled wood fell to the ground. He stared at it as he fought to control the anger he had kept in until they'd gotten back to the keep.

He would tear Conall limb from limb. Or he would drive his sword through his belly. Hundreds of ways to kill the man flashed in his head.

Letting a few deep breaths pass in and out of his lungs, he clenched and unclenched his fists. *'Twill do her no good if ye can't calm yerself.*

Malcolm chimed in, "Ye ken he willnae let her stay here, even if we give him the letter. What would stop us from slitting his throat as soon as she is in our hands?"

Lachlan turned to the men gathered behind him and reined in the roiling emotions overwhelming him. His brother was right, he had to be a leader—they had to think fast. There was not much time to save Maggie.

If the bastard got away with her, he would wed her with all haste, and there would be nothing he could do. He could take on Conall, but the church was another matter. But if he killed him, the church could not stand in the way.

Maggie's sapphire-blue eyes haunted him. Every time he closed his, he saw hers. He was supposed to keep her safe, but he'd failed. It was his fault Conall had come here because of the letter. The bastard had Maggie because he had not kept his guard up. He slammed his fist on the table.

"He can have the blasted letter. He will show his hand soon enough. The priority is getting Maggie to safety." Lachlan closed his eyes and rubbed them, trying to focus, attempting to act as a general instead of the lovestruck fool he was.

"Do ye think he would harm her?" Malcolm asked.

"Aye, he would. He is sick—he wouldnae hesitate to kill her if he thought it would serve his purposes." Lachlan sank into a chair. "He killed a priest for no reason." He looked toward Alan. "He didnae mention Robbie. Could Conall have found him?"

"Nae. No one kens where he is." Alan shook his head.

"Since the MacDonalds arrived earlier, send some extra Cameron men to help those guarding him. For some reason, Conall must ken he isnae here, because he didn't demand the lad as well. As long as he is safe, losing the letter willnae matter."

Lachlan fingered the snippet of Maggie's hair. Shortly before they had stormed back to the castle, Brodie had retrieved it as Lachlan watched Conall pull her into the trees. Elspeth had found a blue ribbon the color of her eyes to tie around it, and he'd pinned it on his plaid, close to his heart.

The hours, meetings, and plans dragged on with uncertainty. Would the other invited lairds arrive today? Where was Maggie's father? And how the hell had the Erskines slipped onto his land? But he was sure of one thing—Conall had become a dead man as soon as he'd struck Maggie.

Early in the morning hours, Lachlan made his way to his empty chamber. He needed to attempt a few hours of rest before facing Conall.

A piece of paper peeking from beneath the bed caught his attention, and he scooped it up. It was to Maggie. His heart dropped when he saw the signature at the bottom of the page—*Yer love, Conall.*

Bile rose in his throat, and his vision blurred. His hands shook, and the paper rattled. He ignored his pounding heart while he read.

> *Dearest Maggie, I am waiting for ye by the forest's edge. I hope ye were able to get what we needed. The thought of ye in Lachlan's arms one more moment is driving me mad. Come to me so I can take ye home. Yer love, Conall.*

Aileen had been a threat, but Maggie had been sent here to destroy him and his people. It was unforgivable—he had put his clan in danger by believing in a lying lass. He thought of the tapestry story he'd overheard her tell little Davina and Alik. Had she known he was there? Had everything been a lie? He was a fool for ever trusting her, for thinking there was more to her, and for believing she was the one for him.

Afraid his legs would give, he sank to the bed. He had trusted her, had given her something he'd sworn to never do again, and she'd taken his offering and ripped his heart to shreds. Black fog spread in his chest, and he found it hard to breathe. She hadn't loved him after all—'twas all a lie to worm her way in and take everything.

He should send his men to attack the camp right away and be done with them all, but he couldn't bring himself to give the order that might see her dead. He had reasonable cause because they were trespassing on his land, but it didn't feel right. The bastard had hit her, but mayhap that had been for show and the arse wouldn't harm her. He tried to push away the memories tearing at him, the ones that said she had cared for him and that they could have a life together, but they were lies—he never wanted to hear her name again. He told himself those things and attempted to let the fury run wild, but it wouldn't come—the despair did. He would have known how to handle the rage, but this ache in his heart, the hole in his soul, would destroy him.

. . .

Maggie sat huddled in the corner of Conall's tent. She made herself as small and inconsequential as she could. The last thing she wanted was to draw his attention.

He had questioned her earlier, and she'd used the head injury excuse to be vague; he was not as adept at perceiving her half-truths as Lachlan. Her head pounded, but it was clear. Thankfully, he was too distracted with plans for tomorrow to pay her any heed.

They hadn't even bothered to bind her, thank the heavens. Meek, scared, and submissive was what they thought of her, and that was exactly what she wanted them to think, but she had no intention of going with them. In the last few hours, she'd decided she would make it to God by way of the nunnery or, if must be, the grave.

Scanning her surroundings, she took stock of anything useful, hoping she would find a way out. There were many claymores lying around, but she was fairly certain she couldn't lift one. She did see a crossbow and a quiver of arrows, but they were across the tent and out of reach.

"If the wench doesn't bring it first, they will. Did you see the way he looked at Margaret? He's a besotted fool." Conall spared her a glance.

"The whore was right, he does love 'er," another man replied.

What whore? Her heart raced as she turned all the words over. *Lachlan doesnae love me.*

"She is a beguiling witch. I'd do almost anything to keep her, too." She kept her face turned down to avoid Conall's gaze, but she wouldn't take her eyes off him. He was unpredictable.

"What do we do when we have it?" asked one of the men who had stood with Conall on the field today. Maggie knew him by his raspy, harsh voice; he was almost constantly coughing or clearing his throat, a rattling sound that grated on her nerves.

"We cannot give them Margaret. She is our only way out of here. We are on his land." He studied her again. "If we turn her over, there is nothing to keep the barbarians from swooping down on us as soon as she's in their hands." Conall leaned back on his haunches and thrummed his fingers together.

"And the boy?" the man asked and coughed so loud and long she thought he might fall over.

What boy?

"The wench says he isn't here, which is why I stalled long enough for her to finish the search. We have to get him, too." Conall's gaze cut back to his friend as he tapped his foot angrily on the dirt.

Maggie's heart sank—they were after Robbie, whom she hadn't seen since they'd arrived at Kentillie. Who would let Conall know where the lad was?

"Do ye think he went back to the church?"

"We shall stop to check on the way home. Probably, but I think we will have to leave a few men here to see if they can find him."

"What do we do if the laird won't let us leave with her?" the gruff voice asked.

"Then we kill him."

Maggie's heart stopped beating at Conall's words and the smug grin plastered on his normally unreadable face. She cringed at the undisguised thrill in his voice, the same one he'd used when he taunted her during his visits to her home.

He wanted Lachlan to refuse. He wanted to kill Lachlan, and he was crazy enough to try it.

The words Lachlan had said that first day rang in her ears—he would never fight for a lass. Probably he wouldn't turn over his precious letter for her, either. But at the same time, he was prideful and wouldn't let Conall take her, even if he no longer wanted her. Men were like that with their toys.

But he had professed some feelings for her, and he was a proud man. She might not have his love, but she was indeed like her mother—her heart beat only for Lachlan. Once she had given her soul and love to him, she could not take it back. The only thing that mattered now was saving Lachlan.

When questioned, she'd told Conall about her original head injury and led him to believe she had been incapacitated for some time. Now all she had to do was make him believe she wanted to go with him.

The discussion with his men ended, and he stalked up to her. "I am not certain you are telling the whole truth, but we will get that straightened out when we get home." He dug his boot into her rib, and she winced.

"I swear, Conall. I havenae lied to ye. I was confused…" She looked directly into his eyes, hoping to make him believe her.

His gaze raked up and down her body. "I will not touch you for now. I want to make sure his seed didn't take hold in you. I will not have one of his babes as my heir." She tried not to let the relief that washed over her show; he didn't need to know he repulsed her.

"Stand," he ordered. The relief disappeared. She was too slow for Conall, and he grabbed her hair to yank her up. Her head didn't like the sudden movement compounded by the blow he'd dealt her earlier, and dizziness assailed her. She almost tipped over, but he caught her at the waist, which made her want to vomit. Thankfully, he let her go as soon as she'd recovered.

"Turn and put your hands behind your back. I have to bind you," he ordered smugly.

"I promise I willnae go anywhere. I willnae leave this tent. I dinnae want to be out there." She was trying to comfort him when what she really wanted was to be back in the keep with Lachlan.

"Just a precaution. Turn." Her pleading had fallen on deaf ears. She winced and attempted to pull away as his fingers dug into the sensitive flesh under her arm. She thought she was going to cry, but she held it in.

It could be worse. Thank God he was not going to force himself on her. What if she was with child? Something she'd not considered before. As the bindings tightened painfully around her wrists, she realized she had not bled since before that first night in Lachlan's bed. For the last few days, she'd felt nauseous and had barely been able to stomach the smell of roasted meats.

Could she have Lachlan's child in her belly? Suddenly, she wanted to wrap her arms around her stomach and shield it from this madness, but she couldn't. Her eyes watered with the need to protect the innocent wee babe growing inside her.

Oh, God, what would she do? Different scenarios played

through her head. Conall would take her home, and when he realized she was with child he would beat her until she lost it. If she got out of this and made it to an abbey, would they let her keep the baby?

If she lived through this, she would have to tell him—she couldn't give away a child she had made with Lachlan. How would he react? Already he had moved on to another woman, but would a bairn change that? She would not take him back out of his sympathy for her, which would only lead to more affairs, more heartbreak.

Conall broke into her thoughts. "Your father will be glad I found you."

She yelped when he pulled and the ropes dug into her skin, hoping he would not tighten the bonds any farther. "Was he worried?" She wished she could take the question back. Even if he was, it was probably more annoyance his plans had fallen through than actual concern for her.

"He and your brothers have been searching all over for you." He spun her back around, and a fresh wave of dizziness hit her, although not as bad as the first.

She steadied herself and asked, "How did you find me?"

"Glenn." Conall mashed his lips, and she thought she saw a hint of sadness in his eyes. The only emotion she'd ever seen on him that did not scare her.

"I thought Lachlan had killed him." She wished he had. If only she'd checked to be certain Conall's men couldn't make it back. Or that she'd listened to her head instead of her heart—she would have gotten a map and planned her route to the abbey and would have been long gone before the snake had come for her.

"He did. Glenn had just long enough to get back home. All he could say was 'Lachlan.' I knew then he had my letter. I had no idea you would be here."

"Will ye take me home to see my family, then? I would

like them to be there for the wedding." She attempted to sound happy about it, and he looked at her, puzzled; maybe she was getting better at this lying.

"No, I have your father's blessing. We will be wed on the way back. I will not be letting you get away again. I've wanted you for too long." He ran his hand down her side and stopped at her rear to cup it. It was a struggle to keep the revulsion that jolted through her off her face. She had to change the subject.

"What is this letter ye need?" Truly, she was curious, Lachlan had not told her what was in it, and she hadn't asked. The diversion worked, because he let go of her and backed up.

"Nothing you need to be concerned with. It's men's business." Now, that made her angry. *Men's business.* If it was men's business, why the hell was she wrapped up in the middle of it? She wanted to scream.

"It becomes my business if you are willing to trade me for it." With effort, she squashed down her anger and attempted to sound hurt.

"I will not trade you. I just need him to think I will. He wants you." His gaze drifted down to rake her appreciatively. "But everyone does. You're the bonniest lass in Scotland. And that is why you will be mine."

"Why wait until tomorrow? Lachlan would have gone for it today."

"Because the Cameron whore and I made a deal. She's already delivered you. She has until tomorrow morning to get me the letter and find out where the boy is." Maggie was having a hard time making sense of what he was saying. Again her head had started throbbing.

"With any luck, I'll be long gone with you and the letter before Lachlan knows what happened."

He snaked his arms around her and pulled her body flush

with his. His erection poked her, and she prayed, *Please, God, dinnae let him touch me*. He dipped his head and bit down hard on her neck. Pain assaulted her as she gasped and tried to pull away, but he had her pinned.

He laughed. It had not been like when Lachlan had playfully nipped at her. This hurt, and he might have drawn blood.

"I cannot wait to have you in my bed." Hot, rancid breath assaulted her as he whispered in her ear. Grabbing her hair, he yanked her head back, forcing her eyes to his. The desire she saw there scared her. It was not what she'd seen in Lachlan's eyes as they'd made love—this was dark and looked more like a need for control than any longing for her.

He sneered at the fear she'd not been able to hide then pushed her down roughly. She landed on her knees—the jolt had been rough. Dizziness assailed her, and she was light-headed again.

"As soon as I know you're not with child, I'll have you. Get some rest. Tomorrow will be a long day." He strode to the other side of the tent and continued to plan tomorrow's events.

Maggie attempted to listen. It was important she learn what was going on, but their words were distant and mumbled. Although she struggled to hear, she had trouble staying focused. Every part of her head vibrated with pain, and her eyes became unfocused. She tried to fight it, but she was no match for the deep, dreamless sleep that took her.

· · ·

After the last lass had betrayed Lachlan, he had come back stronger, and he could do it again; this would be no different. But the hole that had been ripped in his heart this time ached, and he found it a struggle to take each breath. Crushing pain made him want to hunker down in the corner and lick his wounds. But he was laird—he didn't have that choice.

As he stood and straightened his plaid, his fingers brushed across the strands of hair Conall had cut from Maggie's head. He'd forgotten it was there, and he dipped his head to inhale the still present smell of lavender. A devastating grief washed over him as he realized he would never again feel her in his arms or know the pleasure he experienced just from watching her smile. She might as well have stabbed him in the chest and twisted the dirk over and over, because that's what it felt like.

His finger ran down the length of the lock. *To the devil with her.* The anger was back, and he ripped the small bundle loose as a knock sounded at the door. He tossed it onto the bedside table and said, "Enter."

Alan strode in. "The Macleans have arrived."

He was glad Alan had been the one to find him, because he couldn't let anyone else see him like this, so he squared his shoulders. Maybe if he looked like a leader, he would again feel like one.

"She was working with Conall all along. And I fell for it." As he voiced it, his heart lurched. He wished he had the stomach for whisky and could drown the pain, but the thought made his insides turn. There was no drink strong enough to see him through this.

"What do ye mean?" His friend continued forward as he sank to the bed.

"Maggie. She was in league with Conall. They are lovers." He choked on the words, and he started to quake as hurt and anger battled in his chest.

"Nae. She's terrified of the man. Did ye no' see him strike her?"

"I ken, it doesnae make sense." He picked up the letter and passed it to Alan; something about it kept setting an alarm off in his head.

As Alan took it he asked, "What's that smell?" Then he pulled the paper up and read it. "Nae, I dinnae believe it." He sat on the bed and handed it back to Lachlan.

Lachlan's gaze returned to the letters on the page, and his breath caught. "It says Maggie. The bastard called her Margaret." He analyzed the words more closely. "Conall speaks as if he's been around the English too long, but this writing sounds like one of us. The script is different, too. We need to compare it to Conall's letter. I dinnae think 'tis the same."

Could Maggie be innocent? Who would plant something like that? Who would want to drive them apart?

A cloying, sweet smell caught his attention—'twas the same scent that had assaulted him as he'd walked in to find Arabella in his room.

Relief washed over him. Maggie had not deceived him. Why had he not believed in her? And he had decided to let Conall have her. Guilt and desperation warred in his heart. "'Twas Arabella."

"What does she have to do with it?"

"Everything. The note, 'tis from Arabella."

He'd let his own prejudices blind him to the truth. Maggie was innocent and always had been. Never again would he allow his past to taint his belief in someone who had already proven herself in so many ways.

He jumped up and rushed out of the room and downstairs toward the study to compare the handwriting. 'Twould be the final proof that Maggie hadn't betrayed him. Before he could open the door, it swung in. Arabella stood in the frame holding Conall's letter in her hands.

"Ye treacherous, deceitful wench. What are ye doing with that?"

She had the nerve to try to hide it behind her back and attempted to skirt around him, but he blocked her exit, reached behind her, and pulled her arm with Conall's letter back to the front. His eyes drifted to Alan. "Take it."

"Somebody had to get that whore out of here. She is going to destroy everything." Instead of remorse in Arabella's voice, there was anger.

Taking a deep breath to calm the storm that was building inside, his eyes caught movement down the hall. *Finlay.* "Get Malcolm and the rest of the council," he yelled to him, then looked to Alan. "Stay, because I just may be tempted to strangle her."

He guided Arabella back into his study, let go of her, and pointed to a chair. "Sit." Walking to the opposite end of the room to put a little distance between them, he started to pace while Alan took a seat near the door, presumably to block the exit.

The room remained silent until his most trusted men were all assembled. Arabella's gaze shifted erratically around the space as she squirmed under the scrutiny. He turned to her. "Talk."

Standing, she attempted to walk out the door, but Dougal shut it and blocked her path, and she strode toward Lachlan. "She is going to destroy ye. I was just doing it to protect us."

Lachlan held his palm out to stop her advance. "Did ye help the Earl of Lundin's son onto our land?" He was crushed that one of his own people had betrayed the clan.

"Aye." No remorse entered her eyes. "I met him at the tavern on the way to Fort William the night ye said ye were going to send me away. When I told him about that whore and how besotted ye were with her, he offered to take her."

"Och, Arabella, did ye even ken who he was?" When he slammed his hand down on his desk, she jumped.

"Aye, I kenned she had betrayed him, and she would have done the same to ye." Her hand rose to his chest, but he scowled.

"Dinnae touch me."

Her face screwed up with frustration. "All he wanted was some letter and a lad I told him I kenned nothing about."

Thank God he'd kept Robbie's location from everyone but Alan. "Have ye gone mad? Ye are the one who has just betrayed the clan. Take her away. She is no longer a Cameron, and I dinnae want to see her again. The other lairds can decide her fate."

Maggie was innocent.

His Maggie was in that monster's hands, and he was going to do everything he could to get her back. Even if it meant handing over that damned letter.

Chapter Seventeen

Rain lightly pelted Lachlan's face as his horse tromped through the battered grass. Waiting for Conall and his men to join them, he made his way to the middle of the field.

The Erskine men had been camped in a small clearing just on the other side of the trees. They had lit an abundance of fires during the night in a vain attempt to inflate the number of men they actually had with them.

Arabella had guided Conall and his men around the guards to a secluded area of his land, where they had lain in wait for Maggie and the wench's return with the letter and news of Robbie. Since she'd slept with half of them, it hadn't been hard for the traitorous woman to know the location of the scouts so the small band of Erskines could slip past. Likely the bastard didn't have his father's backing or the approval of Argyll, else he would have had more men with him.

The entire night, Lachlan kept the group surrounded. Had they been able to surmise where Maggie was being held, they could have easily infiltrated the camp to find her, but Conall had kept her hidden, the reason they hadn't risked an attack.

Sheets of rain had started to fall in the wee hours of the morning and extinguished the fires, but now it wasn't much more than a trickle. This would be in their favor, as most of Conall's men had little in the way of cover and must be cold and wet. Their spirits would be low, and their location would impede their view of the horde of Royalist clans arriving at Kentillie.

Conall had roughly thirty-five men with him. Nothing compared to the army Lachlan had at hand, with more trickling in all morning for the planned meeting.

Lachlan's heart swelled with pride at the clans coming together in a show of solidarity for Scotland. The timing couldn't have been better. They would witness the traitor's actions, as well as see the missive before he turned it over to Conall. If their presence helped to save Maggie, he would forever be in their debt.

Instead of just a couple of Camerons at his side, he was flanked by at least fifty, with more men spread out in the woods to cut off the intruder's escape. They would not get anywhere with Maggie.

Conall's small force of men looked bedraggled and downtrodden, like mangy stray dogs caked with filth and mud as they came into the clearing. They formed a tight formation and marched forward. Giving his reins to Alan, Lachlan dismounted and strode several paces in front of his men, glaring at them while he waited for Conall.

It didn't take long for the bastard to slink forward. "Where is my missive, Lachlan?" Contempt rolled off his tongue as he ground out the words.

"Where is my woman?" Lachlan countered.

As his jaw ticked, Conall glared, the hatred in his eyes palpable.

Good. An angry enemy didn't keep a clear mind in battle. And this was a battle he intended to win. "I have yer letter.

We agreed to a trade. Where is Maggie?" Lachlan fought to remain calm. He'd not seen Maggie yet, and he ached to know that this monster had not harmed her.

At first, Conall looked confused, then angered. The man obviously did not like Lachlan's familiarity with her. *Good.* The arse was cocky and overconfident, and the rapier at his side was no match for the claymore Lachlan was about to unsheathe.

Conall nodded to a wiry man almost hidden in the shadows at the edge of the woods. He disappeared, and Lachlan held his breath.

Like a ray of sunshine peeking from behind the clouds, Maggie appeared, holding her head high like a princess. The man followed in her wake as if he were a servant. Her fingers twisted in the folds of her skirts, the only outward sign she was affected by the events playing out before her.

"Your woman? You stole her from me. She is to be my wife." His eyes bulged as his face reddened.

Maggie continued forward and looked as if she was going to walk straight across the expanse and into his waiting arms, but the man grabbed her arm and guided her to Conall's side. Lachlan could see a blue and swollen bruise on her face, likely where Conall had struck her, but other than that she appeared unharmed. The mark on her soft, delicate cheek enraged him, and he clenched his fists to keep from charging.

Conall yanked her close. Her body tensed, but there was resilience in his little lass as well. Quickly, she tamped down her fear and replaced it with defiance. She jerked away from the arse's hold and stood proud with her chin in the air. But Conall pulled her back—he was using her as a shield, the cowardly bastard.

"She doesnae want ye. Ye ken that," Lachlan taunted.

"It does not matter what she wants. I have a contract with her father," Conall said smugly.

"How do ye think he is going to feel about that when he finds ye are a traitor to yer religion and yer family? And ye are a coward who would use his defenseless daughter as a shield?"

"Traitor? The Covenanters are trying to bring Scotland together under the true religion."

"Do ye think the other clans will agree? They will see ye imprisoned for what you're doing." Lachlan stood with his feet shoulder-width apart and back straight, ready to strike if the snake caused Maggie one more moment of pain.

Conall glared and said nothing as he kept Maggie pinned to his side.

"I dinnae think yer father will appreciate ye planning his murder," Lachlan added.

"It will be my word against yours, and who will believe you? You're a disreputable thief who took my betrothed hostage," he sneered.

"Do ye want to say that where the other Highland chiefs can hear ye?" Lachlan motioned to several men behind him.

Conall's face pinched into a snarl. "What treachery is this?"

Lachlan nodded at Alan, who gave the word, and several flags were unfurled behind him. Flags of the Maclean, MacDonald, Stewart, and Menzies clans dotted the field in a show of solidarity.

"They have all seen yer incriminating missive. Ye willnae be going home again. Whether ye go to yer death today or with these men is up to ye."

The thunder of horses' hooves sounded as a group of riders approached from the direction of the keep. Heads turned and a path cleared to make way for the newcomers. Lachlan did not recognize the flag they flew, but he did recognize three of the men riding in the front.

Dougal, Finlay, and Gillies had returned with what must

have been a significant army of Murray men. He said a quick prayer for the good timing. Maggie's father would have the truth about his daughter's betrothed.

Conall's eyes widened. His nostrils flared as his gaze darted from Lachlan to Maggie's father and back again. He coiled his arm the rest of the way around Maggie and pulled her in front, so her back was flush with his chest. Then he drew a dirk from his side and held it up to her throat. Her movements stilled as the point of the blade poked at her tender neck.

Christ, not again. He had a flashback to the last time a man had held a knife to her.

"What in God's name are ye doing, Conall?" the Murray asked as he reined in next to Lachlan.

Lachlan recognized Maggie's high cheekbones and regal bearing on the graying head, but that was the only similarity. Her dark hair and pale skin must have come from her mother.

Lowering the knife from Maggie's soft flesh, Conall pointed the tip of the blade at Lachlan. "They have left me no choice, Gavin. She is supposed to be mine. He stole her."

Maybe she knew enough not to rile the beast, because her eyes pleaded with her father, but she didn't call out to him. If they didn't tread carefully here, Conall was likely to hurt her. The Duke of Kirk glanced over to Lachlan and gave him an almost imperceptible nod as if he, too, understood the danger to his daughter.

It stung that she didn't look in his direction, but it was possible she still believed he'd bedded Arabella; he'd see to it that she knew the truth once he had her safe.

"Then your fight is with him. Not a wee lass," the Murray called.

Three men jumped down from their horses and hurried up beside Lachlan. All had swords drawn, and he knew immediately they were her brothers. The older two had her raven's hair, but it was straight, and the younger brother could have been Maggie's twin, with black curls and deep blue eyes.

"Put down the dirk, Conall," Lachlan ordered.

"Destroy the letter. Destroy it, or I will slit her throat." He'd seen that unstable look of desperation in men's eyes on the battlefield—it's what led men to make mistakes. He had to get Maggie out of his arms.

"Ye can have the letter, but ye cannae have Maggie." He held out the parchment, stepped forward, and placed it on the ground, then backed a few paces. Hopefully, in the process of moving toward it, Conall would ease his grip on her.

"Hamish," ordered Conall. "Take her. If he tries anything, kill her."

The man who had walked Maggie out of the woods sidled up and took her arm, but his movements lacked conviction—he didn't have the look of a man who could kill an innocent lass, especially in front of her father. Conall's mistake had been to let go of Maggie. She was safe now. Alan, Malcolm, and Brodie would keep their eyes on her as he fought Conall. No harm would come to her. Lachlan's shoulders relaxed slightly.

Conall strode forward, bent, and snatched up the letter. He inspected it and hunched backward, not taking his eyes off Lachlan. "Stay back. We will release her when we are out of sight."

The youngest of Maggie's brothers almost rushed him, but another held on to him.

Lachlan flexed his fingers, ready to grab hold on the hilt and slide out his own weapon. "Ye ken I cannae let ye do that. Let her go now or be prepared to draw yer sword.

"Halt," Lachlan yelled at Hamish, who had started to move Maggie toward the crazy bastard. The man obeyed, and he turned his focus on Conall. "Ye will never touch her again," he warned with dead calm. "Draw yer weapon or surrender now."

• • •

Maggie watched with horror as Conall drew his rapier and faced Lachlan. She'd heard tales of his prowess with a sword—they had not been exaggerated. Although she had seen Lachlan wield his claymore in two battles, she was terrified for him.

As Lachlan was much larger, he would have the more powerful blows, but Conall would have more agility.

Lachlan unsheathed his claymore with a slow, deliberate ease, which reminded her of a perfected synchronized dance. It was beautiful and deadly.

She spared a glance for her family. They had appeared from nowhere, and she was surprised at how grateful she was to see them. Her brothers looked as if they wanted to pounce on Conall, and her father stared at him with murder in his eyes. Thank the saints, he would believe her now about her betrothed's cruelty.

Conall swung first. He rolled the thin rapier right to left, but Lachlan deftly evaded the move. He swung again in the opposite direction with no results then attacked several more times, and with each thrust, Lachlan sidestepped the blade.

Watching Lachlan evade the moves was like listening to poetry, smooth and comfortable. He had a grace to him she'd never expected; his large size didn't hamper his ability to move effortlessly from one place to another. It was as if he'd been born for this. He'd not made a move toward Conall, who was already panting and struggling to keep his pace.

Stepping forward, Lachlan took a swing of his own. A killing blow. Although Conall was able to block it with his sword, it knocked him off balance. He stumbled but recovered almost as quickly.

"I'm going to bed her every night after you're dead." Conall lashed out with a verbal assault, likely an attempt to divert Lachlan's attention and weaken him, and she prayed the devil's tongue would not affect him.

With ease, Lachlan pivoted to avoid the blow, but she flinched with each new attack.

Conall huffed out, "I'll have her screaming my name." Her breath caught on the threat, but his panting proved he was becoming weak.

Lachlan did not take the bait and stayed deadly calm.

"She'll carry my bairns, not yours." Conall swiped and missed again. When Lachlan came down with another blow, Conall blocked it, but Lachlan followed through. The clash of blades forced Conall's arms into an awkward position. He growled in pain then aimed for Lachlan's midsection, only missing by a hair when Lachlan jumped back.

. . .

Taunts during battle normally did not rile Lachlan, but damn if Conall wasn't getting to him. It was Maggie.

While the two circled each other catching their breaths, he remembered telling Alan he would never fight for a woman. He had been wrong. If he had to, he would fight every day for the rest of his life to keep her.

"Ye'll never touch her again, Conall." He couldn't stop himself after the man's insults; he was getting too emotional. A deep breath calmed him.

He lunged, his claymore coming down just to Conall's left, but the arse dodged the blow and came around to catch Lachlan in the back. Before the rapier could connect, he leaped out of range.

This time he waited. *Be patient.* Lachlan closed his ears to any other taunts from Conall's treacherous lips and focused as the bastard continued to charge at him without success.

Once the man became winded, Lachlan struck hard and fast. His blade swooped down and skimmed his arm. Blood spurted from Conall's shoulder, and his arm went limp while he screamed in pain. "Enough. You win." And he feebly tossed his sword. "I give. You can have her."

Surprised, Lachlan lowered his claymore to his side but kept it at the ready. He'd expected Conall to fight to the death. Still, the man had surrendered, and despite the urge to raise his sword and take off Conall's head, he held still.

Staring at the blood pouring down his bicep, Conall gripped his shoulder and tried to cover the wound. His face went stone cold. In a flash, he reached into his pocket and threw some kind of powder into Lachlan's eyes. Pain seared him. He was blinded.

Chapter Eighteen

Maggie's heart sang when Conall admitted defeat. Lachlan had no choice but to concede, because he couldn't cut down an unarmed man. But Conall was not surrendering—she'd seen that look on his face the day she'd rejected his advances. Dread washed over her as he slowly reached into his breeches then threw what looked like sand into Lachlan's eyes.

In one swift move, she shoved her knee into Hamish's groin. When he doubled over in pain, she grabbed his bow and pulled one arrow from his quiver.

By the time she looked back, Conall had drawn a pistol and pointed it at Lachlan. On instinct, she nocked the arrow, took aim, and let it fly. It connected with Conall's hip just as he pulled the trigger on his small gun.

The impact jolted him, and the bullet flew through the air, missing Lachlan.

She sighed in relief. Heedless of anyone else on the field, she dropped the bow and ran. She needed to feel Lachlan's strong arms around her and know he was safe. Conall writhed on the ground, but her brothers ran in to subdue him.

"I love you," she cried without thinking as she dashed toward Lachlan. He'd straightened and was rubbing at his eyes as she moved in to poke his shoulder with two fingers. "Dinnae ever scare me like that again, Lachlan. I thought he was going to put a bullet in ye." Tears fell down her cheeks as she grabbed his face to look into his eyes, to make sure he was unharmed.

He blinked. "Scare ye, lass? Ye are the one who ran off and got captured by the devil himself. I didnae ken how I was going to get ye away from him." He pulled her in for a tight embrace. She welcomed the feel of him. It was like coming home, but to a home she wanted and needed. Her knees buckled as he claimed her mouth in a kiss that was both possessive and demanding. She moaned and sank into him. It didn't matter that her family stood by watching.

She forgot about everything except Lachlan. Forgot her anger and hurt over his betrayal. She even forgot the crowds surrounding them until the cheers broke through her bliss. She pulled back and straightened in a vain attempt to maintain some modicum of propriety.

Brown spots dotted Lachlan's cheeks and brow. "We need to wash yer eyes. I dinnae ken what he threw at ye." She inspected and rubbed her fingers softly across his cheeks to clear it away.

"Most of it's out. I can see all I need to now."

She melted into him and relief flooded her as he took her hand in his and drew it to his lips.

One of her brothers swooped in and grabbed her around the waist. He twirled her around and embraced her so hard she almost lost her breath. "Roland, I cannae breathe." She could not help but notice the disapproving glare he gave Lachlan.

He then turned his displeasure on her. "Ye have some explaining to do. Where the hell have ye been, Maggie? We were sick with worry."

After squinting at Roland's grip on her waist, Lachlan latched onto Maggie's arm and tugged her back to him. It was possessive, but gentle. She didn't mind. She wanted to feel his touch, to know he was safe and unharmed. "Please join us in the hall. We'll have some food and drink and discuss the future."

Lachlan led her to his horse and lifted her onto its back then jumped up behind her. Drawing her near, he slid his arms around her; it was like being enveloped in a warm cocoon to be in his embrace again, and she relished the feel of his strong muscles as he hugged her close.

She'd not thought she would ever know his touch again. The warm scent of him made her ache to be even closer, and she snuggled in like he was a blanket to keep her warm from the cool night air.

"Woman, dinnae ever run off like that and scare me again. I'll bend ye over my knee and give ye the beating ye deserve." But the harsh words were tempered by the tender way he breathed her in and nuzzled his head against hers.

Had he gone daft? Did he think she ran into Conall on purpose? "I didnae ken he would be there."

"Ye took off without letting me defend myself."

At the mention of the previous morning's events, she stiffened. Aye, he had a point, but she'd been distraught, and no matter what he might have said, she wasn't sure she would have listened. But she didn't want to think of that at this moment, didn't want to remember what he had been doing while she had helped deliver Donella's babe. "Ye have no need to explain yerself to me." She said it, but the words were hollow and tore at her soul.

From the beginning, Lachlan had made sure she knew there could never be anything more than fun between them. He'd never given her any reason to hope for something more.

"I did nothing wrong, but we will discuss it later when we have a moment to ourselves."

She deflated. Her eyes stung. He didn't even regret his tryst with the harlot.

Maggie peeked over her shoulder to see Conall being tied and questioned. His men had all knelt down and surrendered peacefully. "What will happen to Conall?"

"The MacDonald is going to take him and his men. He has a grievance against the Covenanters. I'm sure he will send word to Conall's father of the bastard's whereabouts, but I dinnae ken the man can do him any good."

"I dinnae ever wish to see him again." She shuddered and sank into Lachlan.

"I will make sure ye never do." He kissed her temple. "Dinnae speak of the priest. Robbie wants to stay out of it if he can."

"Aye. I cannae blame him." Like the lad, she wanted to blot Conall from her memory forever.

Maggie's family came up alongside them and thankfully pulled her from her misery. They peppered her with questions as they eyed Lachlan. Trepidation, curiosity, and mistrust were plain in their guarded expressions as they watched the Cameron laird hold her as if he owned her.

"How did ye even come to be here, Maggie?" her oldest brother asked.

For the rest of the ride, she explained how she'd gotten here, omitting Lachlan's attempt to kill her and explaining the head injury as an accident that happened during the skirmish when she'd been knocked backward into a tree. Looking over her shoulder, she was able to see the corner of Lachlan's lip quirk up into a sheepish, guilty smile.

As they rode through the main gate, Arabella was saddling up with several men flanking her, almost as if they were guarding her. She looked as if she'd been crying, and when Maggie made eye contact with her, she froze. The harlot was staring daggers at her, as if she wanted to rip her eyes out. Goose bumps rose on her arms as she tried to shake off the malice the woman aimed her way. For the rest of her time here, she would have to stay away from that woman.

When they dismounted by the keep, Lorna ran over and took her in a punishing embrace. "Ye should have jumped on me horse, Maggie. We could have made it back."

"Nae, he was too close. I had to get ye to safety. I wouldnae have been able to bear him harming another friend of mine." *Friend.* She hugged her once more. "I am so glad ye are safe."

"Aye. I am thankful Lachlan wouldnae let him take off with ye." Lorna released her, and her fingers rose to Maggie's darkening cheek. "Och. Look what the bastard did to ye. Does it hurt?"

"'Tis just tender. 'Twill be fine."

Elspeth pulled her in tight, and when she backed away, Maggie was surprised at the sheen of moisture in her eyes. "I was so afraid for ye, lass. But I knew Lachlan would bring ye home." She took Maggie's hand and pulled her toward the keep, and Maggie felt as if she'd come home.

• • •

A dreadfully long afternoon of negotiations complete, Lachlan finally made the way from his office into the hall. Freezing when he saw Maggie enter with his mother, his heart soared at the mere sight of her. Black curls bobbed playfully as she laughed; her unbruised cheek was pink and flushed. Her presence alone calmed his frayed nerves, and he'd almost gone insane thinking he would never touch her again. He was still tempted to beat Conall for laying a hand on her, but all he could do now was take solace in the knowledge the bastard was gone and would never be able to touch her again.

Hopefully, he would hang for his crimes.

He'd spent the afternoon behind closed doors with other lairds and then Maggie's father and brothers. When the door opened at one point to admit a server with ale, bread, and cheese, Maggie was pacing outside. Although she'd protested and tried to enter the room, her father had held up his hand and said, "This is men's business. We will see ye at the dinner meal." Lachlan was disappointed the man had rebuffed her.

She huffed and stomped away. It had been adorable.

Images of what the evening would bring flashed through his head in vivid detail. He couldn't wait to get her alone and turn that anger into the passion she kept hidden below the surface, just for him. He needed to feel she was real, taste her, and assure himself she would not disappear again.

Pulling himself away from his thoughts, he returned to the conversation with her father. The man was a tyrant, tedious and controlling. Despite his harsh demeanor, Lachlan recognized the care and concern he held for his daughter concealed beneath his hard exterior. He wasn't a man accustomed to letting people know his feelings, which were hidden well behind the wall of a true leader. But the depth in his eyes gave away his true emotions.

· · ·

Pacing at the entrance to the great hall and dreading the news to come from the afternoon her family and Lachlan had spent behind closed doors had been torture. Focusing on the smell of baking bread wafting through the air made her belly rumble, but it kept her from wringing her hands and rushing into Lachlan's study to demand answers. Her thoughts turned to speculation. Her father would take her home, and she'd be forced to marry some other man, or worse yet, they would force Lachlan to wed her, a man who was just like her father, whose love couldn't be won by a single lass.

A deep, instinctive part of her knew she carried Lachlan's child. Did he have other illegitimate heirs running around? Just thinking on it made her queasy again. She wanted to be the only one to carry his babes, but what did it matter? As she was about to give in and demand she be included in their deliberations, Elspeth came up, looped her arm into Maggie's, and drew her into the great hall to walk toward the main table. She gasped at the crowd inside. "'Tis so many."

"Did ye bring yer sisters, then?" It was Brodie talking to a Highlander she'd never seen. She couldn't help the giggle that broke through her lips at his jesting with the man, who growled at Brodie.

Elspeth followed Maggie's gaze. "'Tis Ross Maclean. Those two can get into all kinds of mischief together. Best stay away from both of them this evening."

They made their way through the crowd and settled in their normal spots, but Lachlan wasn't there. Controlling her every move, most likely on her father's command, her brothers, Roland and Ian took the seats beside her and pinned her in so that no one else had access to her. All patience fled, and she couldn't stop herself. "What was decided today?" she asked Roland, knowing he would talk before Ian would give her answers.

"Maggie, ye ken we only want what's best for ye," Roland answered. Dread filled her at the words she'd heard so many times she couldn't count, and she almost missed her father taking the seat next to her brother, with Lachlan on the other side.

"And a week ago that was Conall, so ye will forgive me if I dinnae trust father's judgment?"

Roland's eyes twinkled with mirth, and he gave her a grin she couldn't quite read. Sometimes she thought he riled her up on purpose. "Ye will be happy with our decision."

"Just like I was going to 'grow to love' Conall." She repeated the phrase they had used with her often. She scowled at him, but he only laughed.

Ale was brought to the table, then Maggie's father, Gavin Murray, the Duke of Kirk and most titled man in the room, stood, raised his glass, and silenced the gathered crowd, just as she had seen him do so many times before. Relishing the control he held over the room, he introduced himself and thanked the Camerons for their warm welcome.

"Lachlan and Margaret will be wed in the morn." Too stunned, she didn't hear anything after that moment.

Why had no one warned her? She peered across her family to look at Lachlan. Had he been forced to acquiesce? His stiff jaw twitched, and his brow knit together. Her appetite disappeared. He was being coerced to wed her and was not pleased with the arrangement. She would live with a man she loved who didn't want her. Her father had sentenced her to a lifetime of sorrow like her mother.

Somehow she managed to make it through the meal, picking at her food and moving it around her plate, but she couldn't face Lachlan's frustration tonight. Hoping to slip from the room before he could stop her, she turned to Roland. "I'm tired. Please escort me to bed."

"I am, too. 'Twas a long journey here." He stood and offered her his arm.

He escorted her to the room where she would spend her last night as a single woman. She didn't even try to sleep, just lay there all night lamenting fate for handing her a loveless marriage.

Chapter Nineteen

By the time Lachlan was able to join Maggie at the table, there were no open seats beside her, and it would have been poor manners to ask her family to move so he could sit next to her. The duke had arranged it so that he couldn't get to her, and he felt like a child with a cake placed before him he was not allowed to taste.

Because her father had monopolized all his time, he'd not had a moment alone with Maggie since he'd gotten her back to the keep. Lachlan was already fuming that her father demanded he not have her in his bed until they were wed, and they would have to sleep apart tonight. His fists clenched in frustration as Gavin Murray stood and announced to all what had been decided.

He hadn't wanted her to find out this way. He'd wanted to hold her in his arms after they made love and ask her, to know marriage would please her. Looking at her now, biting her lip and holding back tears, it appeared the news was anything but pleasing. She'd gone pale and silent, not the reaction he'd hoped for. She had never said anything about marriage. What if she did not want him?

The announcement coming from her father had frustrated him. He couldn't wait to marry Maggie and send the man home. He now understood her misgivings about men playing games with other people. The duke was an expert.

All during dinner she kept her eyes averted, and her reaction disconcerted him further. He wanted to growl that he could not get to her, but Gavin had pulled him into one political conversation after another, and when he turned back, she was gone. Her brothers had whisked her away. He'd given them several rooms, and there was no way he could find Maggie without coming right out and asking which one they'd put her in.

They would probably laugh if he did, and he was fair certain they would have the room guarded. They had all made it perfectly clear he would sully her name no longer.

Thank the saints they were able to get Father Fergus to agree to perform the ceremony the next morning.

His mother cornered him after dinner. "She doesnae think ye want her."

"What would give her that idea? I just fought a man for her." Was she daft? Mayhap her head was still addled.

"Have ye told her how ye feel?"

"I havenae been able to get near her since we got back," he ground out between clenched teeth.

"Nae. Before now, have ye given her any indication ye care for her?"

"Aye, I have." But then he thought back to her silent confession while she thought he was sleeping.

She'd professed her love for him, albeit when she didn't intend for him to hear. He'd not missed it when she'd said it again today after saving his life.

He had not said anything to her either time, but damn it, didn't his actions count?

. . .

Maggie rubbed her dry, sore eyes. Sleep had evaded her all night. Between the tears and her youngest brother, Roland, in the bed beside her snoring, she was dead tired. But the worst was remembering the expression on Lachlan's face when her father had announced their wedding. He'd looked as if he'd been given a death sentence.

Lorna and Elspeth had already been in this morning to bring her an elegant yet simple gown of the softest wool she'd ever felt. The cut of the dress was low, and she felt as if too much of her chest was on display, but she had to admit the deep red with lighter stripes running down its length was a good color for her. They helped her dress and then pinned her hair up with matching ribbons. Now she was just waiting for them to tell her it was time.

When the knock came, it startled her. The door swung open without an invitation, and Lachlan loomed in the frame. He walked in slowly and shut the door with an audible click. He turned and locked it.

His brow was stern and crinkled. His golden mane had been meticulously combed, but a lock fell into his face. Although she wanted to reach out and run her hands through the thick strands and feel the silky curls slide through her fingers, she ached that he might not want her any longer and clasped her hands together to fight the urge. She couldn't even begin to guess what emotions his hooded blue eyes were hiding.

After thoroughly scanning her, he smiled. "Och, lass, ye look lovely."

Saddened, she studied him through lowered lashes. Maggie had wanted him to marry her because he loved her, because he wanted no other. Now she only hoped she could make it through this marriage without spending her life utterly heartbroken.

"Thank ye," she finally managed as the painful constriction of her heart and throat eased.

"I didnae get to speak to ye yesterday. There is so much I wanted to say, but I couldnae get away from yer father. The man has a way of taking over."

She couldn't help but giggle at his exasperation, a feeling she'd dealt with her whole life.

"I see it didnae take ye long to get his measure." The easy banter relaxed her as he took her hand and guided her to sit on the bed beside him. Her heart beat faster at his touch.

"Ugh, and yer brothers! They wouldnae let me out of their sight." He rolled his eyes in exasperation. Aye, her brothers could be stubborn, but they looked out for her.

"They can be a wee bit much, too." She smiled.

"Maggie, what I'm trying to say is, I wanted to speak with ye before yer father made the announcement. I didnae even get to hold ye after we got back to the keep." His hands, holding hers, squeezed firmly and his warmth soaked in and relieved some of the tightness that had been eating at her all through the night.

"I was under the impression ye no longer wanted me," she said and looked away.

He gently turned her face back to his. "Listen to what you're saying, Maggie. If I didnae want ye, I wouldnae have fought so hard to get ye back."

"And Arabella?" There, she'd voiced it. Now he'd know how the jealousy clawed at her heart. Wetness filled her eyes. Damn, she had not wanted him to see her water up about it—she looked like a simpering fool.

He gently placed his palms on her cheeks and tilted her face up to look into his blue eyes. She found herself wanting to drown in the earnest emotion she saw there. "I dinnae want her. I want no one but ye. I'm not certain what ye saw, but think back. 'Twas no' what it seemed."

His sincere gaze remained locked on hers. "She went into our room and left a note that made it look like ye were scheming with Conall. She planned it so that ye would think I'd betrayed ye. All along her plan was to send ye out where the bastard could get his hands on ye. I caught her trying to steal the evidence. 'Twas why the bastard wouldnae just exchange ye for the letter on the first day. Arabella was going to take it and then try to turn Robbie over to him. Not only is she a traitor to the clan, she put ye at risk, and I cannae forgive her for either. She is gone and ye'll never have to see her again."

She believed him, but the tears came anyway, dripping down her cheeks.

He caressed them with his thumbs and leaned in to place a soft kiss on her lips. "I swear to ye, Maggie. Ye are the only one."

She fell into him, relishing the feel of his body as she wrapped her arms around him. He was warmth and security and home. Hope blossomed in her chest, but doubts remained, because he had never promised he had any more than passing desire for her, and she didn't delude herself—he might still want her, but he'd sworn he would never marry.

"Ye dinnae have to marry me." The words rushed out before she could stop them.

He pulled back and stared at her. He looked hurt. "Do ye not want me?" Reverently, he carefully drew his fingers along her bruised cheek.

"I want ye like I have never wanted anyone else. Ye are the air I breathe," Maggie managed to say. "Ye cannae let my father force yer hand. Nor the babe. I dinnae want ye if that is why ye are doing this." She motioned to the gown.

His head quirked sideways as if she had shocked him. And she realized too late—he didn't know she carried his child in her womb.

• • •

"Babe?" Lachlan studied Maggie as she closed her eyes and bit her lip, obviously waiting for his response, but he was still trying to wrap his arms about what she'd said.

A bairn. She looked so beautiful, sitting there with her black curls pinned up, a couple of ringlets escaping to frame her heart-shaped face. Her long, dark lashes almost brushed her cheeks, and she looked down as if she were ashamed.

She was carrying his child. Pride swelled somewhere deep within him.

Whether or not she carried his child, she was his. She'd kept it from him—she hadn't wanted him to choose her because she carried his child, and it only made her more beautiful in his eyes.

Finally, she returned his gaze and nodded. Lachlan moved to his knees on the floor right in front of her. She was everything. He had no words to explain how his heart leaped every time he saw her and how she had become his world.

He didn't know how he would face a day without her passion for life and her reckless behavior that drove him to distraction. For her and the babe's safety, he was already running through in his mind what he would no longer allow her to do.

He placed his hand on her still flat abdomen and looked deep into her sapphire-blue eyes. "I cannae say this doesnae make me the happiest man alive. To ken a life we created lives inside ye."

"I dinnae want to be an obligation." Stubborn defiance shown in her eyes.

He laughed. "From the first day, I have kenned ye were the one for me. When I held ye in my arms, it was right. I fought it because I was scared." He'd never admitted to anyone in his life he'd been afraid of anything.

"Why would ye want to tie yer life to me, when I overheard ye swear to Alan never to do so?"

"I was a fool for ever believing that, but when I made that promise, I didnae ken ye."

"I dinnae want ye to marry me because my father says ye have to."

"Yer father has nothing to do with it. I wrote to him last week and made plain my intentions to take ye as my wife. That is why he came. I didnae want to say anything to ye until I had his blessing."

Her eyes lit as his words sank in.

"I love ye, and there will never be another for me."

She smiled at him, a heart-rending, soul-searing smile that left him speechless. "I love ye, too, Lachlan Cameron." She threw her arms around him, and her lips dipped to his for a bold, confident kiss.

"I love ye, Maggie." His fingers lovingly played with the ringlet that tickled her cheek.

"Now, let's go get married. I cannae wait any longer."

Epilogue

"Dinnae even think about it." Maggie turned at her husband's voice as he entered the sick room and saw her about to hoist a bucket of water to take outside and dump.

"'Tis no' so heavy, 'twill be fine."

Staying true to his word, after they had married, he had listed tasks that he didn't want her doing until the babe was born, and the list grew with each day that passed. Knowing he meant well, she tried but scoffed at most of his demands — after all, what was so dangerous about going up to the turrets to look at snow that topped Ben Nevis, the loch as the moon glimmered off the mirrorlike surface, and the stars that filled the sky at night when the clouds stayed away? Last time he'd caught her up there, he'd made her promise to at least not go up without him, and that was just fine, because she adored hearing him talk about the land he loved so much.

"I was looking everywhere for ye. Why are ye out here?"

Maggie hadn't wanted to leave his side, but she'd rushed

in to share the responsibility of preparing for the Epiphany dinner tonight with Elspeth.

"I didnae get a chance to finish my work before dinner." Space in the room was tight, and if she didnae keep things clean, there wasn't enough room to mix up her medicinals for those who needed them.

"Come, I have something to show ye." Taking her hand, Lachlan drew her away from her task and out into the cool night air.

When they passed by the entrance to the great hall, her head tilted to the side. "Where are ye taking me?"

"I have a surprise for ye." 'Twas worth leaving her chores to see the boyish curve of his lips as he smiled.

He pulled her to a stop in front of a tower of the castle that lay unused, the one where she'd spent the night after he discovered her identity.

"Wait here. I'll light a candle." When he disappeared through the door, she shuddered at the loss of the warmth that left with him.

He returned and took her hand, drawing her near, but his smile had left and he seemed more apprehensive.

What had once been a barren, cold room on the first floor was bordered by tables on two sides, and he tugged her closer to one of them. Between the candle and low evening light shining through the windows, she was able to make out glass vials and earthen pots. "What is it?"

"A place for ye to work with yer herbs. Come."

Guiding her toward a small, dark room off to the side, he held the candle up to show ropes strung from the ceiling in planned increments. 'Twas the perfect environment for drying plants and flowers.

"Do ye like it?"

Her heart swelled and her eyes misted at all the effort it must have taken to put this together—for her. "Aye, I love it, husband."

"There's more." Guiding her to the stairs, he led her to the room she'd been locked in the day he discovered her secret. Pausing at the door, he smiled and pointed. "It can no longer be locked from the outside." The bolt that had kept her inside had been removed from the door, and he pushed it open to reveal a room she didn't recognize. A fire blazed in the hearth, the walls were covered with tapestries of couples in various scenes in nature, and a bed covered with plush blue blankets replaced the sad excuse for one that had been there before.

"I didnae want ye to have any bad memories of any part of Kentillie. 'Tis yer home now, and every part of it should feel like it." While he walked over and placed the candle down on a small table by the bed, she stepped into the transformed space and tamped down the happiness that was overwhelming her.

"'Tis my way to say my heart is open to ye. I never thought I would be able to trust again, but ye gave that back to me. Now I plan to give ye everything yer heart desires." Och, she loved this man. "And when ye are here working, I willnae have to drag ye to the other side of the keep to bed ye."

He took her hands and gazed into her eyes. "Do ye like it?"

"I love it." What she didn't know how to put into words was the truth that had bubbled up to the top of her heart—he had restored her faith in men. "I love ye."

In the time they'd been married, not only had his eyes and heart remained faithful to her, but even as her belly grew and she lost her curves, he had made this room for her.

She said it the only way she knew how—raising up on her toes, she kissed his lips, then her free hand pulled the pin from his plaid. "Let's try it out."

Acknowledgments

Special thanks to:

Robin Haseltine for seeing potential, sharing her knowledge and being my partner on this journey. She's a shining star, and I am truly fortunate that our paths crossed.

My husband for his love, support, and belief in me.

My kids for putting up with takeout, dirty dishes and understanding when mother was working.

My parents, Jo Ann and David Bailey, for being here since the beginning and for their faith, support, and unconditional love.

Jennifer R. for being a sounding board and my first reader. I will always be grateful for our friendship.

Toral P. for loving my first book and asking for more.

My writing tribe, along with being great friends, they hold a wealth of knowledge and have shared their wisdom and support with enthusiasm and love of the craft. I will always be eternally grateful to: Harper Kincaid, GG Gabriel, J. Keely Thrall, Taylor Reynolds, MK Meredith, Denny Bryce, Julie Halperson, Angele McQuade, Jennifer McKeone, and Laurel

Wanrow.

The Fox Mill writers who were there when it all started: Julie, Lisa, Sheila, Michele, and Jules.

Robert F. Dorr, a veteran, hero, and mentor, you will be missed.

And for you, the reader who picked up this book and gave a new author a chance to share a piece of her heart.

About the Author

Lori Ann Bailey has a romantic soul and believes the best in everyone. She cries every time she sees a sappy commercial or when one of her kids does something to be proud of. She felt emotionally drained after reading sad books, so she started reading romance for the Happily Ever Afters. She was hooked.

After working in business and years as a stay-at-home mom she has found something to be passionate about besides her family: her books. She lives in Northern Virginia with her real life hero, four kids who keep her on her toes, two dogs that are determined to destroy her house, and two cats that secretly plot the demise of those dogs.

Discover more historical romance...

A False Proposal
by Pamela Mingle

War hero Adam Grey returns home and plans to run for Parliament. But he needs the support of the local baronet, who controls the seat. He learns that his dissolute father has promised him to the baronet's daughter in return for forgiveness of his debts. Adam wants nothing to do with marriage or his father's problems, so he fakes an engagement to Cass Linford—his best friend's sister.

Only an Earl Will Do
by Tamara Gill

The reigning queen of London society, Lady Elizabeth Worthingham, has her future set out for her. Marry well, and marry without love. An easy promise to make and one she owed her family after her near ruinous past that threatened them all. And the rakish scoundrel Henry Andrews, Earl of Muir who's inability to act a gentleman when she needed one most would one day pay for his treachery.

Bayou Nights
by Julie Mulhern

Matthias Blake is as out of place in New Orleans as a raven in a flock of hummingbirds. He has serious work to do and Christine Lambert is a distraction he doesn't need. But how can he resist a lady in distress—even if that lady can win a fight armed with a hat pin? Together they must overcome their pasts and defeat dark forces sent by a shadowy evil. In the process, they just might find the greatest treasure of all...

VISCOUNTESS OF VICE
a *Regency Reformers* novel by Jenny Holiday

Lady Catharine wants a little excitement. Bored of playing the role of the ton's favorite slightly scandalous widow, she jumps at the chance to go undercover as a courtesan. Social reformer James Burnham is conducting a study of vice in England's capital. Catharine is the last sort of woman James should want, but want her he does. When Catharine and James are forced to band together, they'll be drawn into a web of secrets and lies that endangers their lives—and their hearts.

CPSIA information can be obtained
at www.ICGtesting.com
Printed in the USA
LVOW12s1249020117
519400LV00001B/18/P